CW00496165

What Survives

What Survives
Copyright © M. Amelia Eikli 2023
Published by Inkspun Books, Weston-super-Mare

Cover design © M. Amelia Eikli/Thought Library Media Ltd
Edited by Antonica Eikli

Cover fonts: Apothecary Serif and Sabon LT Pro
Content font: Sabon LT Pro, 10.5pt and 18pt

This is a work of fiction. No identification with actual persons (living or deceased), places or events is intended or should be inferred.

This novel includes topics and imagery that some readers might find upsetting.

All rights reserved. For permission requests, write to Thought Library Media at the address below.

Thought Library Media Ltd
contact@thoughtlibrary.co.uk

First edition

ISBN-13: 978-1-912159-09-3

What Survives

M. Amelia Eikli

M Amelia Eikli

Inkspun Books

To my wife, Nica, for all the times you fought for this book.

1

I've named the dog Scram, because no matter how many times I tell him to, he never does. He sits next to me, wagging his tail with an infuriating enthusiasm, and stares at me as if to say, 'Yes! I love "scram"! What a wonderful word! Say it again! Oh, say it again please!' So I do, and he doesn't get it, so Scram has become his name.

The first couple of days, I expected him to leave. I pretended not to notice him so that I wouldn't be disappointed when he wasn't there anymore. But I got used to him; I started looking for him in the mornings and made shelter for him at night. Now, I grab treats for him in every shop we pass. There's always an excellent selection. No one, not even the most paranoid doomsday prepper, thought to empty the shops of dog treats.

He makes walking better. He never growls, and he catches rabbits, pheasants and passing wasps. He chases butterflies and barks excitedly at birds. He's a very good dog.

'Scram?' I say. I speak to him when it gets too quiet. 'Do you think we're in Hamburg now? Do you think we've made it to Hamburg, boy?' I already know we have. I've been following the map closely—and the big '*Wilkommen in Hamburg*' sign is a bit of a tip off.

Big cities creep me out, and the smell of death is everywhere. So far, I've mostly avoided walking into cities at all. But the heel of my boot has a slash in it, I'm almost out of petroleum jelly, and I lost my knife somewhere outside Hanover. I picked up a kitchen knife from an old lady's house, but I need to find one that folds. Big cities mean selection and survival. I can't really say no to that.

Scram barks and jumps. He's running back and forth in front of me, sniffing lampposts, corpses and muck. He loves being in Hamburg like he loves being everywhere. He investigates the hair of a lady who lies in a doorway, but he doesn't disturb her. He never disturbs the dead, and I love him for that.

Here, they've piled up the dead on street corners. They're lying quietly, waiting for the van that never came to pick them up. Sometimes, I try naming the dead as I pass.

Mrs Lying in a Doorway, I think, *had beautiful hair, and held on to the end.*

Mr Bright Green Trainers, I continue, *couldn't outrun the disease, but gave it a good go.*

This way, I can remember them all; I make a space for them inside what I know of the world. But the piles are too big. *Mr... Mr... Mrs...* and I don't know, because they all blend together and ooze into my consciousness as 'this pile' or 'that pile'. It's too harsh. Too toxic. Instead, I try not to look at them, just keep moving north, breathe through my mouth, count my steps, think of something else or nothing at all.

I lean on numbers to make myself keep moving. There were roughly eight billion people in the world. I can't be the only survivor. Even if just 0.1% survived, there should be 80 million of us, wandering about. 80 million people means I'm bound to run into some of us eventually. With 0.01%, it would be slightly harder for us to find each other, but even with 0.001%—80,000 people—and a lifetime of loneliness to fuel the search, I will find others. I'm bound to. I'm hoping, though, that there's a genetic reason I'm still here. That would mean hope for my family.

A stylish family of mannequins—impeccably dressed in wrinkle-free hiking gear—stand in front of pristine tents and unused sleeping bags; this is the shop I'm looking for. They're surrounded by plastic flowers and papier-mâché trees, bird feathers, twigs, a plastic campfire and a stuffed bear. The shop owners get bonus points for effort. I wrap my hand in a towel and set about smashing the window. Even with the emergency hammer I stole from a bus, my arm grows sore and my mind wanders. *Hiking, tents, a kiss in a... no.* It's important that I don't think too much. Security glass is a nightmare. It splinters slowly and in big, heavy sheets. You can make it through, but it takes time. I swear a lot and Scram rests.

When the window finally gives in, I brush the glass away with my foot and step inside. Scram jumps in beside me and sniffs the display. Will he widdle on the fake trees? These are the things that concern me now. He doesn't, of course. Instead, he runs in and out of the tents and plays with a plastic plate that could—by a dog—be confused with a Frisbee. Looking around, my eyes are drawn to a small red light that's blinking inside. For a moment, it makes my stomach jump.

Lights can mean life, my stomach says, tossing and turning in excitement. I settle it at once.

Lights just mean batteries, I think in my sternest tone. *And batteries mean nothing at all.* These truths are important. These truths keep me sane. My stomach needs to arrive at this conclusion before it takes me down with it. I've been walking for more than a month, and *nothing* has, so far, meant life.

The red eye stares at me from the top of an old-fashioned answering machine. The type with a tape and backup batteries that got so popular after the third, or was it the fourth pandemic. The tape rewinds with a loud whirr I haven't heard since I was a kid, but its low-tech squeak still feels excessively futuristic in the dead quiet around me. A frail male voice sputters. It's emotional. Final.

'*Alle Mitarbeiter von Stolze Sport und Freizeit möchten sich bei Ihnen für die Zusammenarbeit bedanken. Das Geschäft bleibt vorerst geschlossen... Vielen Dank.*' I don't pay attention to what he's saying, but the sound of a human voice is comforting. Comforting and painful. Then there is a long pause, and his voice shifts. '*Laura... wenn du irgendwo da draußen bist... Bitte komm doch wieder nach Hause! Alles ist verziehen... Wir... komm wieder nach Hause.*' There is such a soreness to this and I can't help but translate, even though I don't want to know. The German I learned at school rises up through 15 years of neglect and tells me he's asking Laura, whomever she is, to come home. All is forgiven, he says. Come home.

Discomforting. That's what I meant. The sound of a human voice is discomforting. I shiver and start looking around the shop for what I need. The machine continues. '*Sie haben zwei neue Nachrichten.*' There's a beep and an automated message of some sort. A chipper pre-recorded voice tells me something I don't need to know. Whatever it wants me to do, it is most definitely too late.

The shop has a great selection of hiking boots. I'm already dreading breaking in a new pair; not only do the blisters and sores hurt like hell, but they will also slow me down. Ideally, I'd be in Denmark by now, so I'm already behind schedule. But there's nothing to be done, so no point complaining. My current right boot lets water in through the heel, and no amount of duct tape can fix it forever.

My measure of a good day has changed in these past few months. This is a good day, as I've run into the ultimate sign of good fortune: there are no excess doors. The shop kept boxes of shoes in different sizes stacked along the wall. I can find my size without breaking down any warehouse doors, which means fewer calories spent and more walking time today. The machine still drones on, the voice too chipper for this tomb. I start unlacing a pair of purple boots that resemble the ones I already have. For some reason, I'm reluctant to pick any of the most expensive pairs in the shop. They feel out of my league, even though there are no leagues left.

The machine beeps. The second message starts playing. I freeze. Someone is sobbing. A wet, sticky and heartbreaking sound, occasionally broken off by violent, rolling, scraping coughs. Swallow, breathe, swallow. My skin is cold and clammy, and I recognise these coughs. The woman on the tape hasn't got long left at all.

'*Opa...*' the voice croaks. More sobs. More coughs. '*Ich komme...*'

There are no more messages. Just the silence they leave me with, surrounded by shoes for nobody's feet. I throw up in a purple boot and sink to the floor.

Eventually, I wrap the shoes in a plastic bag I find under the counter. The smell of sick makes me gag, but the thought of leaving it exposed for animals to find is worse. Swallow and breathe, swallow and breathe. It strikes me, as I place the shoes in yet another bag and throw them in a bin that will never be emptied, that these messages were important. Opa never heard the message from the girl, whom I can only assume had been Laura. Her words, like all other words from the end of the End, disappeared into nothing until I picked them up. I don't want them. I wish I could erase them and leave them behind. But instead, I play the tape over and over until I'm sure I'll remember them by heart.

I find another pair of shoes that fit even better than the first. They are dull and grey, so I pinch a couple of the fake flowers from the window display and weave them between the laces. It looks all right. I take a couple more and stick them in my hair for good measure. The shop has an impressive display of hunting knives in a big cabinet on the wall. I break the glass with my hammer and choose a big one. It doesn't fold up but it's sleek and long, and the sheath is beautifully decorated with trees and wolves on dark leather. I rub my thumb against it. It's sharp. I suck the small beads of blood between my teeth. It tastes wrong. When I notice how long it takes to stop bleeding, I start counting the weeks since... *Don't think about it, just count.* 14? 15? 18? I have no idea, but I add iron tablets to my mental list of things I need to find. I've got no time for anaemia, and I should be getting my periods back soon.

I grab some freeze-dried camping meals, a new head torch (the one I have is fine, but this one's better), and half a packet of ibuprofen I find in a drawer behind the till. Scram is standing in front of a pack of tennis balls, whimpering slightly.

'Oh, please, can we? Can we?' says his tail, and he turns to me with his tongue out, tilting his head so that his face adds, 'Oh boy! Tennis balls! Come on! You'll love it! Come on!' So I break open the pack and pour four of the five balls into my backpack. The fifth, I hold in my hand until we get out, and then I throw it as far as I can down the street. Scram couldn't be happier. He barks and runs in his weird little way, halfway between a run and a skip. He reminds me of a calf in spring. He runs here and there, always in the general direction of the ball but constantly veering off to this side or that depending on where his skip lands him. I laugh a short laugh. Just a syllable or two. 'Ih ih,' I say. The sound is off, but the intention is there and makes me smile.

I keep moving north. I'll be there in plenty of time for my niece's birthday.

Six weeks ago, I placed the backpack on my bed and closed my eyes. The smell of her still hung in the air like an afterthought. I had the feeling that there was something I meant to say, but I couldn't quite remember what, or why. We had bought this backpack five years earlier, when we were still new and fresh and didn't know who we'd be as a couple. We had hoped we'd be the outdoorsy kind. We spent hundreds of pounds we didn't really have on hiking boots, a tent, head torches, thermoses, walking sticks and softshell jackets. We only went camping once. My feet blistered so much that I couldn't walk the next day. We had to take a taxi home. I wanted so much to be healthy, strong, enduring—but my heavy frame and excess pounds ground my feet against my boots until I bled and oozed and swelled them full. I spent the next year learning to walk. Not the cold march of everyday navigation but the steady, patient gander of a proper hiker. We had been planning to go hiking again, but the backpack still looked brand new.

When the End came, we were scared. We huddled together like frightened sparrows in our little nest. We never stopped watching the news. It was far from our first pandemic, but this one felt different, right from the start. We watched the early reports that said the disease must have originated somewhere in Asia, and the later ones that said the US was more likely the birthplace. We watched the guides on how to protect ourselves—the old classics of face coverings and social distancing, and the specifics of bleach and magnesium. Then, there were endless accounts of incubation times and symptoms. We felt the world grow quiet as more and more experts died before they could tell us how to survive. We heard the howl go up around the world when they said they'd been wrong: contamination had started a year ago; incubation time could be eight months, or even more. The disease was everywhere already. It was too late.

The broadcasts stopped in the middle of the second wave. By then, it had already been dubbed 'The End'. Before the second wave had rolled past, electricity, water, everything had shut down. There simply weren't enough people to keep the world going. There simply weren't enough people to care.

For a while, we thought we were survivors. And for a moment or two, there was calm. We weren't many. Maybe 30 in our town; someone said there were a couple of hundred in the next city over. We all wore face masks and gloves. We followed the guidelines written by those who hadn't made it. Most of us were young. All of us were heart-scared. And we kept to ourselves, most of the time.

She would lean into me when we cuddled, and we'd pretend like the past year and a half—with all its sorrows and uncertainties—hadn't happened. Her fragile body and glittering mind were the only things I cared about. I wanted to protect her, find some way to make her safe and happy. I used to think she had led me back to God, and now, God had left us a new Earth. We were chosen. Or abandoned. Perhaps we were left behind for a reason. We were the righteous, or we were the damned. Either way, we had each other.

We never talked about our parents or our siblings. There were no phones, no trains, no postmen, so we couldn't know if they had made it. Not for certain.

Instead, we read to each other by candlelight and planned to go and see them when things settled down. Her family first. They were just a few hours away by car, near Wales. Then we'd find a way to visit mine, in Norway. We talked about my niece's birthday in October. We'd definitely visit them then. Someone would have figured something out before that—of course someone would. I did what I could to keep our hopes up. I talked about the future, and furniture, and how to get through the next winter if the electricity didn't come back. She tried to make me smile, talked about books and poems and how happy she was that she had found me. Then, after a few weeks, she started coughing, and I knew God was dead, and probably had been for a while.

2

I keep a stone in my pocket. I bring it with me everywhere I go, and I have for five or six years now. I used to keep it in the windowsill, next to my keys, so that whenever I left the house, I would pick it up and place it in whatever jacket or bag I was bringing. She gave it to me a few weeks after the camping trip. My plan was to go on a pilgrimage that summer, walk the Camino de Santiago—the pilgrim route along northern Spain. Every day, I imagined walking the 800 or so kilometres to Santiago de Compostela, sleeping in the *albergues* along the way, meeting other pilgrims, walking my feet sore and red. Every day, I imagined the feeling of being there, of arriving and approaching the Saint on my knees. I imagined the feeling of having landed. Of having made it to the end.

There is an iron cross along the way, half-buried in an enormous pile of pebbles. For decades, people have brought stones with them from all over the world and left them at the base of the *Cruz de Ferro*. Each stone represents your problems, grievances, toil and turmoil. You would bring them to the cross and leave them behind—symbolically and mentally—before continuing towards your goal without them. I'm sure many just did it out of tradition. I'm sure some did it for a laugh.

My stone is T-shaped and gnarly. I touch it every now and then to remind myself that it's there. The pilgrimage was postponed, year after year, until the End came. I always wanted to go, that never changed, but life kept squeezing in between the fantasy of walking and the actual training. She found the stone on a beach and gave it to me with a kiss. She never stopped thinking I would complete my pilgrimage, so I never stopped bringing the stone.

I have moved the stone from pocket to pocket since I left. I make sure it always makes it into a new day. Now, I hold it in my left hand as I throw Scram's ball with the other. The stone is heavy. It grows heavier every day.

I didn't know I was gay when I met her. She turned up in the shadow of Anya, an avant-garde punk feminist, who threw quite a deep shadow, indeed. It was the launch party of a mutual friend's chapbook. We were hipsters, artists and drunks. Anya was like a child, speaking in absolutes and definitives one second, then in imaginative nonsense the next.

'I don't eat meat, fish, poultry, eggs, dairy or honey, and I don't wear silk or wool,' she declared to our group. One boy dared to argue her point about wool, bringing up sheep welfare and purpose-bred breeds. She shot the naysayer down with exasperated declarations about exploitation. 'Besides,' she continued, making an exaggerated pause, 'I think the whole concept of wearing clothes for anything but warmth is a gross tradition, initiated by the patriarchy to perpetuate male control over the female body.' My eyes quickly scanned her exposed cleavage and skin-tight dress. I didn't mean to. I didn't *want* to. She was very clearly in control of her body; she looked confident, sexy, dangerous. Not the way I had pictured feminists, but I didn't really understand feminism back then.

'But men wear clothes too...?' said the boy, who had clearly not learned from his past mistake. She scoffed. But before she could come down on the poor guy and defend her thesis, another man swooped in from the kitchen and Anya disappeared in a cloud of hugs, promises and reunion joy. Someone spoke.

'Do you smoke?' the someone said, and I had to look around several times to find the origin of the voice. The woman had probably been standing next to Anya all along but, like some witch in a fairy tale—at least, that's how it felt—she hadn't chosen to reveal herself to me before now.

'Oh. Uh, no. I've heard cigarettes are bad for you,' I said when I located the round, clever eyes in front of me. The girl looked like images of Cleopatra: a sharp, dark fringe at a perfect right angle to a long bob. Thick eyeliner. Large clunky necklace. Cute button nose. She shrugged and headed towards the door, and it opened an unexpected hole in my chest. A hole that held all the dark secrets I was keeping from myself, a stormy night of a hole that flooded my mind with cold water.

'Don't mind keeping you company, though,' I said, hurrying after her, not wanting to let her go. She gave a brief smile at first. But it lingered, stayed and then grew as we spoke, a sunrise settling my storm, leading me to safe harbour.

We talked about vegetarianism and animal rights. We talked about art, and books we enjoyed, and for all the time we laughed and bickered, she didn't light her cigarette. Our opinions fit each other. They weren't the same—heavens, no, our worlds were too different. But our values aligned, and we were shapes in a picture that neither of us had seen before but both of us instantly recognised.

'That Anya...' I tried. 'Her points are a bit... out there?'

Cleopatra shook her head. A small, measured motion that made my blood bubble and fizz. 'No. *She's* a bit out there, but her points are sound. They're just not realistic.'

'Even about the clothes?'

'*Especially* about the clothes.' She winked at me. We stood quietly for a long while. She smelled of coconut.

Anya stepped out towards us, a pendant rolling steadily atop her cleavage, slowly, hypnotising, mesmerising. I envied her, wanted her or wanted to be her. I could taste my heartbeat with every step she took. She came within ten inches of me, then bent down and kissed the girl who looked like Cleopatra. I was confused and jealous.

'Baby!' Anya said, and put her arm around Cleopatra's shoulders. Once again, the woman who looked like an Egyptian queen was slipping out of view. I struggled to keep her in focus.

'So, what have the two of you been gossiping about?' Anya said. A flash of annoyance across Cleopatra's face.

'She's just convinced me that there are *some* good reasons to go vegan,' I said.

'Great!' Anya replied. Her voice was happy, but she didn't smile. Cleopatra did. I kept my eyes locked on her face. I was certain she'd disappear if I even blinked.

I blinked.

Anya was walking away from me and back into the party. I couldn't see Cleopatra. *Of course they are gay*, I thought. *Of course they are.* My mind tried to make points about not believing in stereotypes, about veganism, feminism... but I didn't care. I just wanted the girl who looked like Cleopatra to come back. The storm was brewing, and I wanted shelter. Stepping back into the party, magic struck: she peered over her shoulder, looking back at me with stories in her eyes.

'It's fine by me if you eat meat,' she said, just loud enough to carry over the music but not loud enough to be a shout. 'Just make sure there's a vegetarian option for me.' She smiled.

'I will!' I said, but she was already gone.

I told my husband about them both, on the phone. We laughed about my girl crush.

Scram barks. I've been staring at the poster for a long time. I haven't seen Anya for years now, but here she is, on a poster in Germany. Her band never made it in the UK, but I had heard through a friend that they'd had some success in Germany. Cüntfückers, they called themselves, good grief and bless my giddy aunt. It had apparently started as a joke, but then they never settled on a new name, and there you go. I think I have a single song by them on my MP3 player. 'Pretentious', it's called. She wrote it about me, I'm fairly sure.

Scram barks again, and I absentmindedly tear down the poster, fold it a couple of times and put it in my pocket. I throw his ball. It's wet and slobbery but I don't care, and neither does he. The smell of corpses is intense here, and I hide my face in my thin scarf. I can hear a swarm of flies nearby. Looking up a side street, I see two big piles of bodies at the end of the block. There's a pharmacy down there as well, but I keep walking and hope to find another. I avoid the dead if I can. I already carry too many.

I find another pharmacy a few streets on. There's broken glass here, but I always expect that with pharmacies so I don't get too excited. Desperate people in the third wave tore down entire hospitals in search of antibiotics and cough syrup. Nothing worked, of course, but you had to try. I brush the glass away for Scram and step inside. The place is a mess, but not picked clean. I grab the largest tub of petroleum jelly I can find and another pack of ibuprofen. I take a look around, smell the creams and ointments with deep breaths, imagine being clean and smelling of soap and lavender. I open a box of sugar-free sweets and put one in my mouth. Peppermint. I leave the box on the shelf and keep browsing. A few packets of blister plasters, yes, these will be useful. I still have a few, but breaking in new boots is never easy. Iron tablets—I pop one right away—and a pack of sanitary pads, just in case.

As I walk, the city closes in. It wraps its arms around me and tightens them around my chest. Parks and bridges, waterways and sculptures, new and old. It is beautiful, but too much.

I stand for a while on a little bridge and look out over a small lake. There are a few people floating in it, but not too many. I don't have to notice, so I try not to. I haven't thought about drowning since I stood on the beach in Dunkirk, but now I do. I imagine sinking down through the water and feeling my clothes become heavy. I imagine the burning pain in my lungs, and the forced breath, right at the end. How my lungs would beg for air and get nothing but water. I wonder what it would taste like. Would it taste like city pond, or like bloated bodies and soggy dead? Would anyone ever find out that I died at a different point in time than the others? Would they know that I chose to die right here, right now? But then again, these bodies may have chosen to die here, too. Many made difficult choices, right at the End. There wasn't much else to do.

I clench the stone in my pocket and wonder if I should leave it here, in the lake. But I don't. Scram discovers a family of ducks resting peacefully on the bank. He barks and snaps and sends them flying. Some days he'll catch one, but today, he's only playing. The sound of their wings as they take off is too loud. Much too loud. They flap and quack and bristle and swish; they are too close to my head, and the flapping blows the air away from me and makes me gasp for breath. I can't breathe. I'm still on the bridge but I'm already drowning. My lungs fill with the stench, and I can taste the bloated corpses on my tongue. I spit again and again but the taste sticks and creeps towards my throat. I gag and start running. I can't breathe. Can't breathe. I try to think of something else.

I had a South African friend, the last few years before the End. Kobus—short for Jakobus—van Niekerk. He was the proudest man I ever knew. He was proud of his curries, his thoughts and his taste in music. He was proud of his ability to sense trouble coming, and his courage to stay standing through difficult times. Kobus van Niekerk was proud of his name.

'I am of no church!' he would say, almost every time we sank down into a second glass of wine. 'I am of no church. It's right there, in my name. I don't belong to any God, I do not pray at any altar. I am a Niekerk—No-Church!' We toasted to that repeatedly throughout our friendship.

I looked up the origin of his name after the second or third of these nights. Van Niekerk: a topographical surname meaning 'by the new church'. This name suited him much better, but I never told him so. No one I'd ever met had built himself a new church quite as strong and sacramental as Kobus's.

He had been a financial journalist back in South Africa, and had a deep-rooted hatred of the middle class. He didn't trust them; he found them appalling. He saw himself as a working-class hero, although his £85,000-per-annum tech job suggested he might have left the working class behind. He didn't see it that way; continued his brimstone braying.

He didn't mind the *upper* class, no, not the slightest. The aristocrats, he reasoned, could do whatever they pleased.

'The fucking old money doesn't count,' he said on these wine-soaked nights. 'It is dream money. Not substantial. It's money mined from fairy tales and stories of kings and queens. It is money off the backs of slaves and caravans and drowned seafarers. And it is important! It gives the likes of you and me something to strive after, something to dream about! Something to hate and loathe but secretly crave.'

If Kobus got to rule for a day—a fantasy he seemed to play out in his mind quite often—he would make the size of your house dependent on how many children you had. One bedroom per resident, tops. Those who wanted to be foster parents, or take in the elderly or infirm—they could get the grand mansions, the five-bedroom villas and the vistas of London. They should be the ones to benefit from the pools and tennis courts. 'But no childless couple with two incomes,' he'd thunder, 'should ever be allowed to have a four-bedroom house all to themselves, all on their Larry lonesomes, no, sir! Never!' He would often stand up at this point, wave his arms in conviction and punch the air for emphasis. Single-room apartments, crowded developments, council estates and run-down tower blocks—that's where the rich should live, he thought. Those were the people who had the means to make those places nice. The means to go on holidays. To escape.

Kobus could work himself up to quite the rage over this. He would pace up and down the floor and deliver his sermons with hellfire in his voice.

'Fucking halfwits with a big fucking job in a big fucking company,' he would fume, swearing with his Afrikaans twang, the way he always did. 'What do they contribute to the world? All right, so you earned an extra two mil' today because you pushed some buttons, sold some junk, screwed over some workers. Congratulations on being great at being awful! Hurray! Now take your fucking pay cheque and feed some hungry people, right? *Right?!*' he would say. And I would nod and smile, although I didn't always agree, and sometimes found his views obnoxious.

Once, he spat on the floor. There was no stopping him when he started these rants, and I never really tried to. I would get comfortable in my pulpit, drink my communion wine and let waves of righteous indignation wash over me from the outside, sanding me down until I became a more faceted person. I didn't mind at all. Of all the friends I ever had, Kobus was probably the most difficult, and one of the ones I loved the most. Because he was kind. He was generous. And he was never, ever boring. That used to mean a lot to me.

Kobus hated a lot of things in addition to the middle class: injustice, capitalism, peas, seagulls and his next-door neighbour, Diane. Everything he hated, he hated for very complicated reasons. Always with a well-thought-out speech to go with it. He hated so many things with his full brain capacity, I sometimes wondered how the entire world didn't burst into flames when he woke up in the morning. He hated with a passion that could melt steel, but the things he loved, he loved even stronger. He loved red wine and spicy curries. He loved reading, and

17th-century England. He had a deep devotion to finding connections in the world. This was the one practice of his religion that I could get behind, and the one trait we truly shared: the wish and ability to see beyond facts and figures, to dive deep, to explore the darkness underneath every concept until we found the silver threads connecting them all. We would throw our chosen facts up in the air and polish each thread until it was clear and shining. Until every single fact was connected through time and circumstance; until we could prove new constellations in the sky.

I loved our little congregation. I loved his stories and questioning mind. Where I could discover a connection, feel the thrill of the moment and then move on, Kobus would spend days—sometimes weeks—weaving it into the tapestry of relations he created for himself. The mission of his mission: to prove that everything was connected to everything else, preferably through 17th-century England. If at all possible, through Sir Thomas Browne.

Kobus was more pessimistic than I am, though. Which is probably why he chose the very first exit, right at the beginning of the End.

I still can't breathe. I gasp and gasp but there is nothing but sound. Hissing. Wheezing. I have run too far, too fast. My backpack is too big. The air is rotten and thick as tar. My lungs are too small and my throat too narrow. With every breath, bits and chunks of all things dead and forgotten force their way inside me. They fill me, push themselves in so tightly I think I might burst; they cut off my oxygen and make me retch. The taste of rotting flesh on my tongue. Pus. Maggots. Bloating. Marshes. I trip and fall, again and again, but I keep getting up until I see grass to my left. It's some kind of park. A green lung in the city. Just what I need: fresh air. I close my eyes and pretend there are no buildings around me. I dig my fingers deep into the cool soil, claw my way forwards, bit by bit. I will my body to smell a forest nearby. I try again and again. I just need a rest. Just need to get my breath back.

Deep breath. Now. I force myself to slow down. I force my mouth to empty of ghosts. I am breathing. That's what's happening now. I'll just get my breath back, and then I'm going to walk over to the forest I can smell nearby, where I'll find a stream and take a swim. In the forest—there, I can smell it, now, deep breaths—I will make a little food for Scram and me, and set up camp for the night. I lie on my stomach and feel the weight of my backpack pushing me into the ground. As I calm down, the lush green grass turns back into the prickly, long stubble of unwatered city, and the smell of the forest turns into the familiar whisper of death.

'Scram?' I mumble. He lies down in front of me, confused by this game. I'm a snail whose house is too small, too wet and too heavy.

'Just a second,' I say, 'okay?'

Scram wags his tail in response.

The girl who looked like Cleopatra kissed me by a small lake, two months after we first met at that ridiculous party. Her lips were cold and soft, and I could barely feel them against mine. Yet, that one brief kiss shattered every illusion I held about going back to my old life. There was a bench there, and we sat staring out over the pond, watching the shards of our old lives glitter on the surface like stars.

It will take me at least a few more hours to get out of the city, and it's too late for that now. This park is the closest thing I have to wilderness, so again, I force my mind to ignore the buildings and dust. I put up the tent as if I'm in a lush clearing, make freeze-dried stew on the small burner and hum a little to myself. I should have grabbed another bottle of gas. I should have found some water. I should have found a belt. But there's no going back; that is my one and only rule. There will be other shops, there will be other towns, but there will never be more time, so there will be no going backwards. I have to keep believing. (Hoping? Wishing? Checking?) I need to make sure, and certainty is moving forward, so that's what I do, too.

I don't really need the burner to get food in the evenings. There's more than enough to burn, and no one to talk about rules or safety. I fantasise about setting a city on fire. Watching the fire spread and consume all that has been forgotten. I wish I could set the world on fire. I won't, but I wish I could.

I pick out the keychain with our photo on and stroke her face with my thumb. She had an affinity for printing fragments of our history on mundane objects. We had pillowcases, cups, plates, credit-card holders, notebooks, keychains and even a calculator with our pictures on.

'If there is something you need, but it doesn't matter to you what it looks like,' she explained when the pillowcases arrived, 'you might as well use it to remember something you don't want to forget.'

I carry some of these things with me in the backpack. There's a cup with the photo of us by a Roman fountain and a keychain with a photo from our first official date. And then there are two notebooks: one with my favourite photo of her, a photo I took on an icy winter's day, when I suddenly got the urge to explore and she came with me. We were laughing and stumbling through the snow, and the faux-fur trim of her hood made her look like an old illustration from a children's book. The photo is only of her face and the hood, and there is so much happiness in her face. I remember seeing the picture for the first time and thinking, *She knows how this story is going to end.* She looked like someone who knew everything would be all right.

It's time for some music. I fish my MP3 player out of the side pocket of my backpack and turn it on. The light is unnaturally bright, and it startles me. I turn the screen brightness down to the minimum and scroll through until I find 'Pretentious' by Cüntfückers. They released a single EP and called it *The Best of Cüntfückers*. I'm sure someone thought it was clever.

Hearing Anya's voice doesn't move me the way I thought it would. We were never close or anything, but I expected it would be harder to hear a voice I knew than the voices of the strangers on the answering machine. Perhaps I don't care so much that Anya is dead. In a way, she's been dead to me for ages.

The song is definitely about me, and I smile as I listen to the lyrics and think of the first time we heard them.

'Do you remember?' I whisper to the keyring. She looks back at me with the same smile as before.

Anya sings: 'The girl was mine, you took her still, you told her I'm contentious, you made her leave my love behind, oh god, you're so pretentious.' The song makes no sense and barely rhymes, and I remember rolling on the floor, wheezing with laughter, listening to it with the girl who looked like Cleopatra. Her skin against mine, her breath in my ear. The song on repeat over and over, because we couldn't stop making out, kissing, clawing, laughing. We were brand new, fresh in the world, a fresh couple after months of pining for each other. I had left my husband, she had left Anya. Neither of us knew how the other felt, but we knew we wanted to feel the way we did when we were together. Tiles against my back, flour in the air. We were meant to be making cupcakes when Anya sent her the song. 'Pretentious'.

I trace the edges of the memory, not letting it become clear enough to hurt, just enough to make me smile. When the song ends, I turn the MP3 player off. It's not that I worry about power; I have an emergency charger with me. The old-fashioned kind you used to get, where two AA batteries got you half an hour of charge. But I can rarely take more than a song or two at a time anymore. There's too much responsibility in choosing which songs will be remembered and which will be forgotten. I wish I'd paid more attention to music when it was alive.

After the second pandemic, or maybe it was the third, MP3 players and analogue answering machines came back into vogue like they'd never left. We all craved ways to keep our music, our photos, our memories and messages in ways that didn't rely on the internet or phone network. We'd seen the value of the old LPs, CDs and battery-operated CD players when all the streaming services went down in the big internet crash. Old iPods were pulled out of desk drawers and people traded music libraries as if they were Pokémon cards. The third was when we stopped thinking, 'This will be the last pandemic.' Everyone had been prepared for the fourth. And the fifth. And the first wave of the End. Everyone had their own music backed up on handy devices. It was a good way of getting to know someone, clicking your way through their music.

I give Scram most of the stew and pull out the second notebook. It's small, not much bigger than a matchbox, and the photo on the front is of the two of us after a fight. My eyes are swollen, hers are red. We look tired. She insisted on taking the picture right after we made up, and she made me the book so I could write down little things that annoyed or frustrated me before they grew into big things. I have filled in the first couple of pages. I flick to page four, dig out a pen and write 'Hamburg' on the first available line. I fiddle with the stone in my pocket. I can smell a forest nearby.

3

I wake up early. Hours later, I'm still not out of the city. I pretend not to notice, just walk through the endless valleys between brick houses, follow the lengths of the gorges, street after street after street. Time moves more freely if I think of it like this. If I reimagine the city as a landscape of craters, mountains and groves—scars on the surface of the Earth—nature I can love. More palatable than buildings, corpses and streets. With my eyes half closed, my surroundings are beautiful. One foot in front of the other, and I'm back on my way. The city is a dark forest, and I know I should stay on the path and not step into the wild. I should walk straight home to Grandma's house, as it were. But I pass a door that's wide open and it's time to make a stop.

Supermarkets and corner shops have almost always been broken into. They're chaotic and out of essentials but overflowing with everything else. Birthday cards, detergent and stock cubes form the leaves in the foliage, while canned goods, rice and toothpaste form the gaps. This shop still has bottled water, which is surprising. The End must have come quickly here. Or perhaps they were just better prepared. Many people had squirreled away enough food and water to get them through a year or two. And toilet paper. We had learned. There's a rustling from across the shop, but I don't really notice. Birds are everywhere these days.

Out of habit, I grab a basket from the stack by the entrance. It makes no sense, I know, but I clutch to this small act of normality like a steel-wired talisman. Energy bars, biscuits, instant pasta, chocolate and some water. I open the first bottle and drink deeply. I carry several packs of iodine tablets and will drink almost anything these days, but this water is clean. I correct myself. It's not *clean,* not the clean of mountain streams back in Norway. Not the cold, clear, pure taste of nature and moss and clouds. No, this water is *clean*, bland and empty—the taste of machines and regulations. I drink more and add a couple of cans of Coke to my haul. Not worth the weight, really, but they remind me of home.

A low, deep growl. I turn around, expecting to see another dog approaching. I grab a full bottle for something to throw. There is no one there. I look to Scram. He's standing stiff as a board, his ears forward and his eyes staring intently at something behind the shelves. I squint, but see nothing. A short growl again. It must have been Scram.

But something is approaching. Tack tack tack tack against the hard floor. It *sounds* like a dog. I raise the bottle above my head, and a wolf steps out and crosses the aisle in front of us. Hundreds of years of fairy tales rush through my veins, and I turn to stone with a fear I've never felt before, ancient and cold. Every single hair on my body stands to attention; I can taste my pulse, I can feel the air against my neck. The wolf stops and turns its head to look at us, and for a long moment, that's all we do—stare at each other. It's taller than I expected it to be, and browner. But it's dark in here, and my vision is coloured by myth. The wolf grows in front of my eyes; its jaws part and extend. It wants to gulp me down and swallow me whole, and there is not a single axe-wielding huntsman about. Not any longer. I am into the woods, but these aren't the woods. No one will hear me fall.

The wolf loses interest and trots on to the next aisle. I grab my basket and back out towards the entrance, eyes fixed between the trees. The shelves. The aisles. Slowly, Scram follows, but he keeps turning his head back, tail between his legs, whimpering slightly. By the till, I make a short detour to grab some more batteries. I hardly dare to turn my head to see what I'm reaching for, and my ears amplify every sound. I worry that my pulse is so loud it might drown out an oncoming attack. There is no movement, but I keep searching for it. I stand with my back pressed against the far wall and stare up along the aisles. There it is again. A grey shadow weaving in and out of the forest of items no one will ever need.

'We'll get dog treats at the next one,' I whisper to Scram, and we leave through the broken door.

Kobus had four daughters with four different mothers, and a lover in Oxfordshire who had two of her own. He referred to them all, mothers and daughters alike, as 'my girls', and he loved them deeply when he didn't hate them. All of his exes were wild. All of his daughters were troubled.

I asked him once why he hadn't moved in with the lover in Oxfordshire. I knew she wanted him to.

'I am 54, and I have been married thrice,' he said. 'This is my fucking last chance to live this life. This free life. This selfish life.' He drank wine in deep swigs and shoved food into his mouth in big scoops. He always ate as if he might be called away at any moment; as if his duties could not stop and wait for dinner.

'If,' he said, spraying rice onto the floor, 'I move in with her, it is going to be "hello, neighbour" and "how are you, neighbour?" and "good day, neighbour".' He swallowed, scooped, chewed.

'And then,' he continued, 'it is fucking "hello, soccer training on Monday", "hello, library event on Thursday".' Garlic naan crumbs everywhere. 'I don't want to have tea with soccer moms,' he said. 'I want to fuck soccer mums, but not have fucking tea with them. I am too...' He chewed loudly and swayed his head from side to side, as if searching for the word in the air.

'Old?' I suggested. He laughed.

'Selfish,' he said, nodding and refilling his glass. 'Besides...' he said a few moments later, 'I could not do that to my other girls. There has been too much in and out of things already. It must be calm now. It must be stable.' He meant this, I believe, and he never moved in with the lover. Instead, he took another lover, a childless Essex woman with a cabin by the sea. It broke the first lover's heart, but they never got around to talking about it.

The wolf leaves the shop a good while after us. It slinks out of the door and doesn't notice me up here, behind a window, across the street. I ignore the bodies in the bed and the smell under the ceiling. Instead, I watch as the wolf steps out into the street, disguised as just another big dog. It has put a collar on and everything. Somehow, it disappoints me. The world goes back to feeling empty.

I walk back into the valley of the dead without looking over my shoulder. Scram begs for another ball but I'm too tired to fish one out of the backpack, which is now heavy with food. We walk towards a large road junction, and I stand for a long time just staring at the dark traffic lights. In my head, I hear my own voice shout, 'Please! Just turn green! Just turn something! Let there be light!' but I seldom say anything out loud these days. I close my eyes until I see the lights, and I walk.

There are many things I miss that I never noticed while the world was alive. I miss the background hum of electric appliances. That hum you only ever heard when the power cut out. Not just the hum of fridges and laptops. But the hum of thousands of thousands of cars, and lights, and suitcases being wheeled across pavements. I miss cold drinks and people with annoying laughs. I miss having to slow down because the person in front of you seems to be moving in a time much slower than yours. I miss meeting the eyes of children in prams and seeing their faces change. I miss there being someone on the other side of... anything.

I tumble out between the last rows of houses and see fields on both sides of the road. The sound from my chest is like a yelp, and I breathe and stumble forward, suddenly terrified of the city behind me, out onto the field—yes, yes, yes! I relax, slow my pace and consider the time. It will be light enough to walk for a few more hours, but I'm tired and my left shin hurts. Must not overdo it. I keep forgetting that I must not overdo it. The stench is gone, or maybe it's just at a level I'm able to ignore. I breathe freely for the first time since entering the city, and hope it will be some time before I have to enter another.

My mind wanders. Sometimes, I wonder if I should try drugs, now that there are no rules left to break. Never did I ever try a single one. Nothing injected, snorted, smoked. Not that I didn't want to; it was simply never allowed. I guess I wasn't much of a risk-taker. How, I wonder, would I find any now? Where? The pharmacies have all sorts of drugs, but I know nothing of their effects and don't feel like risking it. I wish I could find something mild. From the way people talk—talked—about weed, you would think there was a bag in every purse. So far, all I've gotten from purses is a pair of sunglasses and a small collection of MP3 players. There is no music left in the world except whatever I choose to listen to. Or other survivors, of course. Other survivors out there, somewhere. I steer into a field and find a place to put up my tent. Soft, and surrounded by smells I do not recognise. Scram finds a wild rabbit within minutes of stepping off the road. The pride is larger than his body when he brings it back to me.

'Look what I've got!' his face says, and I want to be excited for him. But the rabbit isn't quite dead. It stares at me and whimpers with parts of its guts spilling onto its soft fur.

'I'm sorry...' I croak. Not because I'm emotional, I don't think. My throat is just dry and hasn't been used for a while. The rabbit's ears twitch slightly. I don't blame it. My voice is strange. Not like mine at all. Its ears twist again, and I notice how long they are. And it's skinny. Skinnier than a rabbit. Anorexic and stern-looking. It's a hare.

'I'm sorry,' I say, a little louder. I've never eaten hare, but someone once told me it's delicious, and I used to quite like rabbit, and I imagine it's much the same. I break its neck, awkwardly and much slower than I'd like, and then I make what just might be the only hare stew in the world. Scram eats it happily, every last bite. I think I can hear a wolf howling somewhere, far away or long ago.

We eat, and I watch the landscape. I keep my back to the city, pretending it's already out of sight. I used to imagine the end of the world on dark nights when I was little. I would close my eyes and envision abandoned cars cluttering the roads, doors still open, their drivers fled. I would picture food left out on breakfast tables, steaming teacups hastily abandoned. In every vision I had, the world was abandoned in the middle of its daily chores. Perhaps there would be dead, of course there would. But the dead I imagined were just like the living. The living, stopped in their tracks. I imagined that everyone would just come to an abrupt standstill, never to be piled up on street corners like bin bags, broken furniture or Christmas trees. I never imagined that we would stack our dead in tidy mounds. But now, there's only me abandoned on the road. The cars are parked somewhere else. No one left food on their tables or vacated the world in the middle of their chores. Night-time fell across the Earth, and people parked their cars, put the food away and crept into bed. The sun simply never rose. The dead are forever sleeping and the quiet rings across the landscape. I keep listening for a train in the distance but, of course, the last train has gone. Scram snaps at butterflies in the dying light.

There's a thought that haunts me, and when it visits, I cannot sleep: what if this was a rapture? What if God and the Devil killed off all of humankind and picked their favourites from the dislodged souls? What if I'm left behind because neither wanted mine? This thought is restless and rattles my bones. It falls asleep in the early morning, and I'll probably manage to leave it behind for a day or two before it finds me again. It rides on the smell of death and rests atop the piles of corpses. There are no other ghosts left. Where are all the ghosts?

Every morning, Scram wakes me up when he gets bored of sleeping. He sniffs my face and whimpers softly. He is a very gentle alarm clock, and I never mind. It's still summer, so we can walk early and hard. Hamburg becomes a distant memory and for days, I do not speak. We're headed towards Denmark, and I've run out of words.

Through Belgium, I told him every fairy tale I know—originals, cartoon versions and musicals, when I knew them. I summarised *Hamlet* and *Moby Dick*, *Oliver Twist* and *Wuthering Heights*. For a while, I talked about Roman gods and Greek myths, and all I knew about the Vikings. Back then, I didn't feel the weight of it. I didn't stop to ponder how many books I've never read or how few I remember. I didn't stop to think about all the fairy tales I never heard, and all the cultures whose mythologies were never written down. Now, I don't know how to keep remembering. There are so many stories. How do I choose? I carry one book. It's heavy, and I feel it digging into my back. But that's okay.

I used to carry a Bible, too. It was beautiful, leather-bound, and given to me by my grandparents as proof of my coming of age. My grandparents were beautiful people, and I thought they'd live forever. I remember my grandfather turning 80 and the celebration we had. I was nine, and offended by all these people barging in with new knowledge about him, the man who had been in the house next door my entire life. I remember him turning 90, when I meditated on the fact—for the very first time—that people had known my grandfather for a full 70 years before I was born. This had blown my head open, and for weeks, I couldn't shake the feeling that I never really knew anyone.

I was humbled by his 100th birthday. He held my grandmother's hand through the whole thing, and occasionally he would look at me and nod. He would nod at every face he recognised that didn't break eye contact. A little acknowledgment. 'There you are, I am here. We know each other.' It seemed like a nice habit. I adopted it for a while. He was deaf by the end, and remembered dreams and places as if they were yesterday, and yesterday as if it was a whisper from a long-lost fantasy.

My grandmother prayed for me, sometimes out loud, and I never told her about the girl who looked like Cleopatra. They met, several times, but we called her my English friend and left it at that. My grandmother was the sweetest lady you could ever meet, and her sweetness was a poison that infected anything that wasn't the way she knew it should be. She knew that girls should not kiss girls, and that Hell had room for everyone. I helped her with her mobile phone and read her the obituaries when my grandfather fell asleep. I kept bringing her greetings from my ex-husband until long after he stopped sending them.

I carried their Bible for weeks. I don't know where I left it, and I hardly noticed it was gone.

4

It has been raining for days. My tent smells of rain, my boots smell of rain, the blisters on my feet are grey and the skin around them is crinkled and wet. Squishing, slurping, gurgling, tapping and swooshing. Rain against leaves against dirt against skin. Scram smells of wet dog, and I smell of very little.

I am naked, standing with mud up to my ankles. I let all of Germany's sweat, dust and shame trickle off my body. It's liberating and lonely. I haven't washed in weeks. In the beginning, I carried soap, but I don't any longer. I keep my hair brushed and braided, my fingernails more or less clean and my pubic hair trimmed by old habit. I brush my teeth obediently. I've even started using dental floss—I never did before the End, but now, I take care of everything I cannot fix, my teeth being first on the list. I don't worry so much about smells or vanity.

The rain whips my skin cold. My fingers turn blue and I'm pale beneath my sun-baked skin. I see myself from across the field, tattoos wrapped around my arms and legs, harsh tan lines cutting across my ankles, chest and shoulders. I am thin. I've never been thin before. But now

I'm slim and strong, with a body that shivers and spasms in the cold. Scram lies whimpering under our tarp, waiting for me to come back to my body. He can feel it too. We've been here for a couple of days now, and I know I should be moving. My entire body is aching for movement, and yet, I've decided to wait out the rain. It tastes salty on my cheeks.

The rain makes me think about water and oceans and streams and rivers and falls. I think a lot about whales. A few weeks before the beginning of the End, I watched a documentary about the blue whale.

'The blue whale,' the narrator said, 'is the largest animal ever to live on Earth. Far larger than any known dinosaur.' She talked about all the measurements of the whale's body, none of which interested me except this fact: a baby could crawl through its enormous arteries. This sense of scale amused me; what else would you measure in whether or not a baby could crawl through it?

'There is still much we do not know,' the narrator concluded after a good 40 minutes of whale facts and New Age music, 'but thanks to people like Mark and Caryn, we will hopefully find the answers to all the whale's mysteries.' And this is what I think about. That we didn't know much about the ocean, and now, no one will ever know. No one will ever find out if mermaids exist, or map out the deepest crevasses. Of course, I cannot stop believing there are other people alive. Anything else would be madness; statistics say there must be. But even so. How many survivors would we have to be for it to make sense to start researching the depths of the ocean?

Some people thought the reason the whale song's pitch has been going down for the past 40 years is that they've been combatting the increased noise levels from human seafaring. I wonder if the pitch will go back up. I wonder if it will be easier for them to find each other now, when they are once again the loudest things in the sea. The loudest things in the world, I'd imagine. The loudest things in the universe. Maybe.

I've never seen a blue whale. I saw a minke whale once, outside Reykjavik. I was there on a holiday filled with ash and steam. We went on a harbour safari to see whales and puffins, and we saw hundreds of the latter but only one whale. It wasn't a big whale. It was young, and seemed confused. It swam up to our boat as if asking it for directions, and then swam away in a straight line, suddenly sure of where it was going. I ate puffin that evening. *Adorable birds make for weird meat*, I thought at the time. The chicken that tastes like fish.

'We've had to debate whether or not to keep hunting them,' they told me back then. 'The nests have failed for years and years, and there are fewer than ever before.' It made the meat harder to swallow. Livery lumps of fishy chicken, sticking to my throat, forcing their way back up, weighing on my conscience. No one asked why I left so much on my plate. Now, I wish I had finished every last bit.

I have eaten zebra, kangaroo, snake, alligator, antelope, puffin, whale, cow, sheep, horse, pig, chicken, grouse, quail and a couple of types of bugs. Now, nature is restored to its natural order, and I will never taste interesting meat again. Unless, of course, I find a gun. Or a bow and arrow. Or a book on making snares.

I will never, ever, eat whale.

My blanket is damp, but I huddle up underneath it. Scram stinks, but I let him in for comfort. The world is grey and noisy, so for most of the day, I just sit and think, ignoring my body's restless jerks and twitches. I stand up. I sit down. There is much to think about. In particular: I have forgotten a word. I have searched the far and wide of my memory, I have thought through all the lyrics I can remember. I have brought up conversations, poems, TV shows and arguments until my heart turned raw and sore. I bring up every person I can ever remember having talked to and every death I've not yet grieved, but I cannot find the missing word. So I'll think and think and think, and eventually, I'm sure, I'll find it. Scram licks my cheek and I hold him close to me, bury my face in his fur. The word isn't there. I try to speak, but my voice is strange and soft, drowns in the rain, slammed to the ground by the water and wind.

'What,' I whisper into Scram, 'is that word... for feeling something will not end well... so you are... *something* about it...' I can't remember. It's such a common word. I can't find it in English, and I can't find it in Norwegian. I swallow again and again, trying to wash away the forgetfulness. I have to remember. *Someone* must remember. The word is gone. My mouth tries to speak again, but the rain hammers my voice to the ground and leaves me only a thin croak. I try again and again. I try.

It's been four days, and I need to move. There's time, but not much time. There are miles and miles to go. What if they're dying? What if I would make it there in time if I left right now, but not if I leave tomorrow? What if it is already too late... *No!* I can't think like that. I need to think of...

'Archery!' said the girl who looked like Cleopatra, the week before we kissed. 'You should come!'

I had never touched a bow before, and I knew—beyond all certainty, beyond all doubt—that I would make a complete fool of myself if I tried.

'I've only been doing it for a few months,' she told me in the pub. She smelled of flowers and sat so close that I could feel the heat from her thigh. 'But it's fun!' I didn't believe her. I've never been strong, I've never been good at sports. My big, bloated body would look out of place at the archery range, and I worried that I wouldn't even manage to draw the string taut enough to fire. Anya wouldn't be there, but several of Cleopatra's male admirers would be. How little of a threat they would find me. How little of a threat they would find my skills. But she would be there too, and no matter how hard I tried to turn her down, the sound I made was yes, yes, yes. She sat next to me on the bus there, resting her head against the window and talking quietly about a trip she'd been on to France when she was little. I couldn't stop staring at her hand. The tips of her fingers were inches from mine and the tension between us was so strong, it felt like we were holding hands already.

With beginner's luck, I hit the bullseye more than once. It was a question of steady breathing more than anything.

More than strength. More than weight. Cleopatra never took a deep breath. Each movement of her lungs was light and carefully measured, like everything else about her. She would weave in and out of visibility like a golden thread. When you noticed her, she was stunningly beautiful; when you didn't, it was hard to recall the features of her face.

Everyone projected onto her the personality they most wanted to see. Anya saw a rebel like herself, and reacted with shock every time Cleopatra did something ordinary. Most of her friends saw amplified versions of themselves or each other, a good replacement for the one who got away, a decent substitute for the parent who never called, a functioning proxy for the long-lost sister. And I saw all of that; I saw how she reflected light in every colour. She was a gemstone, cut and polished to such a shine that every side looked like a diamond, and you had to get close enough to peer through her eyes to find out what colour she really was. I wanted to get that close.

I hit close enough to the bullseye twice in a row and then a bullseye exactly. With pride and relief, I spun around and hugged her for a second. Two. Three. She laughed, and I laughed, and the admirers scoffed and sighed. I saw her then, for the first time, clear and brilliant all the way through. A week later, she would kiss me, and the day after that, we would say goodbye through tears, knowing it could never be the two of us; that this was a short-lived thing meant for memories and diaries and deathbed confessions. I had to go back to my husband, figure out how I could have fallen for a girl. She wasn't ready for a relationship. Or so we thought. Or so we said. But I returned to Norway to find everything in flames. I begged my husband to keep me. I asked him again and again.

'You are gay,' he told me. Kindly. 'It wouldn't be fair to either of us.' I wish I had got around to thanking him. He was right, like he always was, or hardly ever was before that point, unless I listened really closely. I always thought I would thank him. Write him a letter. Sing him a song. But he remarried, and I was in love, so the End came and went without any proof of gratitude.

The morning comes with sun and blue skies, but the word is still missing from my mind. I haven't slept. The keyring with the photo of us on is digging into my palm, but I clutch it harder and harder still. I hope against hope that she will send me the word. That she'll send me a sign or a memory.

'What is that word?' I whisper to her over and over, but she never replies. Scram is restless, and I finally agree to pack up our little camp and get going. I'm in a rush, I know that, but it has felt so good to have a home. Even just for a few days. Even just for a moment. My braids are still damp, so I untangle them and let my hair loose in the sunshine; it dries quickly when we start walking. I am surprised at how long it's become. I haven't cut it since the second wave, but somehow that feels both recent and endlessly long ago. Scram barks and looks at me, but I cannot find a tennis ball. We must have left the last one back at camp. For a while, I throw him sticks and branches I find along the way. Soon enough, he loses interest, and we walk quietly through the never-ending space around us.

The map has told me Denmark is only a day or two away. It fills me with excitement. Scandinavia—it's almost home. I wonder what the date is. We stop outside a little town and I dig my mobile phone out of my backpack. I turn it on, check the date, still no signal, disappointed, although I knew there wouldn't be, turn it back off, wrap it in plastic, back in the backpack. Breathe. I make a mark in my notebook. Sooner or later, I know, I will drop the phone, or the battery will run out, or something else will happen to make the date reset or disappear. Eventually, I'll have to get a calendar. Or maybe I won't.

It's the second of August. Both of my wedding anniversaries have come and gone. As far as I can remember, they felt like normal days. One must have been in Belgium. The other near Hamburg, possibly in it. I draw a cake in the dust with a stick and sketch three candles on top. I leave them to burn until the wind blows them out.

August means there's still time to get there and turn around if... if they haven't... if they aren't... August means there's still time. Scram barks at the stick, and I throw it for him. It sails through the air, spinning. Watching it makes me dizzy, nauseous. When did I last eat? When did I last feed Scram? I must remember to eat, I tell myself. Remember to eat, and don't overdo it.

The village is small but has a main street lined with shops. I cannot see a single corpse and, although I can smell them behind their curtains, it's not too bad at all. The corner shop is intact—the first time I've seen that since before the End—and I spend some time getting through the door. I don't feel like breaking the glass of the windows—it feels wrong to spoil something unspoiled. It's an old-fashioned and heavy door, but I don't mind. Nothing is too difficult when you don't have to worry about police or alarms or time. Eventually, I have an opening big enough to enter. The stench isn't too bad. There must not have been deliveries after the first wave here. My nose is runny after the storm, and I pick up a packet of tea, some lozenges, a jar of honey and some lemon juice. I rip open a pack of dog food, and Scram eats way too much.

'I'm sorry, boy,' I whisper. 'I'm really sorry.' I fill my backpack with too much food. I enjoy choosing. I drink a bottle of Coke. The sugar and caffeine hit me like a truck and I have to sit down for a while. I find a whole case of potatoes that aren't rotten at all. A few of them have started growing green sprouts, but most of them look fine. The shop has a row of trolleys, all chained together and nested up nicely. I don't have a coin but use a hammer, and soon I have one beaten apart. I fill the trolley with soft drinks and potatoes, a few onions that don't look too wrinkly, dry pasta and dog food. It takes me hours to make a hole big enough in the security gate to get the trolley out onto the street, and when I do, it's so heavy that I can barely wheel it forwards. But it's only August. August means there's time.

I thought she was planning to leave me most of that autumn. When we left my parents' house in October, after my niece's second birthday, I drew her close to kiss her and felt she had slipped away from me again.

'Love,' I said. 'I'm tired now. I can tell there's something going on and that there has been for months. Please, please tell me what it is.' Instead of joking, like she normally would, she drew a deep breath, drew me closer, and drew me a picture through the look in her eyes.

'I know we said...' she began, then trailed off with tears in her eyes. She had a couple more false starts. Each sharpened her message until it came out pointed and brittle: 'I really want a baby.'

'Okay,' I said, and tightened my grip around her, 'of course. Of course. Let's have a baby.' I wanted a baby, too. I had wanted a baby since the first time my sister placed that little ball of gratitude in my arms and told me her name was Lilly. I had held her so tenderly. I had held her so close. For the first six months that she had grown in my arms, her chubby cheeks made me forget all about the divorce that was happening in the background. She would fall asleep with her entire body pressed to my chest. She would laugh and giggle when I made faces. She became the remedy for everything. And I wanted to love my own. A year later, I was back in England with Cleopatra; two years later, I was planning to propose to her. But all the time, I had wished for a baby, while being terribly scared, terribly scarred. I had been adamant that I never wanted children.

'Of course,' I said again, because there wasn't much else to say. We had just spent four days with the little chatterbox, who loved us for existing, and for bringing her presents with Curious George on, and for spending hours with her on the floor, drawing the same six animals over and over.

'Of course.' Every minute we had spent with Lilly, I had known the time had come.

'I know I said...' I said, kissing her forehead.

'Yeah...' she whispered into my neck.

'But I think it would be okay now... I think I'm... healed, or whatever.'

She looked at me, beaming, and assumed it was she who had healed me. Perhaps it was. Perhaps it had been. We kissed and started doing our research. There was much to learn.

I wheel the trolley for days. It gives me something to focus on, something to do. I try to fill my head with the trolley, allow its edges to become mine until I can't think of anything else. It helps that it isn't perfect. The front left wheel pulls a little to the right and squeaks when I turn to the left. At some point, I cross the Danish border, but I don't really notice. I think of a book I used to love. A father and son walking through a post-apocalyptic landscape. It was dark, very dark, and it made me think the End would be dark. It also made me think the End would have people in it. And I wonder if I would have traded my End for their apocalypse, or not. They had a trolley, I have a trolley, but everything else is different. Separate worlds completely.

In theirs, people ate other people, and the world was cold and ashen. I never look over my shoulder; even if

I found other survivors, I'd have no reason to believe they would hurt me or feel the urge to eat me. There are animals. There are fish—or, at least, I assume there are. There's plant life and nature, even more of it now than there used to be. Already, every village is getting a rough abandoned look. Nothing is neat and orderly anymore. Gardens are wildernesses, parks are fields. Potted plants hanging from lampposts are brown and dried in the sun, but roads stretch through heavy, lush grass. Wild flowers press up through once-neat flowerbeds, and every tree is its own shade of green. The world is wild and beautiful, and nothing is dark but me.

We pass a pet shop, and Scram jumps up and down in excitement.

'Look!' his tail says. 'Look! Look! Look!' And his face adds, 'BALL! BALL!' so I laugh and spend some time breaking the window. It's only a small hole, but the stench that pushes through it is unbelievable. I take a step back and read the sign. They sold pet supplies and tropical fish. I gently pull out all the dog toys I can reach from the window display. Scram is impatient. He follows my hand with his head, up and down, and I'm cruel, saving the ball for last. I squeeze it and it makes a sad little squeaky sound. Scram sits down, tries to give me both paws, lies down, sits up again. More paws, turn around, sit, play dead, all the tricks! All of them! At once! Ball, please. Ball!

'Go!' I shout, and throw the ball down the street. My voice echoes between the buildings and threatens to raise the dead. I hold my breath. My throat hurts. Scram barks from down the road and speeds back with his new favourite toy. I push the trolley forward, and throw the ball when I must.

The baby became everything. We talked to the best of the best and we spent every pound we could spare. We tried for about a year. I took so many hormones that my sense of humour disappeared, and I raged at God and the world and the night for not giving me an easier time. Cleopatra was patient with me, but she looked sadder every time we failed. When we finally saw the two lines on the pregnancy test, we laughed and kissed and cried as if we'd survived impossible odds. My due date was early July. We were to have a little girl. We were to call her Emma. We filled our house with plans for things to buy and make and get.

I cannot be sure, of course. But I think she died from what they all died from. It was right at the end of the first wave, and doctors were few and far between. But we found one, eventually, who could untangle her from my insides and leave us to bury our hopes for the future. Cleopatra didn't cry, and neither did I. Not then, at least. Secretly, I think we were both relieved. Times were so uncertain, and hope was already frail. Neither of us said, 'We will try again.' Neither of us said, 'This is so unfair!' Neither of us said, 'Why us?' We just walked home with our daughter in a cardboard box, and buried her by the pond where Cleopatra and I had first kissed, and where I, the year before, had proposed on an ice-cold bench.

5

I carry grief for so many people. Those I loved, those I knew, those I met. For Laura from the German shop, whomever she was, and her grandfather. For Kobus's girls, for authors I loved, for authors I never read, for celebrities, for acquaintances and ex-colleagues. I carry grief for Cleopatra and our baby daughter. I carry grief for everyone who is no more.

No, not everyone. There are those I don't grieve. Right in the middle of my gut, behind all the sadness, there is a tiny bubble of relief. There are some I'll never have to see again. Never again walk into by coincidence, or see across a crowded street. Those I'll no longer hide from behind bookshelves in shops, or pretend not to see as I pass them. I don't grieve their deaths. It saddens me that I carry them with me at all. I wish I could empty the bubble and use it to carry more of the lovely and good-hearted people I never met. More of the people I never even heard of. In my mind, I think there are a couple of names down there, behind the sadness. A couple of people I do not mourn. But I know there's really only one name. Everyone else, I've forgiven.

I suppose there was a time I wanted children even before I became an aunt. But it's a long time ago now, and I barely remember who I was back then. I was still a virgin, and felt that was important. I was curious about sex; I thought it would be great, awesome, wonderful. I still thought I was straight. Still eagerly looking for love, still thought my lack of success was all about the guys, the chemistry, my state of mind. And I know, if I really think about it—which I never do—that the moment that made the slashes between me and my future was there, right at the end of my 17th year. His name was Lion, and to me, he was the sun.

We met online, because that's what you did back then. He said the sweetest things, and I carved them into my heart in capital letters. I asked him once how many people he had slept with, and he told me, 'Three and a half. The half one didn't really count.'

'You didn't really sleep with her?' I asked.

'No, I did... but it didn't really count.'

I should have left right then. What sort of person dismisses another human being as a half? I. I did. I became half. Like the moon, I was only ever that which he shone upon. The things he didn't see or care about were wiped out, unimportant. I turned my face to him wholeheartedly and turned my back on everyone else. I made myself half the person I used to be and felt more whole than I'd ever been before.

Eventually, he invited me to stay, or I invited myself, or neither. But I was in his small flat, and I shared his small bed.

'Nothing will happen,' he promised me.

'I'm not ready,' I said.

'I know,' he said. 'Nothing will happen.'

'I don't want to,' I said.

'I know...' he said.

'No...' I whimpered. 'You promised.' But he was already...

'So,' Kobus interrupts my thought process, the way he always does, 'I find this thought really interesting...' He walks next to me, right behind Scram. I can hear his typical steps, confident but slow. I don't turn around, but I know he's fixing me with his intense stare. Trying to figure out if I'm listening. Trying to figure out if I 'get it'.

'What?' I say. There's no natural number for how many conversations we've begun this way. The introductory 'So', which would often cut me off in the middle of a sentence or, at the very least, in the middle of a thought. And always, without fail, it was about something he found 'really interesting'. Kobus never found anything very interesting, or kind of interesting, or extremely interesting. Everything was *really* interesting, as if that wasn't a quantifier for the degree of interest but a mark of substance. Things could either be really interesting or not interesting. Real or fake. Substantial or insubstantial. Here or not here. Kobus worked in binaries of his own making.

'I read this article, the other day,' he says, and I can hear him biting his lip in the way that means he hasn't yet fully formed his idea but wants to put it out there.

'Oh yeah?' I say. I'm happy to know the dead can read. Scram looks at me, confused. He wags his tail to check if he's still a good boy. I pat his head and give him a chew toy from the trolley. He carries it enthusiastically.

'Oh yeah?' I repeat, louder, waiting for Kobus to continue. His steps are still there, but he doesn't speak. So I don't either.

...already inside me, and I couldn't think about anything but this: *I am no longer a virgin. My virginity is gone. It is lost. I lost my virginity.* Over and over like a mantra. I didn't cry until after. And he held me close and kissed me softly, and said that I was so hot, he just hadn't been able to help himself. He didn't apologise. He just explained again and again.

'If you want to leave, I understand,' he said. It was 3am and I was six hours from home, in a city where I knew only him. I was 17 and thought the night outside was dangerous and filled with people who wanted to hurt me. I forgot that those people also lived in houses. I forgot that they sometimes went to sleep. I listened to his breath and told myself he loved me. He hadn't said so. But I had. And now...

'So, I find this thing really interesting,' Kobus interrupts again. I don't reply. The silence is too much, and there's a sour taste in my mouth. I miss buses. I miss trains. I miss people arguing and the sound of sirens in the night. I try to whistle. The melody trickles out of me like water, and Scram is ecstatic.

'Oh boy!' his tail says. 'Oh boy! Oh boy! What a beautiful sound! Do it more!' So I do.

'When a panic attack sets in, it's not uncommon for people to shut down all other senses than sight,' Kobus says. 'One simply can't focus on sounds, for example, or some sounds get so amplified that you can't focus on others.'

I keep whistling. The tune is simple, and it doesn't remind me of anything. Diddle diddle di, dam dam dam, duuuuuu, diddle diddle dam, diddle diddle du, diddle diddle di. Over and over.

'And I find it really interesting,' he drones on, 'how in all of Sebald's *Rings of Saturn*, hardly a sound is mentioned. Everything is purely visual.'

Diddle diddle di, dam dam dam.

'And it makes me think,' he says, and I'm starting to recognise this conversation. It's a conversation we had years ago after a class on nature writing. That's how we met. When I signed up for a master's degree in English literature in order to come back to Cleopatra.

We had been arguing about gender and nature. Kobus could be old-fashioned. He didn't think much of women as explorers of the world. He believed that knowledge was masculine and nature was feminine, like everything else meant for conquering. Women, he figured, required translation of the world to fully understand it. Translation of the underlying meanings; translation of the ways things move and stand. He was often eagerly translating. He felt himself capable of greatness.

'It made me think that sight is the masculine sense. It's right there, in our words. "The *male* gaze", "*hawk's* eye", "eying *someone* up", "eye for an eye". The very sense of vision is fucking strong. Masculine.' He spits the words out with anger and bravado, then draws a ghostly breath.

'Green-eyed monster,' I say, for no specific reason. Diddle diddle di.

'Exactly,' he says. 'Whilst hearing, and touching, those are inherently feminine. "A *woman's* touch", "to *lend* an ear".' I can feel his eyes burning into me. 'Or like you, right now.'

'What?' I say.

'Your whistling. In all this nature writing, Sebald, McCarthy, Macfarlane, Thoreau, you have a man conquering the feminine landscape by walking and watching. You, however, are walking and filling the fucking landscape with sound. You can't conquer it with your eyes, because the landscape has turned masculine. And you do not know how to conquer a masculine landscape with your eyes. So instead,' he says, 'you whistle.'

He's wrong. I constantly keep a watchful eye on the horizon, looking for movement or artificial light. I take in all of the overgrown streets, rugged sheep and starving dogs. I keep it all in my head, I try to remember everything. The stench of every dead person I pass is safely stored in the back of my mind. Laura and her grandfather will never be forgotten. Neither will the sight of all those piles, all those towers, all those dead.

Kobus keeps walking with me for a while. He talks about how the landscape, for thousands of years, has been considered feminine, but now, for me, it has turned hostile and male. I whistle louder. Ages ago, I read that the human eye senses movement before it senses colour and shape, and a flicker to my right makes me stop.

'Shut up,' I hiss to Kobus, who doesn't. There are some fat cows on the field and some dead ones in between. What once were dairy cows are now banquets for flies. Some have died quite recently. The fat cows walk in big circles around them, their udders dried up, or perhaps still suckled by one of the two calves I can see out there. It's the same all over Europe. Cows who waited for days to be milked, until the pressure got too much or infection killed them. Then the few who survived. They're behind fences that won't hold through the winter. But then again, neither will the grass. I stare at a bloated cow who's waiting to explode in the baking sun. Flies are already feasting on her glassy, dead eyes, and I wonder if she can see Kobus.

I look past her, across the field, towards the little woods on the other side. A shadow crawls forward on bent legs. Its yellow eyes are piercing me and, at once, it knows everything. I call Scram to me and keep him close as the creature draws closer still.

'Good boy,' I say to Scram. Petting him. 'You're a good boy.' The shadow has a mane like a lion, glistening with a silvery shine. Its fangs drip with venom, or saliva, or blood, as it moves, slowly towards me. Scram whimpers.

'It's going to be okay,' I say. I can feel the creature's breath against my face, rolling in over the field. Warm. It smells of rotten cows and bloated intestines, flies, anger and dung. I hold my breath. This stench cannot enter my lungs, I know that instinctively. It will burn through them, dissolve my stomach and my bones. Like a spider, the creature will drink me dry. Leave behind a dried-out shell that resembles me a little. It's getting close, hobbles between the bloated cattle, the fat cows growing restless, sensing its presence as it passes. Scram whimpers again.

'Anyway,' says Kobus, so loudly it rings in my ears. So loudly I lose track of the creature. 'That's the important thing to remember.'

'What?' I say. Louder, quicker. 'What's the important thing to remember?' But he's already gone. I look down and notice Scram shivering. I've woven my fingers into his fur and I'm squeezing him way too tight. He whimpers, because I'm hurting him and because he doesn't know what he did wrong. I let go. Pet him, stroke him, try to rub away the hurt I just caused.

'Good boy,' I whisper. 'Good boy.' I walk quickly towards the next town. Every few steps, I look back over my shoulder. But neither Kobus nor the creature is there.

Here is the part I can't explain: despite the fact that I lost my virginity with bruises, broken promises and tears, I didn't leave the next day. I stayed for a week, and we had sex every night. I cried in the shower and told myself he loved me, but I didn't leave. I even tried to enjoy it. He went down on me, and he was good at it. He fucked like a rabbit in heat. Hard, fast, quick. Sometimes he wouldn't speak for a while after, just turn to the wall and lie there, quietly. He wouldn't answer when I spoke, he wouldn't comfort me when I cried. But when I was done and started falling asleep, he would turn around and wrap his arm around me. He would nuzzle my neck and stroke my back, and I would tell myself he loved me again until the very next night, when he would prove to me that he didn't.

Four weeks later, he called me his princess. So, naturally, I returned to him. Just one more holiday. Just a short, little break. I was sure he'd explain. I was sure he'd apologise. Instead I was fucked and fell ill. I had to go to A&E. I was in incredible pain, and frightened. They gave me antibiotics and painkillers, and he took me home and put me to bed.

'It's so hard for me to resist you,' he said, 'when you're lying here all warm, and soft, and shiny-eyed.' I couldn't resist him either. I simply wasn't strong enough. He slipped in and out of my feverish consciousness. He slipped in and out of me, over and over, until it was morning, and my fever broke.

All day, I try to think of something else, and I grow tired. I break into a bookshop and roll out my sleeping mat between the shelves. Nearby, the creature growls, searching for me with deep sniffs against the wind. Its belly rumbles and its claws scrape against the cobblestones as it patrols the street outside my door. Occasionally, it looks straight through the windows, and a yellow beam glides across the shelves, scanning the books on them. I've hidden in the back, and I keep myself busy.

I've located a map of Denmark, which is good, because my map of Germany stopped covering my tracks several miles ago. Now I learn that I've walked the wrong way. First of all, I've walked in a huge loop. The trolley has distracted me too much, and I've somehow turned around. It should have been a three-day march or so from the border to where I am now. I've spent six. And that's not even the worst part. The dotted blue line I took to mean a tunnel on the German map isn't a tunnel but a ferry crossing. I have to either swim, find and operate a boat, or make my way to the bridge 80 miles further north.

From the bookshelves, I pick out old friends and read pages here and there. Danish is almost Norwegian, and there are English books too. I skim for the word I've forgotten, but can't find it. Maybe it was never there. Neither the children's nor the non-fiction section has a book about whales, so I flip through a book called *What Can You See Along the Coast?* instead. It features a few rather small whales alongside crabs and gulls.

A squishy sound makes me look up at Scram. He's happily chewing on a teddy bear. This shop doesn't sell toys, and it takes me some time to figure out where he found it. A blue box—the lost and found. 'Did you forget me?' says the yellow note, and there are a pair of mittens and a broken Barbie doll in there. Toys that will never be picked up. They could have been my niece's. The creature outside howls until my blood curdles.

'No, Scram!' I yell and rip the teddy bear out of his mouth. He slouches back, holding a severed plush arm in his mouth. He doesn't growl, just stares at me. The arm hangs limply, dangling, lonely, and I want to take it, but

I'm suddenly scared of him. Scared of his teeth, his claws. Don't know him. Don't trust him. Don't know why this strange dog is my only company in the world. I hug the bear to my chest. 'I'm sorry you lost your arm,' I say. 'I didn't mean to...' I close my eyes. The creature is still howling. I start humming to drown it all out.

'Twinke, twinke, wiwwe staaaa,' my niece sang, making my heart vibrate and my eyes water. 'Wowa wowa hwa oo are.'

She was swaying back and forth, singing at the top of her lungs. She was two years old, and had learned that 'Twinkle, Twinkle, Little Star' had something to do with the shape of stars, but not yet connected the pointy shapes from her books to the glittering dots of the sky. She knew the song in Norwegian, but preferred it in English. She didn't understand a word of either version, she just enjoyed the way the sounds felt in her mouth. The song escaped freely and confidently. She had just unwrapped her present and seen a yellow star. It was the spontaneous reaction of a two-year-old. The velvet squid had pyjamas on. The pyjamas had a star. Do you need any other reason to sing? Isn't that reason enough?

I fall asleep clutching the armless bear. I don't name him, as I suspect he already has a name. But he helps keep the creature at bay and he doesn't seem to mourn his arm.

Neither do I. Throughout the night, I hear Scram creep closer and closer. Eventually he rests his head on my chest, like he always does. I hate that I shouted at him. I worry he will leave me. I stroke his head and whisper, 'Good boy,' but I keep the teddy hidden.

In the morning, I get ready to leave, but someone has been in my trolley. I am sure of it. One of Scram's toys, a couple of potatoes and a chocolate bar are missing. I search the ground for clues and footprints, but of course, there are none.

'Hello?' I call out into the street. My voice echoes and booms between the houses and returns empty like an aimless boomerang.

'Is anyone there?' I try again in Norwegian. It sounds strange and brittle, foreign and familiar. The sound makes my heart bleed, and I wish I was singing.

I push my voice down into my throat as if I've swallowed a sock. It's a child's imitation of Danish, I know, but I'm hoping they'll appreciate the effort. Scram sniffs doors and windows as we search street after street.

'Hallo?' Constantly calling out for the thief, willing a person to appear around the next corner, longing for a sound, a voice, proof. Every now and then, I see the grey shape of the creature dart across roads in front of us or in the corner of my eye. But it doesn't come closer, and I can't tell what it is. I wish I knew. Sometimes it seems to walk on two legs, other times it runs on four. Sometimes its face is long and sharp, other times it seems sunken and gnarled under a thin cowl. A couple of times, I cross its path. Its claws have etched scratches into the pavement, permanent marks of its stalking crawl. I don't have time to hide from it—there might be life in this town! There could be people! I search and call, I cry and beg, but I find no answers or sounds.

Darkness falls, and I start seeing the creature's yellow eyes whenever it peers at me around corners. I decide it's time to return to the shop. No one seems to have touched the trolley since I left it, but I don't stop to inspect it closer. The creature is right behind me now, and I fear it's getting ready to pounce. Tonight, I'll set up my camp closer to the window and keep an eye on the trolley.

The creature doesn't pace aimlessly back and forth like last night. It stands across the street and stares straight through the window. I can see its saliva forming puddles on the ground. Perhaps it's blood, but it makes no difference. I stay crouched behind the shelves and make my way back to my sleeping bag. The teddy is where I left it, and so are the chocolate bar, the potatoes and the chew toy I brought in last night, then forgot. Of course no one has been in my trolley. Of course there's no life in this town.

6

When we had buried our baby in a cardboard box, we stood staring at the grave for a while. The painkillers I had taken were making my head swim; I felt lonely, desperate and faint. I reached for Cleopatra's hand, but found it wasn't empty. She was holding a minuscule pair of socks. Blue, with little multi-coloured stars. Twinkle twinkle, swallow, breathe.

'I bought these...' she said, and looked at me. She felt guilty, I could tell. I nodded. From my purse, I pulled out the blanket I had carried around for weeks. The soft beige fabric was already matted and greyed from me stroking it in my bag. The rabbit's head in the middle winked at us. Stupid pink bows around its ears. Stupid rabbit, swallow, breathe. I picked the bows off and put them back in my purse.

'I...' I said, but the words weren't there. She nodded. I went down on my knees to keep myself from falling and she rested her hand on my shoulder. I wondered if my family was still alive. If they were still praying for the life in my belly. If God would let them know that there was no point in praying anymore. Cleopatra squeezed my shoulder as if she could read my mind. I kissed her hand and rested my head against her. We placed our small offerings on our baby girl's grave and walked home without saying a word. It was only a few weeks later that Cleopatra started coughing. Had I known, I would have said much more. Had I known, I would never have stopped talking.

'So,' Kobus interrupts again. It's early. The morning light is grey and sticky, and keeps me from fully opening my eyes. 'I find it interesting that you should say that.'

'Say what?' I say. Scram looks up at me and slaps the floor with his tail once or twice. He's not used to me waking up before him.

'That you would never have stopped talking. Because, again, we're seeing that strange dynamic between you—female—and sound—female.'

'I have literally no idea what you're talking about,' I say. And I mean that. 'What I was thinking,' I say before he has time to explain, 'is that if I had known she was going to...' But this hurts. I shake my head, sit up and start packing my stuff. Kobus sits in a chair in the corner of the room and talks endlessly about things I've heard him talk about before.

'And that's the thing about curries,' he says. 'The order of the spices matters. And with the lentil curry—you know which one I mean,' he says; I nod to confirm that I do, although he can't see me behind the shelf, 'the order is completely reversed.'

I place the teddy bear in the bottom of my backpack and fold up the map of Denmark. I scan the shelves one more time, looking for the word I lost, but it still isn't there. I rip out three pages of *What Can You See Along the Coast?*, the ones about small whales, and I pour a generous helping of dog food on the floor in front of Scram. The creature is nowhere to be seen, so I sit outside on the pavement, enjoying the grey morning and eating some soup from a tin. It's too salty, but I don't care.

'Kobus?' I call. 'What's that word... you know. When you know something bad is going to happen. Or at least you think it will. Or you're worried it will... so you are this something?'

'Dreading?' he suggests.

'No...' I say. 'That's not it. It's a less certain word I'm looking for.'

It's going to be a very hot day. Too hot, if I think about it, but I choose not to. The further we walk away from the sea, the hotter and damper the land becomes. The sun pounds its rays down on my skull, and the echo runs through my head. I sweat. I swallow. My mouth is dry. Again, I see myself from across the street. My suntanned skin looks like bark, my tan lines cut to white and soft wood. Weak and exposed. It's hard to breathe. Scram slinks along the shadows beside the road, panting. We rest often, and I worry about water. My head is telling me I need much more, but I can't make myself drink my entire reserve. I worry about running out. I worry about having too little. Scram laps up ditch water whenever he can, and lets every stick and ball I toss lie and wait until we catch up to it. My T-shirt sticks to my body and rubs my skin raw.

'So,' Kobus says.

'What is it now?' I snap, but I appreciate his visits, so I gather myself. 'Sorry,' I mumble, 'I'm just really warm.'

'Remember we talked about vision being the male sense?' I can't hear his steps anywhere.

'I remember *you* talked about that, yes.' I have to stop again. I lean over the trolley and shade my head with my arms.

'Is it not really interesting to you,' he says, sitting with his legs crossed on my shoulders, 'that despite being the only one here, you are still shielding yourself from the male gaze?'

I laugh hoarsely.

'Yeah,' I say. 'It really fucking is.' I strip off my T-shirt and shorts, and, after a second's hesitation, my underwear. These panties have long since played out their role anyway, and I leave them behind on the road. I have two more pairs in my backpack. I've been washing them in streams with my socks, a rotation system with increasingly long cycles. I walk on, naked except for my necklace and boots. Three steps later, I can feel the sun scorching the skin on my back. The deep contrast between my hands and my thighs makes me laugh again. My suncream is right at the bottom of my pack; I haven't used it for weeks. It burps and sputters as I squeeze out its last drops. My entire body is sticky and smells sweetly of coconut. Scram tries to lick my legs, and I have to push him away again and again.

'Here!' I say, and toss his little green ball as far as I can. He doesn't run, but keeps his eyes on it. The trolley squeaks and I think of nothing, just watch how the landscape rolls out around me. I can't see any movement except for birds and bees and a few shaggy sheep in the distance. I look back over my shoulder once, and I see the creature creeping down the road behind me. But it's far away, and moves slowly. Perhaps it is knocked out by the heat, too.

I sing. An old Frank Sinatra song, I think. Or maybe it was Judy Garland. I giggle and put extra vibrato on every word. The lyrics are sad, but the tune is chipper. My voice bends into pretend-opera, loud and round. It may have been Nina Simone.

My breasts have lost both shape and volume since I began walking, and soon it's uncomfortable to let them hang. But instead of putting my bra back on, I tear up a dry T-shirt and tie them up. A single tube of supportive fabric.

I keep singing. My sound is '60s jazz. Sweet and sugary, then deep and growly.

Scram is too hot. When we catch up with the ball, he seems to consider it for a moment or two before he picks it up in his mouth. He walks next to me, drooling and wagging his tail steadily, but low and slow. 'Hey...' it seems to say to me. 'Hey... can we, like... chill... hey...? I will, like... walk with you as long as you are walking, but, like... could we, like... chill?' A small stream cuts through the field to my right. We walk across to drink and fill my water bottles.

The creature is still far behind us and seems to be taking a break in the shadows. For a second, I worry about it, wonder if I should leave it some water. Then I remember the howl and the godawful stench of its breath, and think much better of it. It begins to move. I can see it out of the corner of my eye. Moving faster. Maybe. Quickly, I crush iodine tablets into all the bottles, just in case. Leave them to work, knowing I will have safe water in half an hour or so. But despite this caution, I crouch down on all fours and suck up as much water as I can swallow right from the stream. So thirsty. Thirsty now. The water is warm and soft. Down my throat. Into my belly. So hungry. Have I eaten? Has Scram? He jumps around downstream, chasing a little fish or a frog in the water. He splashes around happily. The grey shadow is picking up speed now, moving ever faster, straight towards me. I let Scram know we have to go. I don't feel like singing anymore, but I do it anyway.

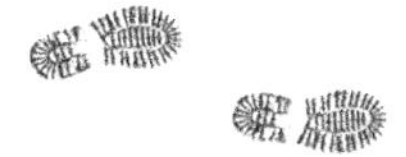

I can't remember which song it was, but I sang it slowly and softly. Cleopatra swayed gently in front of me. It was the closest she came to dancing, and I found it immensely sexy.

I had stopped bleeding. It had been over a month since the operation and only now had my body healed. The pain was gone. Or, at least, it had drowned in the pool of other pain, and I could no longer feel it. We decided to make it a celebration. To ignore the people dying around us. To celebrate survival. Celebrate health. The bottle in Cleopatra's hand was almost empty, but for each shirt button she undid, she took another deep swig. She was never particularly confident in her body. She couldn't see how incredibly perfect she was. The round bum, the perky breasts, her wide hips and slim waist. Her intense intelligence, her radiant smile, her humour, her wits, her kindness—it shone through her body and made me want her, always. She was the girl I used to draw when I was 15. She was the woman I imagined when I closed my eyes.

My long silk shirt was like a dress on her. Unbuttoned fully, now. Hanging open and revealing that little dark patch of hair, the little muffin-top. She was wearing her high stilettos. The ones that pushed her bum up and drove me crazy. She walked over to me, slowly, did a little twirl in front of me, and I reached for her. Pulled her in. Her thighs were smooth and warm against my hands. I kept humming the song as I lay down a trail of kisses across her belly. She snorted.

'It tickles when you hum like that.'

'Sorry,' I mumbled. I placed my lips firmly against her skin and wrapped my arms around her. Then I hummed loudly into her stomach. Blew a raspberry. Nibbled her side. That was who we were. We had fun. We were weird. I would make up small songs about her body, tickle her, make her giggle. She would trace my body with her fingers, give each part a new nickname, and play tic-tac-toe on my stomach, against herself and with her tongue.

'Stop, stop, stop, stop,' she said, screeching and wriggling out of my arms. She playfully slapped away my hands. Left my grip. Pushed me away. Gasped for breath. And then coughed. A deep cough. A sudden cough. A cough with an edge to it. We both froze. My arms fell. Her face fell. Everything I knew...

'So,' Kobus interrupts. I can hear his steps in the tall grass next to the road now. Rustling and bustling to keep up with me.

'Shut up,' I say, and keep singing. He doesn't.

'Go away, Kobus!' I shout. My voice echoes through me. Sheep raise their heads and stare at me. The creature howls. It's really close now.

Everything I knew shattered and jingled against the ground.

'No,' I said out loud. 'It may just have been a normal cough. Dust from the carpet. The strain of being tickled. The extreme awkwardness of that little striptease dance you did there... Let's not scare ourselves. Let's not.' She leaned into my kiss and I leaned into hers. We fucked as if it was our very last time. We experimented and played. We used our toys and our tongues and our fingers. I tried to memorise every inch of her body onto every inch of mine. We kissed each other deeply and madly. Clawed at each other. Bit at each other. Attempted to devour each other completely, merge together and become one being of pleasure and pain.

Afterwards, we made a little nest of all our pillows and blankets, and curled up in the middle like baby rabbits. She placed her head on my belly and I read to her for hours. When my voice gave in, she read to me, and we fell asleep knotted together.

'I love you endlessly,' I whispered.

'I love you more,' she replied. That night, she woke up

shivering with a fever. I gave her a mix of ibuprofen and paracetamol, and held her close until dawn.

'It might just be a cold,' I said. 'It might just be a cold.'

'Kobus?' I say, but there's no answer. The creature's claws drag through the mud behind me, a muffled metallic sound. It doesn't leap. It doesn't pounce. But it is growling and breathing heavily. Scram is still carrying his ball and, although I wish he'd chase the creature away, he doesn't seem to mind it. The stench of its breath makes me retch and tense, but I don't run. My back itches with its presence. I eventually have to crouch down behind a bush to have a wee. It watches me but I refuse to look at it. My urine is thick and brown, and smells like an old man's. I need to drink more. Much more. I stopped sweating a while ago and I know that's a bad sign. Not too far down the road, there's a village. If I'm lucky, they'll have a shop there. My mouth imagines bubbles and fizz; I would really like a soft drink. Or some juice. Water, milk, soft drink, cordial, soup, I don't care. My throat is parched and my body aches. The creature skulks ahead of me and hides somewhere in the village, lying in wait, out of the sun.

'So,' says Kobus. 'I find it really interesting how we, as humans, form relationships.'

'Oh yeah?' I say. I'm happy he's back, but I make sure not to show him. I dig out my last water bottle from the trolley and take a few sips. The water is burning hot. It must be at least 35 degrees out here, probably more in the sun. Who even knew Denmark could get this hot?

'Yeah. So. With you and me,' Kobus says, walking right next to me, now. I can almost make out his arms swinging by his sides. If I were to turn my head just a little, I'd see his feet, his beard, his glasses. 'The relationship is very mutual. You get something, I get something, and neither of us needs to screw the other over. We are equal. In a way,' he says.

'In a way,' I nod.

'But with my ex-wife. Fucking hell. We rubbed each other in all the wrong directions. Every day, sparks flying. The bloody fire brigade couldn't keep us cooled off. And yet, we stayed together for 12 fucking years. Why do you think? Why?'

I frown. 'Because you loved her?'

'No,' he says. 'Or yes. I did. But that's not why.'

'Why?' I say. My mouth is dry, and my tongue makes an uncomfortable sticky sound when I try to run it over my lips.

'Because... Actually... Fuck if I know! We shouldn't have, that's why. It wasn't even fun in the beginning. But it was fiery. And we drove each other crazy. You know?'

'Yeah,' I say. But I don't really.

'Neither of us got what we wanted from the relationship. Except we both did, because we wanted to be miserable.'

'Oh.'

'Fuck,' he says, and I can hear him light a cigarette.

'You started smoking again?' I'm surprised. He had always talked about how it had taken him years to quit, and how his health was so much better after.

'Doesn't make much of a difference now,' he says. I can hear him smiling his most triumphant smile. 'Everyone should have a vice. And an ex who drives them up the wall and turns them crazy.'

'Well... My loss,' I say. 'Too late for that, isn't it...?' I turn around to face him, but of course he isn't there.

We never really fought. Not really. My ridiculously high expectations sometimes made her feel small and useless, and her extreme sensitivity sometimes made me feel big and brutish. But we always talked it through. We talked a lot. I asked too many questions.

'Do you like this photo?' I'd ask her.

'I love it! I especially love what you've done here,' she'd say, and point to the light, or the corners, or a detail in the photo.

'Do you like it better than the one I showed you yesterday?'

'Which one?'

'I only showed you one yesterday.'

'I don't remember.'

'The one with the bird.'

'The blue bird?'

'No! It was black and white!'

'I'm sorry.'

'It's okay.' I'd show her the photo with the bird and let her look at it again.

'I like them both,' she'd say. Quieter now.

'Which do you like more?'

'Hm... the bird, maybe?'

'Why?'

'I don't know... I just do.'

'But what do you like about it?'

'The composition, the light...' And when she said this, suggesting things she thought I wanted to hear, I'd sigh. Dramatically.

'And you don't like the composition and light in this one?'

'Yes, I do... but...'

'So why do you like the bird one better, then?'

As these conversations went on, I knew I was being a bitch. I was pushing her up against the wall with my questions, not giving her time to breathe. I'd bring up photos I had shown her months ago. Knowing full well she couldn't remember them all. And then I'd ask her to compare.

I never did this to be mean and demanding, but I used to run on praise. I needed validation. Constantly.

'Please,' I would think, 'please like it. Please find me fascinating and creative. Please.' Somewhere, somewhere deep, I knew I didn't have to. She loved my work. She loved me. She adored me, looked up to me, bragged about my work at parties. She'd squeal with delight when I got a big commission. When I lost my footing, she'd talk me back, explain to me why my work was special, why my photographic 'eye' was different, why the world needed me. The praise charged me, fuelled me, filled me up. Then it would drain away. I'd empty. Desperately craving more. It all seems silly now. Such a waste of time.

Cleopatra coughed until her back hurt too much and all that escaped her were thin wheezes. Most of the time, she was curled up in my arms. Naked, warm and soft. I wished that I could wrap myself around her and keep her safe. I wished that I could drain her lungs of stickiness and fill them with fresh air. I wished I could make her feel better, wished I could save her life. But all I could do was hope, and pray, and pour water into her mouth. I tried to keep her fever down and carried her to the loo when she needed it. With a soft flannel, I washed her body clean of sweat and tears, and I hid my own whenever I could.

She drifted in and out of sleep, and when she woke, she asked questions. She asked about our baby girl, and I told her I had felt her kicking just a few moments ago. Twice, she woke up crying for her mother. She begged me to call her up.

'I just want to hear her voice,' she sobbed, 'please, I miss her so... Please.' Her pleases were sore and childish. They scratched deep in my heart and made my blood feel too hot for my body.

'Soon, baby,' I would say. 'Please. You just need to rest a little. Please, just rest.' My pleases were desperate and hollow. They carried nothing but noise and did nothing to soothe her. I would make her lie back down and drift away from me again.

On the third day, I started reading to her. Page after page after page after page. She slept through most of it, but when she was awake, she would silently mouth words she knew were coming. I read all of her favourite books. I read until I fell asleep myself. When she woke me up, coughing, I would reach for the book and keep going until sleep washed over me again.

'I wish I didn't have to leave you soon,' she whispered as the sun went down on the fifth day.

'You're not going anywhere,' I said, and kissed her forehead.

'You're lying,' she said and looked at me. 'I love you endlessly...' She started gliding down into sleep again. 'But you are lying.'

'In a way,' I whispered when I was sure she wouldn't hear me. 'But not really.'

7

There are two corpses outside the shop. They're slouched against the wall, like teenagers waiting for adulthood to roll up and let them get into the passenger seat. I think one of them was a woman. There's gold and silver glimmering around her skeletal neck, and two metal disks on her shoulders that I think were once earrings. These bodies are picked clean by weather and animals. Only a few slivers of tissue here and there remain. Slightly more beneath what's left of their clothes, but even the clothes are mostly torn and shredded, perhaps now the padding of a thousand rats' nests. The girl's left leg is missing. There are tooth marks on the bone that pokes out from her skirt. I look at Scram, who looks back at me, innocent as the sun. He never disturbs the bodies. He wouldn't disturb these two. At least they don't smell much.

I use a stick to grab her bag. I'm relieved I can't find a name inside, because I don't want to remember. There's an MP3 player, though; I put it in my pocket. Her makeup bag is full of expensive-looking stuff and a handful of miniature perfume bottles. Lipsticks range from bright coral to dark plum, but the eyeshadows are all variations of beige. She doesn't need her name inside the bag, I realise—her name is Lone. It shines at me from her neck, gold cursive caught by the sun. Her hair is long and brown, and all I know about her is that she cared a lot about her appearance. I wish her hair wasn't torn off her head and spread across the parking lot. I wish her leg wasn't missing. On a whim, I open one of the perfume bottles and let a few drops fall onto her body. There's nothing left of her to put makeup on, but I slip a tube of lipstick into my backpack and put the rest of them back in her bag. Her perfume lingers in the air.

I wonder how old she was. Her clothes suggest 18, but I've been fooled before. I wonder if she ever had a Lion. If she ever moved her life from one city to the next, hoping to get closer, hoping that she loved him. Maybe she found a small flat in a quiet street and maybe she took a job she hated, loathed with every fibre of her being, just so she could stay. Just so she could try out her new personality in a new city. Somewhere no one knew her. Somewhere no one cared.

I wonder if she found herself lonely. If she found that her Lion didn't answer his phone or come to see her a single time. I wonder if she had a miscarriage and was too scared to call for help. Maybe she woke up on the living room floor, bloody and faint and alone. Maybe she found a tiny, tiny foetus in her underwear. A little alien with little hands and little fingers. Perhaps she, too, wondered what to do with it, couldn't make herself flush it, and ended up burying it in the flowerbed of a nice woman up the street, because everywhere else seemed too hostile. Or perhaps that was just me.

Perhaps it was just me who felt relief and sadness to be one and the same. Sad because I had lost something I didn't know I wanted. Relieved because of all the things it would have crushed and torn apart.

Perhaps it was just me who told myself, 'I don't want children. Not now. Not ever,' so loudly and often that I believed it to be true. Maybe she never was too young to recognise the difference between a baby being impractical at this point in her life, and a baby being impractical forever and ever and ever. I'm sure she'd have made a wonderful mum. I'm sure it was just me.

I open one can of every soft drink in the supermarket. Take a little sip of each. I sort them in order of flavour, drink the worst ones first, save the best for last, the way I've always done—then I think better of it and get some more of the best ones. I grab a mixing bowl from a shelf and pour in two bottles of water for Scram. He tries to empty it, which worries me, so I tip it all out and add just a little at a time. We stay for hours, drinking slowly. The creature isn't here, but occasionally I hear its scratchy steps on the flat roof above us, slowly baking in the sun.

The shop is big and cool. The concrete walls keep the heat out while huge skylights let the light pour in. I wade through the rows of shelves and read names out loud, familiar and strange. Most of the displayed cheeses are long gone. Thick blankets of mould stretch under cling film and plastic wrap. Some of them bulge and threaten to burst. But there are a couple of huge waxed wheels on display, and I cut through the first with great hope. It's mature. Very mature. But it's the best thing I've eaten in days, weeks, months. I find a couple of jars of olives and some beef jerky. Stack the cheese wheels by the door with bottles and bottles of water and soft drinks.

'We've got to keep hydrated,' I tell Scram. 'Otherwise we'll die.' He's gnawing on a treat I gave him and doesn't look up.

'This is important, Scram. Are you listening?' I ask. He looks up at the sound of his name, and that's good enough for me.

'Good,' I say. 'Good boy.' He would make a great picture right now. The natural light, the slight sway in his back. I miss my camera, but only a little.

I read magazines and gather food. Every now and then, I go outside to check the temperature, but it's still too hot to walk. My bum sticks to the cold floor in the shop, and every inch of me is covered in goosebumps, so I get dressed again. I expect Kobus to say something about it, but he hasn't said a word for a while.

'I also don't think we eat enough,' I say to Scram. 'I'll bring some more food, but you have to help me remember. I don't know when you get hungry. So you have to say.'

I walk down the baking aisle, open bags of flour and pinch it between my fingers. Pick the ones I like the best, some sachets of dried yeast and a big box of salt.

'I'm going to start making us some bread,' I say. Scram is still by the entrance, so I raise my voice a little. 'We have cheese now, so we can have proper pilgrims' lunches. With fresh bread. Won't that be nice?' My voice sounds loud and light in the cold room. I hear Scram's tail thumping against the floor in response.

They have a good selection of mixing bowls, and I pick a light one. My backpack's getting too heavy and the trolley's slowing me down. It doesn't matter, yet, but it will.

'Good,' I say again. 'Good boy. And what would a pilgrimage be without some wine?'

I automatically go for the mid-range, then change my mind. I search for a 2008 Rioja, my favourite year, but they don't have any, so I settle for a 2017 and a 2021, still vintage but not as grand. I stack them on top of the cheese wheels. There's way too much food. The trolley will be too heavy, I know, but I can't pick out anything to leave behind.

The sun is lower and a mild breeze kicks up. I load the trolley with all my treasures and walk. Looking back a couple of times, I see the creature is still on the roof, struggling to get down. It's still really warm, and I decide, again, to walk in the nude. I feel good. If I could get another tattoo right now, I would. Something to commemorate this moment. I would get myself drawn naked but still in my heavy hiking boots, pushing a trolley full of loot, singing at the top of my lungs. Singing? Yes. I imagine the tattoo, my mouth clearly open, my head thrown back and my chest full, singing. I sing and sing, all the songs I remember.

The evening is long and warm this far north. The moon is full and white, and I could walk all night if I wanted to. But I stop at the side of the road and make some bread dough. I weigh the flour carefully in my hand, stir in the yeast and some salt. I do the water by eye measure and mix with my hands. A sticky, gloopy mess. It glues my fingers together and makes me feel dirty. But I persevere. And then—magic happens.

'I like giving the dough time to grow up,' my father said. 'You were quite wobbly yourself when you were a baby.' He stretched the dough, folded it back on itself, turned it 90 degrees and repeated the motions. Over and over and over and over.

'Bread needs some time to be a baby, then a toddler, and then a teenager,' he said. 'And that's when you leave it to figure things out by itself for a while.'

I sat on the kitchen counter, dangling my feet. This was my favourite part of watching him bake; it always had been. The rhythmic, steady kneading was comforting, hypnotic, and I loved watching the magic happen. The dough started off like lumpy mud. Thick and sticky and loose. Then, slowly, with each new pull and each new fold, it became smoother and more elastic. In the beginning, it would tear a little with every stretch; now, it held together in long strands. My dad patted it together and dropped the smooth dough back into its bowl. The surface was even and sleek like a mushroom cap. He looked at me and took a deep breath. His beard was streaked white with flour and age. He looked small.

'If this is what you need to do,' he said, 'this is what you do. If this makes you happy, we will be happy too. It will take some time getting used to, I think. And... well... You know it's not what we would choose for you.' He closed his eyes and wiped his forehead with the back of his hand. Flour and dough left a trail along his wrinkles. It made him look older than he was. I wanted to yell at him to clean it off, but I bit my lip.

'Okay,' I said. 'You can have time. Of course you can.' He wrapped the bowl in plastic and left it to prove.

'With bread,' he said, 'it is often like this. You leave the dough to figure things out, and when you come back, it is big and inflated, but things aren't properly distributed inside, and it looks nothing like bread at all. Of course it doesn't. When you just leave the dough, it only grows; it doesn't stop and consider what shape it is meant to be. So you have to knock it back a little, shape it and let it rise back into its real shape. That's how you get good bread.'

I smile. 'You think I'm ready for my second proving, Dad?' I ask him.

'It seems like it...' he says and starts wiping off the counter. 'So... you are sure about this?' I am staring down into the bread bowl, trying to catch the dough rising.

'Yeah...' I say. 'I am.'

'And you wouldn't consider... staying married to David?'

'No,' I say. But this is a lie. I asked him to keep me. More than once. 'It wouldn't be fair on either of us,' I say after a little while.

'I suppose not,' he says. Then sighs and tosses a new handful of flour onto the counter. 'I think I'll make some rolls too.' I knew he would do just that.

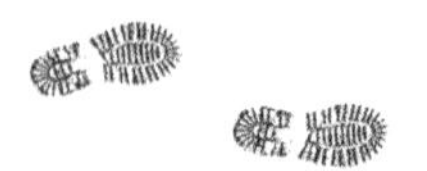

I leave the dough in my new bowl to rise. I didn't grab any cling film, so I just put one of the cheese wheels on top. There's a small wooded area nearby, and I gather sticks and twigs to build a fire. There's a deer grazing a bit further up in the field. I can see her clearly in the moonlight, but she seems to think I can't, and just looks up occasionally to check we aren't coming closer. Scram eventually can't take the excitement and shoots after her.

'No!' I yell, and he cowers for a fraction of a second, but other instincts are much stronger than the respect he holds for my voice. The deer runs; Scram runs. I'm so lonely it could break my heart. I stand absolutely still and stare into the darkness, hoping that every crack and creak I hear is Scram returning. The bundle of firewood grows heavier by the minute, but I can't make myself go back to the road without him. Not yet.

It grows darker. A pair of yellow eyes is approaching between the trees, and this is what I need to get moving. I run back to camp and get the fire going, keeping a heavy branch nearby just in case I need to defend myself. Just in case.

I prefer to make bread with cold water rather than the lukewarm water every recipe asks for. Cold water makes the dough rise more slowly, and that's good. You never want to rush your dough; the flavour is there in the waiting. But now, the waiting leaves me idle and frustrated. I try to fill the empty space inside me with wine. It works for a while, but I can smell the creature now.

'Kobus?' I say out into the air. 'Kobus?' I imagine the scene. Centre stage: a lone, naked wanderer in the woods. Stage left: a beast approaching. This is the beginning of a story I don't want to hear. With my eyes firmly shut, I try to remember the traditional story of *Little Red Riding Hood*. The only version I can bring to the surface is the soft version, the version with the happy ending. The wine is running through the cracks in my mind, highlighting all the holes and empty spaces. How can I keep carrying with me a story I don't remember? Sorrow and grief for all the stories I've lost. The ones I never knew. Swallow. Breathe. The creature's breath is warm against my neck. I hear it open its mouth. Now it'll bite, I think. I shiver and feel my body arch away from its jaws. My neck feels cold. I can't straighten out my arms or sit upright. Arch away. Huddle together. Any second now, it will all be over. This second is my last, so is this, so is this. But then the bread dough has reached twice its size, so I shake myself free from the terror and knock it back into the bowl.

My father was so many things. A farmer from the day he was born, destined to take over his father's farm, his grandfather's legacy, his great-grandfather's life's work. He was a maths teacher when 'progress' thought it time for farmers to go big or go home. A farmer and a teacher for a while. Then a passionate hobbyist baker, a yacht salesman, team leader and—for a few brief months that haunted us for years—a ventriloquist. He was many things, my father, but a Christian over all.

He loved his literature. He delved into Ibsen and Hamsun and all the great Norwegian depths. But nothing in English. Few things translated. He raised me on quotes from *Peer Gynt*, and taught me to appreciate the priest's sermon with a deep and heartfelt love, even before I knew what a sermon was, even before I understood the significance of the sermon in *Peer Gynt*'s story.

My father baked bread every Sunday. Enough for all of us, enough for the week. I would sit on the counter and watch him, and sometimes I'd help him shape the rolls, or brush the breads with egg-wash or milk. He'd tell me the same stories over and over. This meant I knew exactly where to laugh, where to make intelligent comments; it made me feel like he was proud of me for 'getting it'.

'And then there's this scene after Peer meets the mysterious passenger—' he would start, and I knew what was coming. The drowning baker. '—where Peer and the baker are both holding onto the wreckage of the stern, after the ship has sunk. They battle over who should survive...' I nod. I know. I've heard this all before. 'The baker has children he needs to feed, and he begs Peer to show mercy. But Peer manages to shove the baker into the water, because Peer is a selfish man and cares about no one but himself.

'"I'm drowning," the baker says, and Peer holds him up by the hair on his neck and says, "Quick! Pray the Lord's Prayer. You don't have long, so you should probably skip to the important bits."' My father would scoff and shake his head at this stupidity, so I would too, without knowing why.

'But the poor baker can't remember,' he'd continue, 'so he says the only bit that comes to mind. "Give us this day our..." he starts, and Peer mocks him for it. The baker is drowning, after all; bread hardly seems important.

"Give us this day our daily..." the poor baker repeats, because it's the only part he remembers. "It's easy to see you were a baker," Peer sneers at him. And as the baker is going down, he gasps, "Give us this day..." and then he disappears in the waves. Peer says, "Amen lad! You were yourself up to the end."

'But maybe,' my father would say, and I could mouth the rest with him if I wanted to, 'the baker had made peace with all the other bits of the prayer. Maybe he was not worried about temptation or forgiveness, or the return of the kingdom. Maybe the only thing he worried about was food for his children. When you don't know where your next bite of bread is coming from,' my father would sigh—this pondering usually coincided with the bread dough receiving its last few folds, smooth and ready to prove, 'it sure stays on your mind.' I would nod and smile as if I understood, but I wouldn't for many years. Unless you've been really hungry—the type of hungry that runs through your body and eats off your soul—there's a lot you won't understand.

A few years later, I read *Peer Gynt* myself for the first time. I kept waiting for the baker to appear—one of the most important characters, from my understanding of the text. But when he finally showed up, he wasn't a baker at all. He was an insignificant cook, who came and went in a matter of pages, but drowned without remembering the Lord's Prayer. I never confronted my father with this. It would have changed too many things.

I leave a flat stone in the fire until it's scorching hot. I stretch small balls of bread thin and flat, and bake them on its surface. They pop up like naans and are sweet and chewy with just the slightest taste of charcoal. I eat two right away and pack up the rest for tomorrow. I should pick up a bigger saucepan. It won't be so hard to bring one with me now that I have a trolley.

I think of my father's baker's oven. He made it himself for his 60th birthday. Put it together in the cellar, brick by brick. Then he immediately started building a smaller one in the garden, just for fun. I think about fresh-from-the-oven bread with honey. I think about my mum's strawberry jam. I think about Cleopatra's nose, kissing in the rain, and Facebook, and fast food, and Lilly, Lilly, Lilly. Before I know it, I'm crying like a baby. I reach for Scram, who isn't there. I open my second bottle of wine.

'I love... you baby,' Cleopatra whispered. Her breath caught between words and there was a constant gurgle from her chest. But it was a good moment. Hours before, she had stared at me in terror, crying and begging.

'Please,' she had whispered. Looking over her shoulder as if Death himself was standing in the corner and she didn't want him to hear. 'Please. Help me!' I held her as she started sobbing, fighting back the tears in my eyes.

'Why aren't you helping me?' she croaked, weeping and coughing herself exhausted. 'I don't want to die.' I kissed her forehead and held her tighter, desperate, hurting, tearing apart. 'Please, don't let me die.'

'I'm sorry, baby,' I whispered. Almost without a sound. 'I'm so sorry.'

'Please,' she begged again, and I held her and rocked her and whispered the same things over and over: I know, baby, I know. I'm sorry, baby, I'm sorry. I was all out of lies and could do nothing but wait. Wait for her to fall back asleep. Wait for her to not wake up.

Now, however, she seemed awake. Clearer and brighter and present. She was burning up despite the ibuprofen I'd made her swallow, her eyes were shiny and her cheeks deep red. For the first time in a while, she managed a proper cough. Deep and rattling from the bottom of her lungs. She gagged on the phlegm and mucus.

'I love you too,' I said. 'More than anything. I love you.' She brushed my cheek with a limp hand.

'Read me one more book?' she whispered. I nodded. Swallowed. Nodded again.

'Which one?' I asked. My voice was almost steady. She took a long time to answer. When she did, the answer came rolling from far away and way beyond.

'You choose...' she said. 'I don't mind.' I looked for the longest book I could find. I looked for her favourites. I looked for mine. Every second spent by the bookshelf was a grain of sand slipping through my fingers. *Choose a book. Any book.* I grabbed *The Hobbit*, it would do, and I curled up next to her in our tattered nest.

'Here we go,' I said, and cleared my throat. I think I heard her whisper, 'My love, my love,' but I cannot say for certain.

At night, I pray for a different ending. I pray for the world to have gone down in flaming screams of despair, instead. To have left nothing and no one behind. I beg any god that still lingers around to turn back time and start over.

Earthquakes. Super volcanoes. Zombie apocalypse. Nuclear war—let us wipe ourselves out, I think. *Let the polar caps melt and the oceans wash over us. Let there be asteroids. There are so many horrible ways you could kill us all,* I repeat, over and over, *pick an option. Any option. Just please, please, pick again.* But all the gods have crept up to their mountains and, like me, they run on recognition, appreciation and praise. They will get none from me. They've starved themselves thin and transparent. I see through their lies and their promises. But like all politicians, they refuse to back down.

'What is done is done,' they seem to say.

'But there is no one left to believe in you,' I rage at the sky.

'You're left,' says God. I can hear her voice clearly like a thunderous skip in my heartbeat. 'We only really need one.'

'Psychopaths,' I mumble. We've had this discussion before.

8

I expect Scram to be there when I wake up, but by mid-day, he has still not returned. Denmark has already taken too much of my time, I have to move on, but I find myself frozen to the ground, lying on my side, unable to stir or stand. The creature is resting its fangs on my neck and I'm too scared to take a deep breath. What if it wakes up and remembers itself? What if it breaks through my skin? Its breath makes me shiver, sending currents of impossible fear through my body. Even my shadow hides, and everything is white and still. I stand up, not looking, not thinking, not feeling. Nothing moves but me.

Packing up takes longer than usual. My body is heavy and wine-soaked and waiting. Everything I move from the ground to the trolley is as heavy as lead. I drink Coke and water, eat bread and cheese. Should walk, should be walking, should have been walking, but I wait and wait and wait. The creature is biting down slowly, slowly.

'Scram?' I try to call, but it comes out as a whimper. I am angry he's left me. Scared he won't come back.

With every page I read, Cleopatra's breathing became slower and wetter. I didn't put the book down, not for a second, just read and read and read. Her breath grew so faint I could barely hear it. A hoarse groan, a rasping shiver, a gurgled whisper, then nothing at all. I didn't look up from the pages. The world grew quiet and the only sound left was my thick, croaky voice, reading louder and louder, telling myself the volume was drowning out the sound of her dwindling breaths. I clutched her hand in mine. It was limp and pale and hers and cold. With every sentence, it grew colder and colder, but I didn't let go.

Every character had its own voice. Some I made speak slowly and deeply, others were fast-paced and high-pitched. Dwarves had resounding voices and a slight Welsh accent; the elves' accent was softer and rounder. They pronounced each word like a little treat. But even the elves slowed down and whispered away as the truth got harder and harder to muffle. When I got to the final chapter, the thought of the end being just a few pages away overwhelmed me. I clutched her hand and screamed.

I screamed until I didn't have a single sound left inside me.

I screamed until there was no scream, just a sound that turned quiet and breathless.

I gasped for air as my heart shattered, broke and splintered, then crashed.

The world was filled with broken hearts, so there was no room for mine. The shards filled my lungs and cut me like needles, ripped me apart and pinned me to the ground. I screamed until my mouth filled with blood and my soul called out for death or salvation. There wasn't a tear left in the sky, and none of the gods were listening. There was no compassion left on Earth, no one to care but me.

'I'm sorry for your loss,' says Kobus. He's sitting on the back of the creature, pulling it away from me.

'Thank you… I'm sorry for yours,' I say. The creature growls and snaps at him. I can hear them wrestling but I don't turn around.

'Thanks,' he pants. 'But it was different for me. You know that.' His voice is strange. I can't quite remember its cadence or tone.

'Oh yeah…' I say. 'Can I… Do you need a hand?' He doesn't reply right away. It sounds like he's losing.

'You decide,' he says. His voice is like my father's. There's no South African twang left. None of his arrogant certainty.

'Do you remember—' I say out loud. The creature snarls. '—the time we went on that walk with our class?' It's the first thing that comes to mind. It's not a strong memory, but I go with it. 'I was falling behind, because I was too heavy and slow.'

'I remember,' Kobus gasps. Or perhaps it's the creature.

'Our teacher had a dodgy map, or perhaps dodgy navigation skills, who knows, and we were walking the long way around. We should have been back ages ago. Everyone was hungry and grumpy.'

'Yes,' something hisses.

'You stayed behind with me, and we shared the oatmeal cookies Cleopatra had made me and the orange you'd brought. It was sunny. The orange was the sweetest I'd ever tasted, and we talked about going on pilgrimages. We talked about walking the Icknield Way.'

'Do you remember?' I say. I get no answer.

'I remember,' I say louder.

'Good,' says Kobus. He sounds like himself again. Thick accent, definitive answers. The way I like him. The way he annoys me.

'This is kind of a pilgrimage,' I say.

'Really?'

'Yeah. Kind of. You know... I'm putting into my body what my soul wants to achieve, and making my body do what my soul can't. Or something.'

'Aha,' says Kobus, in that way that signals he is completely uninterested, and has something else on his mind. 'So,' he says, as I knew he would, 'I find it really interesting that you are so scared of forgetting.'

'I don't want to talk about it,' I say.

'Then why am I here?' he says. And because he has a point, and because I don't know where the creature went, I decide it's time to get going. I keep my eyes wide open, look for any sign of movement. The day is quiet and still. I clutch the stone in my pocket, and walk.

I clung to her body for a long while. I kissed her cheeks and lips and forehead, and stroked her neck the way she liked.

'Come back to me,' I whispered. It came out as a whimper. I cried and begged again.

'Come back to me. Please. Please come back.' She had salty flakes on her cheeks from where my tears had dried on her skin. Everything was too quiet and my lungs were leaking air. A constant pressure where my heart had been. A shrinking, pressing, cutting feeling, like drowning or losing your breath.

'Come back to me. Please. Please. Come back.'

Several times, I thought I saw her eyes flicker, sensed small movements under her papery eyelids. I shook her and begged her to wake up.

Maybe, I thought, this was the nightmare. Perhaps she was awake in our real life, waiting for me to wake up. Waiting for our baby girl to be born. Waiting for summer to come. Perhaps all I needed to do was wake up, and then our life would go on like before. Wake up. Wake up. I pinched myself until I bruised. I slapped my cheeks and splashed water in my face. Eventually, it did wake me up, and I realised I hadn't slept for days. I rested my head on her chest and wrapped her arms around me, crying myself into restless sleep. I slept until all hope was lost.

When I woke up, the girl who looked like Cleopatra was no longer there. The dead body's eyes had sunk into their sockets and its cheeks were hollow and pale. I tried to move its arms but they were frozen in place, awkwardly angled where they had fallen off me during the night. I felt nothing, and there were things I needed to do. Things that had to be done. The body would start smelling soon—or perhaps it already had. I heaved it out of our nest. Cleopatra's space was empty and cold, and I didn't want the body anywhere near it.

By now, the third wave had spread across our town and left it breathless. There had been no one but me at the last two town meetings, so when I stepped outside and met no one else, I knew the world had become impossibly big.

It was a lovely day. Our neighbour's ginger cat ran up to me and rubbed its head against my legs. Cleopatra used to love him, so I took the time to stop and pet his head a couple of times.

'She's gone,' I said, and he pushed his nose against my fingers in sympathy. Birds were singing at the tops of their lungs and, at the end of the street, a murder of crows was picking merrily at a corpse. Wild rabbits shot across the path in front of me as I made my way to our baby daughter's grave. The small blue socks marked the spot. Digging was slow, but I quite enjoyed it. Within minutes, I was sweaty and sore. I dug through the soil, which smelled strongly of early summer, hacked at roots, made the walls as sharp as I could, moved away rocks and gravel. These are good graves, I thought. Good graves.

It had grown dark long before I finished. I considered going home and continuing in the morning. Going home now, so I wouldn't have to walk home alone in the night. But what threat did the night pose, now? No one would be hiding in the shadows. No one would be lurking with sinister motives. There would be no drunkards, rapists or thieves.

The thought of allowing the body to spend another night in the flat was chilling, and I felt sure Cleopatra wouldn't have wanted it. She was always so concerned with keeping it tidy and clean. I certainly didn't want the body there, so I kept digging until I was ready, kept digging until I could bury her right.

I kick up stones as I walk and steer the trolley over the biggest potholes I can see. I need to make sure there's sound or movement that isn't my own, that isn't just me. Denmark is easy to walk through.

When you grow up in Norway, there are a few things you know about Denmark from the day you are born. Denmark is flat, you know. Its highest point is no higher than the average Norwegian mole hill. Denmark has red hot dogs and bright red salami. Danish people have the reddest faces and their red soda is sweeter than sugar. Denmark has liquorice toppings for ice cream, and rests on the other side of a really exciting ferry ride.

On the ferry, you can get change from your parents to play slot machines. There are overly salty chips served by smiling ladies who speak a mixture of all the Scandinavian languages at once. Red-faced Danes will stumble into you, burp in your face, and give you a handful of sticky money not to tell your parents. The same people will often throw up in the halls, if the sea is rough or the hour is late. You know that Denmark has more bacon than Norway. So much, so much more. I think about these things as I walk. When I have thought them once, I think them again. The sun is too slow, grinding across the sky.

I eat my lunch on a car that's parked by the road. Its roof is burning hot, and I feel like I'm being grilled. All of my water is warm, and my hangover makes it feel thick and gluey in my throat. The roof of the car heats up my bread, and I nibble at olives and cheese. Birds and bees and a really fat squirrel fill the landscape with movement and sound. I take pictures in my mind, and think about nothing and nothing else. Scram is approaching in the distance.

Scram is approaching in the distance! I rub my eyes and sit up straight. It's him! It's him! It's him! He's not alone. There's another dog behind him—a smaller dog, but another dog, still. I stay on the roof until they're almost here. Then I stand in the middle of the road, towering as they approach.

'Hnnnnnnnnnn?' I say. Just a low growl as they step closer. 'Hnnnnn?' Scram dips. He comes forward with his head down and his tail between his legs.

'Nnnnnnnnnnnnn?' I say again, and he lies down in front of me, rolls over on his side, exposing his bulging belly. He doesn't meet my eye. There is blood in his fur, and brambles; it's going to take me forever to get them all out. I'm so happy to see him, I don't mind the upcoming grooming time.

We get the greetings out of the way. The other dog stares at me, takes a step forward. Two. She is absolutely beautiful. Short-haired and sleek. She's wearing a collar, something Scram has never done. I stare her straight in the eyes. She breaks eye contact. Lowers her head. Sits down and stays there, looking to the side. I sit down between them. Ruffle Scram's fur.

'I missed you, boy,' I say. 'I really, really missed you.' He licks my hands and cheeks, and the stench of raw meat makes me nauseous. I name the newcomer Lady. She looks proper, refined—a well-educated dog.

'Hello, Lady,' I say and stretch out my hand. She's cautious. Smells my hand for a long time. I don't reach for her. We have all the time in the world. 'Do you want to come with us for a while?' I pour them some water and they both drink greedily.

Lady eventually lets me pat her a little, but she won't let me touch her collar. She snaps at my hand and gives a brief bark. The anger I feel comes from nowhere and I push her to the ground, growling and showing my teeth. As soon as she calms down, I let her go.

'I'm sorry, girl,' I say. 'I'm sorry.' I fish out the tag dangling from her collar. She doesn't snap at me this time, but eyes me suspiciously. It has no name, just a phone number. I turn on my phone and try to call it three times. It doesn't even dial. It doesn't even beep. I open a tin of liver and place it in front of her to make up. The blood around their mouths makes me think they don't need it, but I don't know what else I can do. I wonder if she'll be able to keep up with us. She's shorter than Scram, and preened. She doesn't look sturdy or strong. But what do I know, really? Who am I to judge? I rolled out of Britain obese and lacking. *Look at me now*, I think as they eat. *Look at me now.*

'So, what would you want me to do with you?' I asked Cleopatra as soon as I got through the door. It was pitch black, so I lit all the candles I could find. We had tried to use them sensibly, save them up so we would have light in winter. This was not the time to care.

The body was softer now, and its limbs lay heavy on the floor. I dragged it into the bathroom and pushed it into the tub. I washed its hair with her favourite shampoo and washed the body in bottled water. Soaped and rinsed until the last week's illness and sweat ran down the drain. I wrapped the body in towels and dried it off slowly. The bathroom smelled faintly of bath bombs, and the wisp of memory made me smile.

She would draw me a bath every Sunday. We'd drink red wine and talk about my photos and writing. Projects I was planning and places I wanted to go. Whenever I sold a new story or got a new commission, she'd buy me bath bombs as rewards.

I poured myself a glass of wine and got back to work. I tried to think of something to talk about, but my words had dried up completely. I looked through our drawers for her best underwear. I didn't go for comfort. She would want to look good. I chose the red bustier I got her for our anniversary. She had said she felt sexy in it. And she was. A black garter belt, the laced one with red bows. Black lace panties and a new pair of stockings. They were still unwrapped and never worn.

'What would you want to wear?' I called into the bathroom. The clothes all looked the same in the darkness. The only thing that stood out was the silvery sheen of the grey dress. The one she had worn on our first date. It was a concert in Glasgow. We had been sitting on a bus all night long. Slept on each other's shoulders, feeling close and strange. I had been back in Norway for months, but what we had thought was our final goodbye had turned into a loud 'maybe' as my marriage fell apart. The maybe became a possibly, and the possibly became a probably, then a probably soon, then a definitely tomorrow, and then we had arrived in Glasgow without knowing what to do. We checked into the hotel, and when we got to the room, we both pretended not to see the double bed. It was just there. A piece of furniture holding no hope or meaning.

We had bagels for breakfast, went back for a nap, got ready for the evening's concert. She had stopped my heart when she came out of the bathroom wearing her dress. She looked like a fantasy. Something I had made up. She was cute, and sexy. Proper and wild. My stomach fluttered, my hands were clammy, I could feel my smile reach my eyes.

We left for the concert, a bit nervous and shy. We were tense, and she was beautiful. We were going to see my favourite artist. Cleopatra had been falling in love with her and me at the same time. I had never seen her live before, and was worried the strangeness of it all would make me too self-conscious to enjoy it. But it didn't. Cleopatra held my hand, and we were suddenly gay in public. My heart could have burst with all the feelings of the night, but it didn't, not then, it just soared. We talked about Cleopatra's painting and how she wanted to go to Ethiopia to volunteer at a maternal health clinic her aunt worked at. We talked about her dream of becoming a journalist, and the many different ways she wanted to make the world better. I listened in ways I didn't know I could, and admired in ways I'd never tried before.

'The grey dress?' I called again. She didn't answer, so I assumed it was okay. Pink cardigan, too. I didn't want her to be cold. I dressed the body slowly. It was much more difficult than I had imagined, and soon I was frustrated, sweaty and hot. The stockings stuck to still-damp legs. The bustier required me to tip the body over and wrap my arms around it to fasten the clasps in the back. But I didn't stop. She never left the house without double and triple-checking her appearance. She was never vain. Just self-conscious. I didn't want to let her down.

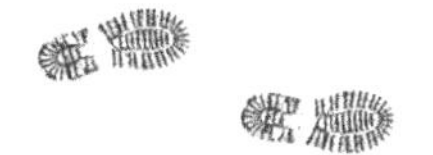

We walk until night falls. I know, somewhere inside me, that I'm punishing Scram for running away; that I want him to feel all the miles we need to make up for, the time we've lost. Lady whines a little, but she doesn't fall behind. I throw them sticks and feed them snacks, and I tell them all about *The Longest Journey.* I don't know where the memory of that film comes from, and I know the memory is fragmented and flawed. Even as I talk, I know I've forgotten crucial parts of the story, as I'm fairly sure there was a homecoming involved, or possibly a brown van. They don't mind. Lady isn't listening, and Scram doesn't care. He just looks at me and wags his tail whenever I start speaking.

'We are such good friends,' his tail says. 'Right?' And as I keep talking, he keeps wagging.

'Oh yes,' he wags, 'we are such good friends. Nothing bad has happened, we are A-OK. Oh yes! I'm a lucky boy.'

I tell the story slowly. One small fragment after one small fragment in the order I remember them, chronology be damned. Scram gets easily distracted by smells and sounds, but he always seems to return to listening. I wonder what breed of dog he is. I wonder about so many things.

There is much I miss from the world that was—much and more and many. But the internet... Good God, I think, if you'd only return the internet to me... I remember how we used to say that whatever you put online would stay there forever. That all the information in the world was available at a keystroke, and nothing would ever truly go away. But where, I wonder, is it all now?

'Kobus?' I say, without thinking it through. 'Do you remember you showed me how you could search every digitised book ever published in that huge, big... eh... data database-thing?' I was never too clear on the specifics.

'Yes, BigQuery?' he says. I remember the name as he says it.

'Could you find something out for me, now?'

'No.'

'Why not?'

'Because we didn't find it out for you then.'

'Oh, yeah.' We walk on in silence a little while. Lady keeps turning her head as if she can sense Kobus there.

'What did you want to know?' he says, eventually.

'Nothing. I was just wondering,' I say. And it's almost all the way true.

9

I tried to put the makeup on as close to her own way as possible. I always preferred her without any makeup at all, and would tell her so, often. And she would laugh, and tell me that she wasn't wearing makeup for me, but because it made her feel better. It made her feel better about her spotty chin, and the way her jawline was soft and wide. This always made me feel inferior. I exclusively wore makeup so she would like me more. What a waste those conversations were.

The paleness of the body's skin made it hard to cover it evenly, but I brushed it smooth with foundation, doing the best I could. I applied her mascara in thin layers. It was so intimate and tender that it made me anxious and sad. The lipstick next. She liked wearing lipstick and often did, but I was never good at hiding my distaste for it. I didn't like the way it made her look too good for me. I didn't like the way it turned her into a pretty lady instead of my cute, hipster girlfriend. I didn't like the way it made her ration her kisses. All of these were horrible reasons. All of these reasons were vain and selfish. Now, I felt guilty, and there was nothing I could do. I applied the lipstick with extra care, making it even and full in her darkest shade. The one I hated the most.

Getting the body to the grave was hard. I was tired, worn and disoriented; grieving, confused and broken. I got the body downstairs by wrapping it in our duvet and rolling it down, step by step. Outside, I lifted it onto my back, grabbed the arms and pulled them over my shoulders, bent forward, tried to walk, but I couldn't move like that. Besides, I had forgotten to put shoes on the body, and would have to go and get some. My brain was screaming at me with a solution, but I was too tired to listen. I put her finest shoes on the body's feet and tried dragging it along on the duvet. I tried carrying it over my shoulder. I tried screaming at the body in frustration.

Eventually, I hoisted the body onto my back again, tied its legs together in front of me with a belt, holding its arms down, holding them tight. The body was a backpack of sorts. Uneven and clunky and fragile. Sometimes, the weight got too much and I fell to the ground. My knees and the heels of my hands bruised and bled. But I kept going, slowly, all through the night, until the earliest grey of morning came to keep me company.

I lowered her body slowly into the grave, crossed her arms over her chest and smoothed her clothes out. She looked gorgeous. Together. Like our very first date and my dreams, combined. One of her stockings had come loose from the garters and I felt a small thrill as I reached out to fasten it. The thrill made me lonely. It felt like a ghost.

My head torch flickered and I turned it off. It was dawn now, anyway. I brushed as much dirt off my body as possible, then jumped into the grave and lay down. I took a deep breath, and waited for my own first cough to arrive.

The evening is warm, and we cross the first bridge. The map of Denmark is carved into my mind. We have to cross this bridge, the island on the other side, another bridge, then a second island, and then yet another bridge. A long one. A very long one. But then, finally, we'll be in Sweden. It must be eight weeks, at least, since I left home. And four more, or less, until I'm home. My other home. Home where I came from.

I can imagine my parents' farm easily. I know each nook and cranny, every secret spot and hiding place. They're all part of the magical world of childhood, and they're all mapped out in my heart. Every squeak and creak of the house I loved so much echoes in my ears. And now it's near. It's right there. Across three bridges and a country. I can smell my father's bakes, I can taste my mother's jam. *I'm coming home*, I think with every step. *I'm coming home.*

But I also know, because more and more words are slipping my mind, that home doesn't mean a thing. It's a direction, not a place. Going home, going north, going forward—they're all the same.

The bridge stretches from the Danish peninsula to one of its large islands. There's a slight breeze and the sea is quiet. Scram and Lady are uncomfortable with the limited road width and limited view. I pet them every now and then but most of the time, they walk uneasily behind me. There's a narrow staircase going up the side of the bridge. A poster telling me I'm not allowed to walk up there unless part of an official walking tour. I pour some dog treats by the trolley and tell Scram to wait. I want to see the sea.

The stairs are easy to climb and the sea is far, far below me. I stand on the edge and stare at its movement; there is nothing to stop me from jumping. I walk the narrow path on top the bridge and I can see forever, and forever is a very lonely place. But there is life. Right beneath me, a dorsal fin, or two—no, three! I can barely make out their shapes in the dusk. The book has told me to expect this. Harbour porpoises. They're common here. Their smooth backs glide in and out of sight. Polished mountain ridges in the calm and rolling sea. Sudden bursts of water and air. Endlessly calm. Endlessly swimming. I feel like swimming too.

For a second, I close my eyes and lean forward. Feel the railing against my thighs, the wind against my face. Why should I not lean forward just a bit more? How would it feel? Which parts of my life would go through my head on the way down? I imagine myself detaching from the bridge like ripe fruit, falling away from the safety up here. My eyes would be open, I'm certain of that, at least most of the way, for sure. What would it feel like to hit the surface? I may let go. I may let myself... I may... Then a sudden and violent sound shakes me to my core.

The body began to rot, but I still hadn't coughed. I had to chase off rats and scoop out maggots. It smelled worse than I could ever have imagined. Constant waves of panic washed through me. The body next to me was going. And I was not.

One morning left me no choice. The smell made me gag until I threw up, and I couldn't even look at it anymore. I buried her quickly, without ceremony. I had to fill in the entire grave and dig myself a new one. My plan had been to lie beside her. Make us our own little subterranean bed. We would be cuddled up next to each other forever, right next door to our baby girl. But the body in the grave was not mine to cuddle. It was being reclaimed by forces that didn't care at all about eternal rest. The image had etched itself into the back of my eyelids. I couldn't remember what Cleopatra's face looked like without things gouging through her skin. Without runny, maggoty eyes.

I waited for days.

'I'll be back in a little while,' I whispered to her grave so as not to wake her up. 'I'm just going to get a new book.'

The first time I left, I went home. I looked around the familiar place and felt her absence completely. The second time, I decided to break into the bookshop instead. There was no one around to mind. Getting through the shopping centre entrance was the hard part. It became a project. Two mornings in a row, I walked from my grave to the centre. Two days I spent trying to find the best way to get through the thick security glass. The solution, as it turned out, was not in the glass at all, but in the staff entrance around the corner. It took me only an hour or two. I cut myself on the sharp metal, but I still felt an enormous sense of triumph when I finally got in.

Cleopatra had once worked in this bookshop. Not for long, just a few months while we were trying to get our bearings. We revelled in discounts and the creative people who passed through. She had loved the people, hated the hours of standing, and was happy and sad when she got a 'real' job instead. I thought of these things as I entered the shop and saw familiar shapes inside. For a moment, I thought I could still catch her scent lingering on the dusty pages.

There was very little light. The innermost corners were darker than night—the children's section was invisible. Just as well, I thought, just as well. There were so many books to choose from. Classics here, science-fiction there. I ran my finger across the classics and read the titles out loud. I had read many of them, a quarter, maybe more. Some, I hadn't even heard of.

It struck me then for the first time: all that would now be forgotten. All that was already lost. Even if I spent the rest of my life in that bookshop, there would be millions of other books on other shelves, fading away into nothing. The truth of it blinded me. All of the books looked exactly the same: unbearably special, intolerably unique. Authors had bled their hearts and souls onto these pages, now to be forgotten like the rest of us. Transformed into mere mortals, nothing and dust.

I grabbed *Pride and Prejudice*, and left the bookshop in such a rush that I cut my hoodie open on the broken window. Shards of glass shattered across the display. I had made a frightful mess. Blood seeped down my arm and in between the pages of the book. Dark dots and smudges across the cover and spine. I ran until I reached the graves and flung the book down into mine. Tore my hoodie off and pressed it against the cuts. Why? Why not lie down and bleed out? The question wasn't in my head, and I couldn't figure out why it shouldn't be.

'Why?' I said again. 'Why not?' It had been six days since Cleopatra died. Six days without so much as a hoarse clearing of my throat. Not a cough. Not a sneeze. And maybe, just maybe, it wouldn't happen. How long should I wait?

'But why wouldn't I die?' It felt good hearing my voice out loud. Something to break up the aggressive chitter chatter of gossiping birds.

'Maybe... Maybe it's in my blood.' I didn't believe it. Not for a second. I had thought the thought before and dismissed it as wishful thinking. But hearing it said made it real. You shouldn't believe everything you hear, but surely some of it's true. So why not this? Maybe there was something in my blood that had kept me immune to this disease. And if it was in my blood, *maybe*, the rest of my family was immune too.

There was no conscious decision. No grand moment of change or resolution. I just found myself walking back to the flat with a pair of baby socks in my pocket, and Cleopatra's silver heart and engagement ring dangling around my neck. I didn't say goodbye. She wasn't really there.

An explosion. I heard an explosion! I scan the muddy darkness for the source of the sound, a big bang, human-made, I'm sure of it. Carefully, I climb down from the railing and hold myself steady. Scram and Lady are barking at the unseen, which makes me even more certain: I did not imagine this. This was real. It must have been fireworks… it must have been. Surely? So loud and clear and unexpected. Nothing like nature at all. I stare and stare, hoping for a sign. Hoping for a brilliant flash of light or smoke, or just another loud bang.

When I get it, my heart stops. It's the most beautiful thing I've ever seen. A strike of white, a flash of red, then silver dust gliding through the air. It's a beautiful flower, painted in light. The first sign of life. Someone is out there!

'Hey!' I call at the top of my lungs. I wave my arms towards the beach on the other side.

'Hoy!' someone calls back. It's far away. Faint. But I cry and scream and whistle.

'Hey! Heeeeey!' Someone! Someone! There are shouts and calls from the other side, I shout, they shout, and this is real and outside my head, and I shout and shout and shout. I make my way down the stairs with trembling knees. My heart sings, my fingers vibrate. I'm the most nervous I have ever been, pushing the trolley as fast as I can. Scram and Lady run next to me, looking at me in excitement.

'Good boy!' I call to Scram. 'Good girl!' to Lady. 'Come on!' When I can't run any longer, I walk as fast as my feet will carry me. I consider abandoning my trolley and going back for it later, but I can't make myself take even a second off from walking towards the sound on the other side.

Every now and then, I call out, 'I'm on my way!' and every now and then, the someone sends up another bottle rocket. They're small flashes of hope and guide me towards salvation. My Christmas star. My lighthouse. Or, at the very least, a someone. When I get to the end of the bridge, I see a fire on a beach nearby. A beacon, calling me close.

'Hoy!' I hear someone say. There! There! In front of me! He's running towards me, arms outstretched. There isn't a single moment's hesitation, I run to greet him. We collide in a hug so close and hard, it makes us both gasp for breath. It's not a hug of friendship, there's no love or lust. There's just the absolute need to make sure—in as big an area as possible—that we're no longer alone. I'm not alone, he's not alone, we're here, we're both here, he's real and so am I. I take him in with my entire body. He is there, and close, and near and breathing and pulsating and warm—so warm. He sobs against my shoulder and I sob into his chest. Scram and Lady are barking and dancing around our feet. The creature is watching me from the dark.

When we finally pull apart, we keep clinging to each other's arms. Terrified the other will fade away into just another nightmare. He starts talking to me in Danish, fast and hurried. Our languages are similar but not the same, and I don't understand much of what he's saying.

'I am sorry,' I say in Norwegian. 'I don't understand. My hearing is a bit rusty, what?' And I laugh, and he laughs, and the sound is wonderful. We try for a while, slowly and carefully, but we end up using English, because we have so much to say.

'I'm Georg,' he says, 'I am so happy to see you, welcome. Welcome! Come! Are you hungry? So good to see you. Please, stay for a bit. Are you hungry? You must be hungry. Where are you from? What are you doing here? Have you met others? Where are you going?'

And while he says this, I say, 'I'm so glad to see you. Are you from here? Have you seen others? Do you know if there are more survivors up north? Is that your bonfire? Are you alone here? So happy to meet you. I think I am losing it a little... No, Scram! Get down! So glad to meet you. Yes, I am hungry. So glad. So glad.' And we keep laughing, and he pushes the trolley with me, because we don't let go of each other's hands.

When we get into the light of the fire, we laugh again, shyly this time. Neither of us is wearing clothes. I'm shy. I feel a desperate urge to get dressed and shave my legs. But I don't, because I don't know how long this moment will last, and I have so many questions and so much to say. A voice! How wonderfully beautiful and magical it is to hear someone's voice.

There was one other time, right after I got to France, that I thought I had found another survivor. It was dusk, and everything smelled strongly of lavender. I was walking towards a hill and suddenly, right in front of me, the outline of a man was gliding towards me in the mist.

'Oh! Oh! Hello!' I said, and waved my arms, jumping into the air. Something with the perspective didn't add up, and my stomach churned as the outline became the real thing. I threw up. I hadn't seen as much back then, and death still made me think of Cleopatra's body and its maggoty eyes. Things would change, but they hadn't yet, and what came towards me felt horrible. Horrifying.

It was a horse. The horse walked along the edge of the road. Nipping at grass and straw, and completely ignoring the remains on its back. There wasn't much left. Just the completely shrivelled remains of someone who had gone for a last riding trip. The wrists were tied to the reins. One of them had on a hospital wristband, yellow plastic against the decay.

I thought of the mummified arm that dangled from a church wall in Prague. Legend said that a thief had been attempting to steal from the offerings when a statue of the Virgin Mary came to life and grabbed him by the wrist. The next morning, monks had to cut his arm off to liberate him, as the statue refused to let go. The arm had been swaying from the wall of the draughty church ever since, a warning to other thieves and miscreants. Every time I've been to Prague, I've stopped by to pay my respects.

The woman—I guessed, based on the small hands and boots—who once rode this horse had tried to steal a few more moments on its back. She would have already been exhausted, already dying. I don't know how I knew, but I did. The hospital bracelet. The way she had tied herself to the horse. I wondered where the rest of her was. Perhaps she had gradually fallen off as rot and decay made her fragile and runny. Perhaps the horse had scraped her off against trees and branches. The saddle was still there. And her leg bones, sticking out of two small riding boots firmly clasped to the stirrups.

The horse was sore and blistered along the edge of the saddle, and I knew I couldn't leave him like that, not really, not now, not with her remains still there. I approached him carefully, with my arm outstretched the way my father had taught me. He didn't seem to mind me; he hadn't yet forgotten people, and there was plenty of straw for him to nip at as I loosened the girth.

He winced when I started pulling it off. The saddle stuck in places, the whole area a chafed-down sore, infected and oozing with pus. But it wasn't deep, and he would be all right. I let the saddle drop, the leg and boot still in place. The bridle had dug into the horse's skin and the throat lash had snapped in two. It had been years—20, at least—since I'd last touched a horse, but I worked it out, step by step. The nose band had dug itself a deep gorge. Definitely infected. It smelled horrible. I expected the horse to whinny and rear up when I started detaching it, but he just shivered and shook.

'You understand, don't you, boy?' I whispered, stroking his forehead. 'You understand she didn't mean to leave you in this mess. She's probably very sorry. Now, we'll let you loose. It will feel better soon. I'm sure of it. There you go. There.'

The bit was green and slimy and worn. I felt bad for him, but at least he was alive. At least he was strong. At least there were more like him out there. I let him walk away, slowly grazing his way into the darkness. The saddle pouch held a blue MP3 player and a letter. Nothing else. The letter was in French and I didn't try to read it. I just shoved it in my backpack with the rest of my things. I threw one last look at the abandoned boot and leg, and the reined-in shrivelled hands. Only when I started walking again did the disappointment wash over me. For a moment, I thought I had found someone else. For a moment, I thought I wasn't alone. I don't think I cried, but I might have.

10

It's getting chilly, so we both put on our T-shirts and shorts. Georg has blankets, and I wrap myself up and sit across the fire from him. I feel like I could sleep for a hundred years.

'I saw you up there,' Georg says, 'purely by coincidence. I've been shooting up fireworks every evening, but usually I wait until it's a little darker. Bigger impact, you know?' I nod. I have thought about it myself. How useful it would be to have a flare or two or three. A way to signal to people far away that I'm out here.

'But then I saw you up there. Thought I imagined it at first. You know... well... I am sure you know how it gets. Things get different... after a while.'

'Yeah...' I say. We don't meet each other's eyes, but we both know what we're talking about. The shadows, the whispers, the endless possibilities, needing to treat each mirage as a maybe.

'But usually, my binoculars don't lie, and you were standing all swaying with your arms out. And I thought, 'Shit, Georg. The only other person in the world may jump to her death if you don't get your finger out of your ass and light some goddamn fireworks.'

'I wasn't going to jump. I was just thinking about it,' I say.

'Sure, sure, but... you know. Couldn't take the chance.'

'There were porpoises down there,' I say. He doesn't understand the word. I think. 'Like sort of stubby dolphins?'

'Ah! *Marsvin*!' he says, and I burst out laughing.

'No, silly, in the water!'

'Yes?' So I show him the pages from the book and notice something I'd never noticed before. The Danish word for harbour porpoise is *marsvin*.

'Wow,' I say. '*Marsvin*, in Norwegian, means guinea-pig.'

'Yeah, it means that too... in Danish.'

'Why?' I say. It sounds impractical. He shrugs.

'And when I shot off the first rocket, I instantly regretted it. Because you seemed to startle so, I was worried I would scare you off the bridge completely.'

'You almost did.'

'Sorry,' he says.

We drink beer and eat deer with the rest of my bread. I don't think about how he's caught the deer, I just appreciate the smell and taste. He shares generously with Scram and Lady. Scram seems to like him, which makes me calm, but I have this little nagging feeling, now that we're all sat down. The truth is, I don't know much about Georg. I don't know what he's like. I know he is a man, and that I am a woman. An hour ago, that didn't matter, but maybe it will, later. Maybe it matters already. The thought is undressing in my mind, slowly and deliberately, as if it's trying not to startle me. Georg may be the *only* other person in the world, but he may not be a *good* person. He might not even be kind.

'Do you sleep out here?' I say.

'Most nights. If it doesn't rain. It's too... you know. My house is a bit busy. Too many things in there.' I understand.

'Do you want to listen to some music?' I say. He brightens up a little. I drag out the little speaker and the bag of MP3 players.

'Wow!' he says. 'How many have you got?'

'13,' I answer, 'so far.'

'Why?'

I don't answer but pick one I haven't used before. A purple player of a brand I don't know. I found it in Belgium, in a purse that someone had left in a bus stop. It takes me a little while to figure out how it works but, eventually, I get it charged enough to skim through the music.

'Beatles, Sex Pistols, Frankie Goes to Hollywood,' I chant. 'Wow... that's a combination.' He laughs. 'Metallica, *RENT* soundtrack, Britney Spears...' I keep reading the names of artists I know, and some I don't. I see my favourite artist on there, but I don't tell Georg. I don't want to think about Cleopatra right now, don't want to be sad, need to be alert.

'Oh!' he exclaims, and I try to figure out what I just read.

'Rush?' He nods enthusiastically. 'Any particular song? There's a "best-of" album and two—'

'Just play the best-of,' he says, so I do.

'This—' he says, and shakes his hand towards the music. His beer spills a little, his head bops from side to side. '—is my holy trinity.' I smile. I've met Rushers before. His childish enthusiasm and the way he plucks his air guitar are extremely reassuring to me. This is a nerd. He is my kind. I feel laughter bubbling through my body, and I play air drums as we rock the night away. It's true, I think: some things never change. I forget about the creature completely.

I am guilty. Kobus rang our doorbell at the beginning of the second wave. Our baby girl would hold onto my innards for two more days, and Cleopatra's skin was still pink and warm. We didn't hug when he entered. For weeks, the TV and radio had told us it was absolutely paramount that we didn't. Preferably, we wouldn't even see each other, talk or walk outside. But Kobus's face told me this was important, so I didn't even think of the risks. He came carrying two large Tupperware tubs, a bottle of wine and a cloud of thunder.

'Hey, sweetie,' I said, like I always did. Because although everything was changing, everything still felt the same. 'Norway's lost phone connection.'

'Fuck! I'm sorry to hear that... Don't think we'll have it much longer ourselves.' He smelled faintly of red wine.

'Want a drink?' I asked—some things never change—and we soon made our way through the bottle. We talked about the newest developments. Talked about how I wished I could go home to Norway and check on my family, talked about how I wished we could check on Cleopatra's mum. Talked about how everything was all messed up and we worried about the baby.

'They've put up notes everywhere,' he told me, 'saying that if you start exhibiting symptoms and you're already alone, you should open your hallway door. They're sending out groups of volunteers to help collect the sick and infirm. People to help you wipe your fucking bum, to help you eat and drag your body out of your house when you're gone.'

'Sounds like the only way to go. I'm sure there will be too many for the NHS to handle if this wave is anything like the last.'

'Fuck the NHS.' Kobus refilled his glass. 'There is no NHS. There never was. The NHS, like the police, like the House of Lords, like the fucking parliament and the fucking soccer teams, they're all there as long as there are people to believe in them. There aren't anymore. This is it,' he said, waving his arms vaguely into the air. 'This is the end.'

'We don't know that,' I said. I have always been a natural optimist, and even then, I thought there was still hope.

'Know what I heard on the radio today?' he said, staring straight through me. 'That the incubation time must be at least a year and that we seem to be contagious the entire period. If you've got it, you're contagious. Symptoms or no symptoms. You get it, you carry it, spread it around, and then die.'

'Shit…' I said, because sometimes you have to swear, and that felt like one of those moments.

'And the irony—' he said. More wine. New bottle. '—is that half a year ago, when there were so many isolated cases and the scientists started fretting. Remember? When we still thought super-strength antibiotics could kill this fucking thing? Back then, they sent people to the Amazon. To Tibet. To the far reaches of the world. First, they sent scientists to test and measure. Trying to figure out where this stuff came from. Then, when the disease spread like wildfire, they sent fucking saviours out. Saviours with flu jabs and antibiotics and pamphlets about staying the hell away from big cities. And so it was that we spread our disease everywhere. What the British Empire couldn't do in 350 years, WHO did in six months. They made the entire world the same.'

'I heard the disease probably originated in Morocco or the US,' I said for something to say.

'Likely. Or some fucking country like that. Easy access to antibiotics. That's how you make sure your diseases mutate into monsters.' Couldn't really argue with that.

I try to keep myself awake until I'm sure Georg is sleeping, but the makeshift bed he has made up for me is soft and comfortable, Scram is resting his head on my belly and Lady is resting her head on him. Suddenly and without warning, I wake up to a new day.

Georg is already awake, rustling about over by the fire. I can feel his eyes on me. Taking me in from head to toe. His gaze makes every hair on my body stand on end, sensing the air, feeling for danger. But when I open my eyes, he isn't even looking. The feeling of being watched is nothing but regular fear.

He blows on lazy embers to make some twigs catch fire, then he wades out into the sea to wash himself. He glances over at me, then, but doesn't see me looking back. He chooses to wash himself with his back towards me, and I wonder if I should get dressed. Scram is snapping at the water falling off Georg, and playing in the shallow waves. Lady lies next to me, still asleep. Her little paws are running through the air, trying to catch up with the way things used to be. I'm falling in love with her, this little strange thing. She doesn't love me the way Scram does, but she needs to be loved all the same.

I don't get dressed. Instead, I walk down until the water touches my ankles.

'It's freezing!' I say.

'It's the North Sea!' he laughs. I jump in, in that stupid way you do when the water is too cold, and you're shy about your body, unsure how deep it is and unsure of who's looking. I jump in with the silly walk of a 15-year-old. Three long, unsteady strides then down on my stomach, despite the fact that it isn't very deep at all. Flailing madly with arms and legs, my face contracting into a grimace, my breathing fast and shallow, cold, cold, cold, oh goodness, so cold.

'Oh my god!' I squeak, and I feel so alive, like being fifteen and twelve and five, and experiencing the ocean for the first time each year. I swivel manically until I get used to the temperature and find peace in the clear, fresh water. I can taste the salt on my lips and feel the weight of my braids. I forget all about Georg and turn over onto my back to float quietly. The soft waves dip me up and down. Up to the skies, then a little bit down, up to the skies, and down again. I imagine the ocean is a pump. Every little movement pushes me higher and higher, more up than down every time. Soon, I'll be right under the sky, touching the soft clouds with my hands. I'll be able to see all the way to Norway, I'll be able to see my parents' farm. Find out once and for all if there's a point to this walking. Then I'll keep on rising, until I can touch the stars and kiss the moon on her big fat lips. Georg can come if he wants to. Scram will go where I go. Lady... well. We'll see.

I stay in the water until my body starts shivering violently from the cold and my teeth clatter like castanets.

'Breakfast!' Georg calls, and I clamber up onto the beach and do jumping jacks in the sun.

'That was amazing,' I say. 'I haven't had a swim in so long.' He smiles.

'Yeah, I'll tell her later.'

'What?' I say, but he turns his face away and blushes.

'I said, do you want a cup of coffee?'

'Sure,' I say. I don't like coffee, but right now, I want nothing more.

'There is no hope,' Kobus said. He hadn't lifted his glass for a couple of minutes and silence had spread from his words. 'This is it. And I have made some decisions.'

'Oh?' I said. I held Cleopatra's hand and I could feel her anxiety. I feared that she might believe him, that she would think there was no hope. The thought scared me, and I think it scared the baby. I felt her fear as a little shiver, or the flutters of a butterfly, somewhere deep inside or right beneath my skin.

'I have made a curry,' he said. 'A big one. A really big one.' He pointed to the Tupperware. One did unmistakably contain curry. Naan and chutney jars could be glimpsed through the plastic of the other.

'I have invited all my girls for dinner tonight.'

'What?' I said.

'All of them. I have lied and blackmailed and used every fucking card up my sleeve to get them all there at seven tonight. And when they come, I'll lock them in if I have to. Push them through the door. Slash their tires and steal their car keys. Say that there is no reason why all of us can't sit down for a meal. "Just in case something happens to me," I'll say. "Just in case." And I will beg and plead until my daughters say yes, and then they will make their mums say yes. Four daughters, four exes, my lover and her two daughters. All will ignore each other and eat my curry.'

'What about the Essex woman?'

'She's gone,' he said, and I wished I hadn't asked.

'Okay... so... it's like the last supper?' I asked. As a joke, mostly.

'Exactly,' he said. 'It is the last fucking supper.' I didn't think too much of this at first. But I noticed something strange in his face, and my brain started looking for connections.

'It sounds nice,' said Cleopatra. 'I hope they'll all behave.'

He shrugged. Deeply. 'That's not important. They only need to eat with me.'

'Kobus...?' I said. The word came out slow and strange. It meant something different this time, but I couldn't quite put my finger on what. 'When they leave, what will you do?'

I thought he was going to kill himself; I thought he wanted to die. He looked at me, slow and strange. His look meant something different too, but I couldn't quite...

'I'm going to make them stay for a while,' he said. 'This is the only way I know to protect them. To care for my girls. I love or have loved them all. And I've hated them, when the love ran out. They drive me fucking crazy, and they drive each other crazy. But Eliza and Bella haven't even met. How twisted is that? They both have a sister they've never met. And their fucking mums, man, they fill their heads with all sorts of lies. We only get one more chance to put things right. And I'm taking it.' He drained his wine glass.

'And I made you this,' he said. Patting the lid of the curry box. The thump thump thump made the knot in my stomach tighten and churn. The baby fluttered again. 'Because I love you too. And you know,' he smiled, 'I always make curry for people I love.'

I nodded. He had made me many curries. Probably more than I could count. Thinking about them made me sad. I wished that I could hold on to him and make him stay with us. That I could talk him out of this plan he had made. I wished I didn't understand.

'I wish we could spend more time discussing books and articles. There are so many topics we haven't covered yet,' I said. He shrugged.

He got up to leave. Said goodbye to Cleopatra. I walked him out.

'Kobus?' I said when he was about to close the door. 'When... when your last supper is over... Where would your girls find your car keys? Like... if they needed a car and really wanted to get home... or something? Or go for a long drive? Where would they find your car keys?'

He looked at me with that annoying smile, for a long time. Then he nodded and placed his car keys on the windowsill. 'I am feeling a bit too drunk to drive. Mind if I leave my car here for tomorrow?'

'Not at all.'

'I fucking love you,' he said.

'I fucking love you too.'

'Bye bye, then...' he said. I didn't reply. I went back into the living room and picked up the curry.

'You hungry?' said Cleopatra.

'No,' I said, and wrapped the curry in several layers of plastic and carried it out to the bins. They were overflowing, a small rubbish mountain where rats and mice had a constant feast. I shrugged and buried the box in the heap. Rats, I figured, are smart enough, and I couldn't worry about them too.

Kobus's car was small and bright yellow. I nodded at it before I went back in. Cleopatra stared at me. Looking for the curry. Trying to piece the puzzle together.

'He's going to kill them, isn't he?' She bit her lip and it bled the way it so often had in the last few weeks. 'He's going to kill them... and you knew... You understood. You let him go.'

I brought our glasses out into the kitchen, because I couldn't find anything to say. A few hours later, the power cut out. Ten days later, it stopped coming back, and my baby was buried under two blue socks. I felt terribly guilty.

Kobus is sitting next to me by the fire.

'A fucking economist,' he scoffs. 'What good is your fucking ivory tower now, Mr Money?' he says to Georg, who—of course—can't hear him. I smile into my coffee. It's thick with sugar to mask the taste and runs through my veins, warming me up. Georg talks about his old job, his hobbies and his ex-wife. He tells me about his new girlfriend, and how he was planning to propose to her.

It's easy to talk to Georg. We know so much about each other, there is much we don't need to say.

'Everyone I ever loved is probably dead,' neither of us says.

'Oh... me too,' neither of us has to reply.

'I have no idea what to do now,' neither of us admits.

'Me neither... and I'm piss scared,' the other doesn't say. We're past that. There are questions I hope we can get to. I want to ask him if he's seen the creature. If he knows what it is or why it's following me. I want to ask if he knows why it didn't bite when it could have. But we aren't there yet. We're at the stage of intimate friends who empty our souls to make sure someone knows. We admit our deepest secrets to make sure we're not alone. Georg has been unfaithful. I tell him about Kobus's girls and how I let him poison them when I could have tried to stop him.

He tells me he smothered his daughter the second day she was ill, only so he wouldn't have to watch her die.

I tell him how I slept next to Cleopatra's rotting body and struggle to remember what she looked like.

He tells me he talks to his girlfriend. And that his daughter sometimes cries at night, and he searches but can't find her.

I tell him I'm carrying 13 people's MP3 players in my backpack to make sure they're not forgotten. It's a long, slow morning, and I make no effort to leave.

I make a bread dough for later and teach him how to get the dough just right. I tell him about my father, and how we hadn't spoken much the last few months before the first wave hit, but then talked every day until the phones cut out. Georg asks questions about *Peer Gynt*, and we discuss how weird it is to be used to the smell of corpses. We feel the same about how quiet the world is. We both feel the wind is colder. We both think the sky is clearer than before. We're both in awe of the stars. And we both agree that none of it fucking matters because every day is all the same, and nothing is ever going to change again.

'Do you ever think about ending it?' I ask. We're eating bread straight from a hot garden tile, topped with cheese and thin slices of venison.

'Every day,' he says.

'Do you think you'll do it?'

'Every day.'

'But do you think you'll do it... actually?'

He thinks about this for a while, eats in silence and then shrugs.

'Eventually,' he says. We're quiet for a while.

'Me too,' I say. 'You know... unless my family...'

'Yeah,' he says. 'I know.'

I dream that God comes swimming up to me and whispers in my ear. She tells me how everything will end soon, and it makes me smile. She's fat and happy and moves through the water like a sleek mountain, just breaking the surface for air.

'The most important thing,' she says, 'is that you let go. Let everything go. Let everything fall down into the abyss, until there is only you.'

'But it hurts,' I say. 'I don't want to.'

'Darling,' she says, and blows the hair out of my eyes the way my mother did when I was little. 'This is Hell. This is your eternal punishment for straying. It is meant to hurt.' Her breath is scalding hot and blasts the flesh off my bones. My skull is scorched and full of maggots. I cannot feel my eyes. Georg wakes me up because I'm screaming. When I wake, I cannot breathe or see or make my heart stop racing.

'Demons?' he says when I finally calm down. 'Ghosts? Zombies? Your ex?'

'God,' I sob. 'She hates me.'

'No, she doesn't,' he says and pats my back. 'She doesn't care enough about you to hate you. She doesn't care about you at all.'

When he has fallen back to sleep, I lie on my back and look out into the endless universe. There are so many stars. I think about how much of history has had a view like this. This was how the stories started, of heroes and monsters and gods. I think about how some of these stars have been lost for the last 100 years, or so. How even Africa's night sky became streamlined and dull as industry and light wiped out the darkness. I think about the stars I recognise, and I study the ones I don't.

'Dear God,' I whisper. 'If you still love me, give me a sign.' The sky is endless and dark, with thousands and thousands of stars. Every single one of them twinkles and winks at me. But they would have done that anyway, so I just go back to sleep. The universe feels empty and cold.

11

I stared at the backpack for a long while. Tried to imagine what I should bring. What I *could* bring. I had already put *The Hobbit* in there. The last chapter was still unread. My plan was to swing by Cleopatra's grave and read it to her before I left. Now, I thought, I might as well read it to her anywhere. I tried to pack all my survival gear, some clothes, two of my cameras, notebooks and photo albums. I filled my backpack and my suitcase and Cleopatra's suitcase. After all, I had Kobus's car.

But what about the Channel Tunnel? I remembered reading something after the Global Solar Flare Defence Initiative was put in place. That the Channel Tunnel would survive two or three months without electricity. It had been six weeks or so now, so I didn't have long if I wanted to be sure I could get through. I doubted I'd be able to get the car to the other side. Even if I managed to drive along the train tracks, I didn't know if it would even be wide enough the whole way. What if I got stuck or ran out of petrol halfway through; what if there were barriers or trains stuck along the way? I looked at all the things I was bringing, and knew I had to think differently. Maybe

I'd have to swap cars multiple times, or walk a little while between each mode of transportation. It would have to be the backpack. I would have to start over.

I didn't need to bring the photo albums. Maybe just a couple of individual pictures. I sorted through them, picked out the ones I couldn't do without. 57. Too many. 32, still too many.

I threw them all in the bin and grabbed the keyring, thermo-mug and notebooks. That would do. I also had a photo of my niece folded into my wallet. I took it out, without looking, and tossed the wallet on the floor. I slipped the photo in between the pages of *The Hobbit*. A little something to remind me where I'm going. A little something to remember where I'm from. All my other needs were eventually reduced to my knife, a torch, some extra batteries, two pairs of trousers, some shorts and three T-shirts. My softshell jacket for warmth, my sleeping bag for comfort, my tent for shelter. I had forgotten about socks and underwear, so I ran my finger over the sea of options and chose the most practical panties I could find. No bows, no lace, no crotchless crotches. Just cotton and comfortable elastics. Three pairs of socks.

I packed toiletries—deodorant, soap, shampoo, conditioner, my favourite perfume and mascara. Then I walked through the flat, whispering my goodbyes. To the things we had bought together, to the things I had brought with me, to the remnants of my previous marriage, and the results of my new life. I looked through some of the magazines. Looked at the photos I'd taken and the articles I'd sold. The silence was overwhelming, so I plugged a little speaker into my MP3 player and listened to my favourite songs. I decided to bring it with me. Decided to bring hers, too. The music was making it harder, but I kept walking through our rooms, making sure I would remember everything. All our lovely books. All our lovely memories. All our unfinished love.

Georg shows me his house and the two graves in the garden. I've brought small shells from the beach and place them on the graves as a sign of respect. He watches me from the window but doesn't come out. His house is sweet, and filled with pictures and toys; everything has smudges of pink paint or glitter, gold stars and unicorns.

'I guess I was a bit...' he says when he catches me smiling at a tankard shaped like a Viking's helmet that has pink glitter stains on each horn and some plastic jewels glued to the front.

'Less concerned about keeping the myth of the horned helmet than pleasing your daughter?' I say.

'Something like that.' Being here is making him uncomfortable. His eyes keep darting into the shadows and he whispers to himself. I wonder what he sees, but I don't ask. Whatever it is, it scares him, but I have enough trouble keeping my own monster at bay.

He shows me everything but his daughter's room. Then we walk into town as if this is a Sunday and we're going for papers and pastries. We chat about very small things. Dragonflies and words that are different in Norwegian and Danish. The sun is friendlier here than it has been for a few days, and my giggles are light and transparent.

He's already moved most of the useful goods from the shop to the shore. But we walk around town anyway, looking for bits and bobs that might make a nice meal. The smells disturb me. Two nights by the sea and I've already forgotten the decay on land.

'I'll have to go soon,' I say as we make our way back to the beach. 'I can't waste too much time before I go home... If there's anyone left, I need to know.' He is quiet for a while. Throws tennis balls for Lady and Scram. Lady only barks, but Scram chases them eagerly.

'You know...' he says, but he doesn't continue. I start thinking about something else, and it takes a while before I respond.

'I know what?' I say.

'The next bridge is much harder to cross. Windy. Quite temperamental. And it's a long way to walk to Copenhagen from here, if you're planning to cross for Sweden...'

'Yes, but I don't have much choice,' I say, 'I can't swim that far...' I try to make it sound like a joke. It sounds like a genuine regret.

'I could drive you there,' he says. 'I could drive you to Copenhagen. Spend a few more days with me here, and I'll drive you to the start of the bridge.'

'Could you not... take me over? Or come with me?' I'm surprised by the hope in my voice and the disappointment I feel when he shakes his head.

'I don't think so... I need to be here. But I'll take you to the bridge. I'll trade you the ride for a few days of company. Deal?'

I chew on his words and look for any underlying currents or threats. I can't find any. 'Deal,' I say. But I remind myself where my knife is. And I pat Scram's head to remind him he's mine.

'Good boy,' I say, and we all walk on in silence.

Truth be told, I had never driven a car. Well, I tried, once. Right after I turned 16, my father took me out to practise. We came to a crossing, and he said, 'Stop,' so I stopped.

'Don't stop completely!' he yelled. 'Go! Go! Go!' So I took us home and we left it at that. The chemistry just wasn't right.

I was always planning to get my licence someday. When I finished uni, or when I was done with this project, at the end of my MA, when I got home from Italy, when I finished this new project I'd just started, or before I had kids. When the End came, it was too late. But I thought I understood the basics. There was a pedal to get you forwards, a pedal to make you stop. Then there was something about changing gears, but how hard could that be? I didn't have to worry about speeding, or hitting other cars, or even getting caught by the police. All I needed to do was... yes. Here we go.

I didn't move fast, but I moved forward. I circled the car park a couple of times, only snubbing the corner of a hedge once or twice. Kobus wouldn't mind. I wanted to spend a few days learning to drive, but I didn't know how much petrol I had, or if there was any chance of getting more. I couldn't get the hang of reverse, but I figured I wouldn't really need it.

The car was small, but I couldn't for the life of me figure out how to open the boot. I remembered Kobus showing it to me, proud of the ingenious hiding place of the button, but at the time I hadn't taken notice. I'd been too busy thinking how typical it was that someone like Kobus would find a hidden button interesting. Something hidden that should be plain. It was such a Kobus thing to do that I didn't bother looking; I knew he'd show me again and again.

I placed the backpack in the passenger seat instead, buckling it in to make sure it wouldn't tip over and make me panic. I left the car running outside the shopping centre, ran into the bookshop and dug until I found a road map of England. They had a thick book of maps of Europe, too, and I brought it, because I hadn't really thought that far ahead.

Big fat raindrops fell thickly against the windshield. There wasn't much to see except road and rain, but I was relieved when I got the windshield wipers moving. As I made my way down onto the motorway, confidence and speed built on top of each other. The swishing of water under the tires made me drowsy, but I blasted music through my MP3 player and tried to focus on the lyrics to stay awake.

Nena sang about *Luftballons* in German, and I sang something similar. I thought about hot air balloons. I'd always wanted to go on a balloon ride, preferably in Namibia. Silently gliding high above the red desert, looking down on the ocean of sand and the waves of dust and heat. Ever since I was a child, I would stare at hot air balloons in the sky, following them on their ride, imagining myself from above. I've always loved to feel small.

I'm getting tipsy, or something.

'So,' I say. 'Do you, like... Are you trying to hide that you really... Do you, like, think we should...' I don't know how to continue the sentence. I hope he doesn't hear me.

'What?' he says, because he's sitting right next to me and I'm talking with my drunk volume, so of course he hears me.

'I don't know,' I say, and drink some more. I'm not there yet. Not enough wine. 'Repopulate,' I say, eventually. 'Do you think it's our sacred duty or something? Are you going to say that, and then make me carry your children? I've seen the way you look at me. You're planning something, aren't you?' I try to bite down on the words as they crawl out of my mouth. I don't mean this. Not really. But the words are sticky and stubborn and keep crawling. They inch out between my teeth and topple like maggots to the ground. He stares at me in absolute astonishment.

'No!' he says. 'What? Whatever gave you that idea?'

'I don't know... You're a man, I'm a woman. I thought maybe you were planning to keep me here and impregnate me and raise your little army of followers or... or something... you know... like in films and stuff.' My cheeks are burning. He doesn't answer me. Just shakes his head. He seems hurt.

'I'm sorry,' I say. 'I don't know why I said that...'

'You said that for the same reason you keep your knife in your sleeping bag.'

'Oh...'

'I wouldn't hurt you, you know.' His dark beard has streaks of grey in it. He seems so old right now. So fragile.

'I'm sorry.'

'I murdered my daughter while my beloved was dying in the room next door,' he says. 'I haven't really put much thought into fucking or screwing lately. Have you?'

I don't answer. Don't know how.

'And as for carrying my children,' he says, 'my children are dead. I wasn't planning on bringing any new ones into this mess. I'm much closer to suggesting we kill each other than screw each other, to be honest, because I am *one* man, and you are *one* woman. One.' He looks bitter. Angry. 'Let's just say you're not my type. I've got a headache. Kids don't figure into my life plans right now. Don't think I'd be a good parent. Don't have protection ready. Am celibate. Don't want to.'

'I'm sorry,' I say again. 'I am really sorry. I am just scared.'

'Yeah,' he says. We are quiet for a long time. His eyes tell me he isn't really here, and I can't tell where he is, or what he's doing there, but it's not making him happy.

'I lost a child,' I say.

'I know, you told me,' he snaps.

'No...' I swallow. 'Not Emma. Before that.' He doesn't say anything, so I just continue. 'There was this guy... And I thought... I thought many things. But he wasn't very kind. He did things to me.' I swallow again. My throat's tight and there's something in the way. My nose feels clogged and my eyes are burning with the smoke from the fire, or anger, or loss. 'And somehow, in all that misery, although he didn't love me, although I didn't really love him, a little part of him ran away with a little part of me, and they merged and started to grow. I didn't notice. I thought I was protected. He didn't notice, because he had stopped talking to me by then.' I study Georg's face for proof that he's heard me. He's not looking at me, but his face is soft.

'But then... without warning, they broke up in there. I had just moved to his city, hoping things would work out for me. I had run away from home and everything I knew, just to be somewhere else. And the only thing I knew there was him, and he was gone. So really...' I can hear that I make no sense, so I swallow again and again until my thoughts line up.

'The bits of him and me broke up and stormed out on each other. There was blood everywhere, and I was all alone. I could feel myself giving up on dealing with it, so I just fainted on the living room floor. When I woke up, I found this tiny little...' A false start. I swallow thrice.

'In my underwear, there was this little...' I clear my throat.

'I buried the foetus, I mopped up all the blood. And I thought about other things than Jacob for the rest of my life,' I say.

'Jacob?' Georg is still not watching me, but he's been listening. He is forgiving me.

'That would have been his name. I don't know how I know. I just do. He visited me, for years. I dreamed about him every December. I dreamed about him arriving on a long train. He would get off at the station and we'd laugh and play until the train whistle blew. Then I had to hand him back. He'd get older and older every time I dreamed of him. Until he stopped showing up.'

'I don't believe that,' Georg says.

'I don't really either. But it is still true.' He doesn't answer. 'I'm really sorry, Georg. You're a nice guy. I'm glad I met you.' He nods, and we leave it at that.

I swapped to the English version of the song, slowly, one click at a time to keep my eyes on the road. I was scared. My entire body was in red alert, interpreting every movement of the car as a disaster about to happen. It was going better, though. The car was humming, and I was singing, and I'd get there in just a little while. Not too far away from Kent. Not too far at all.

Nena insisted we'd spent time in a toy shop, and I sang along as best I could. My foot dared to push the accelerator down a little. I picked up a little speed, was getting there faster. The wipers were singing with me, for a while keeping exact beat with the song. A few beats off. Then back on track.

I lost control of everything. The road was suddenly not the road anymore. It was something slippery and unconnected, lifting the car across the sky and sliding it over the water that covered half of the turn in front of me. It was a road, it was a puddle, it was a deep, impossible pond. I couldn't steer so I hit the brakes, but nothing happened until the slam.

There were no lingering car horns, no sirens in the distance. Sticky blood dripped from my face, and I barely had time to ask myself: would blood show up against the sands of Namibia? Then everything went quiet, and not even Nena could reach me in her luftballon.

Georg and I continue like before. We bathe in the morning and chat all day. We eat and drink and dance. We listen our way through one MP3 player after the other and walk into town when it's time to get more batteries. We only pick up a couple each time, as it's nice to have something to do. Scram and Lady relax on the beach, and when it rains, we all huddle under a tarp and look at the waves. We see many more porpoises, and finally, a whale. It is unmistakable. The big curved back and the jet of water. I can't breathe.

'Georg!' I call. 'Look!' A small pointed dorsal fin, a colossal jump. I scream in delight.

'A whale!' I shout. 'A whale! A whale!'

Georg laughs at my enthusiasm. He has seen them many times before, but to me, this moment is fresh and new. The only thing that is fresh and new. Perhaps the very last. I dig out the pages of my book and study the drawings closely.

'It's a minke whale,' Georg says, but I study the drawing still. Just to make sure. Just to know that I know.

'Hello!' I call to the whale out there. It jumps again to greet me, then disappears completely. I sob like a child.

'A whale,' I cry. 'A whale!' Georg strokes my head and makes shushing sounds. I feel so very small.

12

Tomorrow morning, we are driving to Copenhagen. It has affected the mood somewhat, and all day, we've taken turns being sullen or asking too many questions. Now, we're quiet. We're staring into the flames and listening to the ocean. There's a light drizzle in the air, but not enough to make us care. Not enough to even notice, really.

'Have you seen it...?' I ask. The question makes me scared and shy, but time is running out, and I need to ask him before we leave.

'Seen what?' Georg says, as I knew he would.

'Fucking economist,' Kobus grumbles in my ear, 'sitting here pretending to be all stable in his own mind. Like fuck he is. Like fuck.' I ignore him. I haven't replied to him since I got here.

'There's something following me.' I say. True. 'It's kind of like a wolf.' True. 'And kind of like a man.' Also true. 'It has really long teeth and its breath smells of... It smells really bad.' All true. I weigh each word as it comes out, make sure it fits, make sure it's not too dangerous.

'I'm not sure if it's really... you know... real.' Not true. I do know.

He looks at me, and I can't really read his face.

'No,' he says. 'I haven't.'

'Oh...' I say, and blush a little. 'That's okay.'

'Well, I've seen it,' says Kobus.

'Yeah, but you're...' I say, then stop myself. I think I was speaking out loud. Georg knows better than to comment. Or maybe he didn't notice.

'There is...' Georg says, tasting the words as he speaks, 'something.'

I wait for a long time.

'Something?'

'Yeah. In my old house. Kind of like a shadow. I only ever see it there. It crawls on the walls and stares at me. Its face is just darkness, but I know it's staring straight at me, always fixed on me. Follows me around the house. Makes me think it will attack at any moment. Hisses and snarls and raises its claws to jump when I pass... But it never does.' He stares straight down into the ground.

'Mine crept up to me while I was lying in camp one night... It crept up and placed its fangs on my neck. I could feel its warm breath, and the tension in its jaw. But it didn't bite... just threatened to.' Having said it out loud doesn't make me feel better.

'I think,' he says. Slowly. 'We are imagining our beasts.' I can see that he doesn't really believe it.

'So do I,' I say. But I don't believe it either.

I could stay. I could. Could talk myself into accepting that the odds of my family being there are not in my favour. They're barely odds at all. Georg has checked on his entire family. Not an uncle, not a cousin, not a distant relative alive.

But walking is active. It's doing something. Sitting here, like he does, isn't big enough for me. I need to see my house again. Need to say goodbye. I want to hug my mum and tell her everything will be okay. We could make jam. If I hurry, there may still be mushrooms. All I need to do is hurry.

In my mind, she'll be standing on the stairs when I get there. Tears in her eyes.

'Nice to see you. Oh, we've missed you. Your father's well. We're okay.' But even as I think this thought, I can hear her voice is mine, and no matter how many times I try, I cannot make it change. Have I forgotten? Have I forgotten my mother's voice?

The creature howls that night for the first time since I found Georg. I can hear its growling steps circle around me, just out of reach of the flames of the fire. Sometimes, I get a glimpse of its hooded face, its thick fur, its bright and constant yellow eyes. I don't think Georg can see it, but I think he senses it's there.

'Are you okay?' he asks, eventually.

'Yeah...' I say. 'Just thinking about tomorrow. Thinking about the next month.'

He clears his throat. 'I was thinking,' he says. And I get the familiar sinking feeling. A vague suspicion something isn't right. But I'm wrong again, as I knew I would be.

'If your family aren't there... and I really hope they are, you know that?'

I nod. 'Of course.'

'If they're not there. What are you going to do?'

'I don't know, I haven't thought about it,' I say, and it's almost true.

'Well… We had a summer house in the south of Spain,' he says. 'We had just put it on the market, so it's all empty now, but I was thinking of going there when it gets too cold up here.'

'Oh yeah?' I say.

'Yeah. And, if you wanted to, you could come visit me there.' He looks up. 'There are plenty of bedrooms,' he adds.

'Maybe,' I say, 'If they're not there.'

He smiles. 'Even if they are… Well, winter can be brutal up north. Or so I hear. You'd be more than welcome to bring them. It's warmer there. Easier to live.'

I smile. 'Maybe,' I say. 'If they want to.'

I returned to my body centimetre by centimetre. My head hurt, my neck hurt, and as my consciousness fell into my shoulders and back, I wasn't all too surprised to find that they hurt, too. I had a terrible ache across my chest and abdomen. My knees and my legs were sore. It seemed my entire body had taken a bit of a pounding, but as far as I could tell, nothing was broken. Nothing was lost. Except, of course, everything was.

It took me ages to unbuckle the seatbelt. Another age to open the door. I toppled out of the car. Ice-cold water seeped through my clothes, but I could barely feel it at all. After four tries, I managed to haul myself upright by leaning on the car.

'Okay,' I said to myself. 'Okay!'

I noticed how thirsty I was. How my throat had turned to sandpaper. How long had I been asleep? I wobbled over to the passenger side, where my backpack sat upright and patiently waiting. There were a couple of bloodstains on the right pocket, but I pretended not to notice. It's not polite to stare. Instead, I dug into the side pockets and drank my way through one of the water bottles. I washed away dried blood from inside my mouth, and ignored the small flakes running down my throat. Smells. There were smells now. I looked down and realised there was sick on my T-shirt. I seemed to have soiled myself as well. Shame and fear fought for space inside me. I shivered and blushed and tried not to cry.

'It's fine,' I said out loud. 'It's fine. You're just a bit banged up after the crash. It's okay. Just... We need to get you washed and changed.' My voice was soothing, stern but kind.

'Okay,' I whispered.

'Come on now. There's a village right over there. Leave your pack. You can come back for it.'

I took a few steps backwards, away from the car. It looked horrible. The right side was wrinkled and squished. The hood was scrunched up like paper. I stared at the spot where I'd just been sitting. The window looked like a spider's web, droplets of blood sticking like insects to the fractures and lines. I could have died. Could have been stuck. Could have been stuck until I died. I imagined this clearly. Sitting there for days, hoping someone would turn up to help me. Wishing for the pain to stop and quiet to come. Not being able to get out of the car, being stuck against the wheel with my legs crushed underneath me. Stuck until I starved to death on the taste of dried blood in my mouth.

My stomach revolted. I retched again and again until there was nothing but bile left anywhere inside me. This could have been it. What a stupid, stupid way to go. For all I knew, I could be the last person on Earth. What a stupid risk to take. What a stupid, stupid, stupid...

'This is pointless.' I raised my voice to myself. 'We need to get you cleaned up and changed. We need to find more water and some food, then we need to find the entrance to the goddamn tunnel. Get going.' There wasn't as much confidence in my voice this time, but it had the desired effect. I left my backpack in the broken car and headed towards the nearest village. I wished it was still raining so I wouldn't have to smell the stench of my own frail body. I smelled like one of the dead.

'You know,' I say to Georg. I feel drunk, but I haven't been drinking. 'I always thought I'd be a playwright.' We're lying on our backs and watching the stars glide past above our heads. We've been talking about the darkness, and how we're now living like cave people. I'm resting my head on his arm. We have found a balance between the physical comfort of someone else's presence and the intimacy we both have craved but don't want to find.

'Really?' he says.

'Yeah. I thought I would write plays and musicals. Maybe even an opera. I wanted to write for TV and movies—things people would watch.' I chew on my lip.

'So... did you ever write a play?' he asks.

'Yes. I wrote many. A hundred, probably.'

'Oh! Which ones? Sarah loved the theatre, I may have seen something you wrote. Wouldn't that be strange?' he laughs. He sounds drunk.

'None you will ever have heard of. I never tried to get any of them on stage.' I roll over to my side. The fire is dying down but I can still make out Georg's face in the glow. It's strange how soon he has become familiar. How soon his little expressions have become the script of a language I can read and understand.

'I don't get it,' he says. 'What do you mean?'

'I was waiting, you see,' I say. 'To be good enough. Waiting to be a writer worthy of being put on the stage. And while I was waiting, I took pictures. I have always been good at taking pictures, but it wasn't something I had a passion for. So I started taking pictures, and I wasn't scared to put them out into the world. They weren't my real talent, so I didn't care if people liked them.' I hear a splash from the ocean and wonder if it's a porpoise or another whale. Mice are rustling around in the tall grass and nocturnal birds are hooting. The world is quiet and full of sounds.

'But people did like my pictures, and I liked travelling, so I started travelling with my camera. I sold moments of war and love and dance, fragments of cultures from all over the world. I just snapped them up, and sold them.'

'Strange way of saying it,' he says.

'Yes, but that's what it felt like. And to ease my own bad conscience, I started writing articles to go along with them. Thought it would be a good way to get writing experience. But again, I didn't want to become a journalist, so I didn't care too much if people didn't like what I wrote, and therefore I wasn't scared to submit them. People read my articles, people liked my articles, and I thought—*soon*, really soon, I will try to get a play published.'

'But you didn't?'

'No. I just kept waiting. To be good enough, for the right time, for a play that felt right. Most of my articles were fairly political—eco-criticism, war, that sort of thing. They had to match the pictures, and that was what I photographed. So I waited for an idea for that sort of play. And in the meantime, I wrote play after play after play for practise. Waiting to start following my dream.'

'Shit,' says Georg. It makes me giggle. I haven't heard him swear before.

'Yeah. A bit late now. And I never even started smoking weed. I always thought I would do that. I thought I was the type of person who should smoke weed, lying on her back, like this. Looking at the stars and saying really stupid things, but finding them really beautiful.'

He laughs.

'I've got weed,' he says.

'You do?'

'Yeah. Plenty. I've picked out every house in the entire village. Have enough to last me a year. And if I run out,

I'll go to Copenhagen. Pick through Christiania—the bohemian quarter. Will find enough to last me a lifetime. Do you want some?'

'Nah,' I say. 'I'm too tired.' In reality, I just don't want to cough and sputter. I don't want to inhale hot smoke and see the creature coming at me. I don't want to risk it. Don't want to try.

'Okay,' he says, as I lie back down on his arm. 'Can you tell me a story? Like... make one up?'

I swallow hard. The thought hurts. 'Sure,' I say, and do it anyway. Even though I feel like the world can't contain another story. Even though everywhere I look, I see the world filled to the brim with all that used to be. But I like Georg, and I want to make him happy.

I make up a story with characters and plot twists. I put on voices, like I would do when I read to my niece or Cleopatra. I make Georg laugh, and I love him then. For a brief second, I love him and his dorky laughter. As I notice he grows tired, I move the story into a forest. I tell it slowly, softly, darkly. I let him drift away. When he's fast asleep, I make up an ending. Everyone dies, and there's no one left to grieve.

I washed myself in a cafe. The windows were already broken so I simply stepped over the shards. I gathered some bottles of water and brought them into the ladies' room. I didn't even consider using the men's. These days I don't care, but back then, I didn't think. Everything came about by habit. The face in the mirror scared me enough that I let out a small yelp of fear. My mind took a step back.

'Just figure out what the damage is,' I said to myself. 'Think of it as someone else. It isn't you. It is a someone. Now, state what is wrong. Come on!'

There were shards of glass sticking out of my skin. Two deep slashes weaving from my forehead and back through my hair, disappearing somewhere in a clotted mess of hair and blood and muddy water. The pattern repeated itself. Once through my hair, once across my face.

My cheek was swollen and purple. My lip had been bleeding too. I tried to take in each detail, figure out what I had to do. I started from the top. My head hurt. I cleaned myself with toilet paper, bottled water and hand soap. I was fairly sure my head needed stitches, but I hadn't brought a sewing kit. *Worry about that later*, I thought. When I had rinsed out most of the blood, I braided the hair across the gashes. Braided it into two tight plaits, picking hair from both sides of the wounds, pulling the skin close, as tightly as I could without sewing. I hoped my hair wouldn't stick in the open sore as the gashes began to heal. I couldn't quite figure out what the glass was from. Too thin to be window. Too thick to be mirror. But what did I know, really?

I fixed myself as best I could, and then I fell away.

13

When Georg sleeps, I think about evil; it's been on my mind since I started walking. We used to talk about evil as part of the world. As something that was out there, waiting, lurking and calling. I grew up knowing it was a corrupting influence, something that would distort people's hearts, perhaps stain their souls, but it wasn't part of people themselves. Not as such. When I thought I was the only person left in the world, could I have done something evil? I don't know for sure.

If I kicked Scram whenever he disobeyed me, if I made him suffer, would that be evil? There's nothing to stop him running away from me, nothing to keep him from biting me or tearing me apart. He isn't my dog. I know that. He isn't my dog at all. He is big, and he is strong, so I think it would be a fair fight. Kicking him would be cruel, sure. Unwise and unkind, definitely. But evil?

Perhaps if I poisoned a lake, or a well, and hundreds of animals died. With strong enough poison, I could leave an entire area desolate. Would that be evil? Would it matter? I have seen how nature creeps back. How it has already reclaimed cities and towns, fields and gardens.

Building a city used to mean wiping out nature, but now that the cities are no longer kept, would I even leave permanent scars?

Would it matter if an area turned brown and charred and broken for a decade? Nature has stood by for centuries, eager and ready to reconquer what it once lost—or maybe lent us. Surely, the poisoned well would have less of an impact than all of our cities and airports?

Killing animals isn't evil. Or at least, it wasn't evil before. We killed hundreds of thousands of millions of chickens, pigs, cows, sheep and deer. What would make this different? I wouldn't be killing them for food, that's true, but we've always killed more than we ate. Mountains of meat ended up spoiled and wasted, rotting in cling film or left on the plate.

Besides, when poisoning this hypothetical well, I wouldn't be killing animals that were bred to die by my hand. Neither would I be killing animals I had kept in captivity, tortured, neglected, branded or owned. No, if I poisoned a lake, the animals killed would be animals in the wild, living their natural lives, dying one of many possible deaths. It wouldn't be evil, just pointless and dumb.

But now, there is Georg. Another human. All the acts of evil are back on the table, but I cannot figure out why. What difference does it make, to the world, to my soul, if I split open his guts and roast him over the fire? What difference does it make, to salvation or damnation, that he, like me, wishes he was dead like the rest? Would it not be a kindness, even, to reunite him with his daughter and girlfriend and wife?

'God?' I whisper. Scram lifts his head and looks at me, but doesn't reply. 'Is there any evil left I can do?' There is silence, and a light sprinkle of rain. 'Was there ever?' And I know the truth of that. There was, there was, there might have been, and it might be out there, still.

Every morning, you access your basic information. Who you are, where you are and how you got there. It keeps you sane. Keeps you grounded. Helps you ignore that you're a soft, fleshy being in a world full of hard edges. We name ourselves to feel bigger, name our surroundings so we don't feel lost.

I woke up. In the first few moments, everything felt normal and calm. I tried to access my grounding information, but I came up empty, time and time again. There was nothing but a gap in my mind where the past few weeks should have been. A gap, pulsating and raw, sucking in information from my surroundings. Cuts, blood, a taste of iron in my mouth. An accident. I had to have been in an accident.

'Cleopatra?' I called.

'Hello?' I wasn't at home, I was nowhere I knew.

'Please! Help! Someone? Can someone call an ambulance?' Then a flash of memory. Myself, in front of a mirror, picking shards of glass out of my skin.

'Hello?' Sitting in Kobus's car.

'Kobus?' Sitting in Kobus's car alone.

'Cleopatra?' A cough, a fever, a grave, maggoty eyes, my Cleopatra... Oh no... Oh no. No!

'No' ran through my body like a thunderous church bell.

'No' called me to mourn.

'No' called me to wed my new reality.

'No' was harsh and cold, couldn't breathe, couldn't stay, couldn't go. Alone! Curling up into a ball, it hurt, but I did it anyway. Squeezed small, squeezed tight, tried to implode into myself and slip into the gap in my head. Every muscle tense and taut, every breath a gust of wind through the cracks in the surface. Have to breathe. Have to release. Get a grip.

'You are okay,' I said eventually, my voice an anxious squeak, 'you are okay. Just breathe.'

That's what she used to tell me, whenever the world got too much and I couldn't handle it. When I'd panic or rage, cry and scream. 'Just breathe,' she would tell me, 'just breathe.'

'Just breathe,' I told myself. My voice caught and sputtered, and there was a soreness to it I'd almost forgotten I had. Slowly, deliberately, layer after layer of calm breathing began to wrap up the soreness and fear.

'You're okay. You'll be okay. Just breathe. Just breathe. Just breathe.'

Packed up, labelled and pushed aside. Needed to understand and find answers.

I looked around. Somehow, I had made my way to the tunnel. How? Mud on my shoes, sore legs, tracks in the mud, I had walked.

My backpack was with me. I went through the pockets and checked that everything was there. I pressed the keyring to my cheek and noticed new, fresh cuts on my arms. Must have been somewhere, done something, between now and the cafe.

'Do you think I should start walking now, or wait until I feel better?' I asked her smiling face on the keyring. She didn't reply, but she looked at me with that little smile that told me I had to stop and think.

'You're right,' I said. 'I don't have food or water. I used to have water. I wonder where my bottles have gone.'

The keyring felt comfortable in my hand, so I kept it there. I walked aimlessly, crossing track after track. But all I found were new fences, new obstacles. She kept smiling at me from the photo, and I took that to be a good sign.

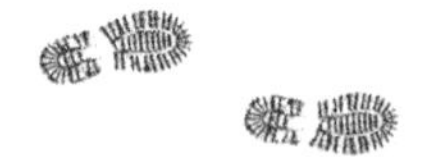

We're quiet in the car. The road is wide and open; there's not a single car but ours. We could drive fast, but Georg doesn't. He drives carefully, slowly, stretching out the distance as much as he can. I don't mind. I'm eager to get home to Norway, find the truth of things. But still, I worry about the creature, the loneliness and what's waiting for me once Georg turns around and leaves. I'm in no hurry to leave him.

'Georg?' I say, and the sound startles both of us. 'Why don't you come with me? Why don't we drive to the farm together? And then... well, you can stay with us, or go home. Or we can come with you to Spain. Either way... why don't you?' The question is a difficult one. Partly, I don't want him to come. If my family is... if they're all... Certain things are better experienced alone. But on the other hand, things will be different in Sweden. The distances are longer. It's further between towns and cities. It will be harder to find shops and food, and there are wolves in the forests. Wolves I used to hear about, and now will have to listen out for.

'I can't,' he says, after a very long time. 'I am waiting.'

'For what?'

'For my son.'

I don't reply right away. I skim through my memories of the past few days. Try to replay all our conversations in double speed. But nothing. No. This is new information.

'I didn't know you had a son?' I say. I let the words out low and soft; give him the option to pretend he doesn't hear me. He runs his large hand through his beard. He rubs his forehead and sighs.

'Well...' he says, eventually. 'His name is Martin. He's 24. Bright boy. One of those bleeding-heart, save-the-world types, you know. But not naive! No, no, he studied political science.' Each sentence comes separated from the previous one. As if he's defining his son by listing the parameters. Trying to draw out an accurate picture in the air.

'And when it all began, he was travelling. Bali, last I talked to him.' Georg bites his lip nervously, blinks, swallows. I turn my head away and stare out of the window. Try to give him a minute of privacy.

'He called me, when things were already really bad. He was scared. Said he had met a couple of people who owned a small plane. They were going to get him to Thailand. And he'd make his way from there.

'"I don't know if I will make it, Dad," he said. "Everyone is dying. I don't know what to do." And I told him. "You'll be fine," I said. "Just keep moving. Come home. I will wait here, no matter what happens. I will wait. I will wait until it gets too cold to stay in Denmark, and then I'll go to the summer house. Considering the circumstances, I think we should keep it. You, keep moving. I'll see you soon. Call me when you get to Thailand." And he said he would.' He goes quiet.

'He never called?'

Georg turns to me. He's dark. 'We don't know that,' he says. 'Maybe they had to turn the network off earlier there than here. Maybe he tried to call but the signal was blocked. Maybe he lost his phone. Maybe someone offered to drive him somewhere, and he was planning to call when he got there, and then got distracted. We don't know anything.'

'No,' I say. 'We don't know. After all, *I* made it all the way here,' I say. He smiles.

'Yes, you did. When you came across the bridge, I thought for a moment...' He clears his throat.

'Oh...' I say. 'I'm sorry.' And I am. He shrugs.

'Didn't last long,' he says. 'My son doesn't have as much hair as you do.' He smiles a sad little smile and pulls on one of my braids for emphasis. It is a tender act. Familiar. So I smile, and he smiles, and we love each other for another moment.

'I hope your son finds you,' I say.

'He will,' he says.

'If my family isn't...' I swallow. Start again. 'I may come join you in Spain, if I don't find my family.'

'That would be nice.' The corners of his mouth bob up and down, a smile, a truth, a smile, a truth. He winks at me. 'No repopulating, I promise.'

The bridge seems endlessly long, but I know it isn't. It's eight kilometres, hardly anything at all compared with how far I've walked already. Scram and Lady are eager to get out of the car. They jump around themselves, dart up and down the road. They bark and play around my feet. I've taken a liking to Lady. She listens when I call, and she's fonder of being petted and cuddled than Scram is. I often feel I need a cuddle, and maybe she does too.

'All right,' Georg says, hauling my trolley out of his van. He tried to convince me we could pick up a new one in Copenhagen, but I insisted we had to bring my old one. I know this trolley. I know its squeaks and creaks, and I know which way its wheels pull. I call it home. Georg has oiled and brushed and rubbed and tightened everything he could get his hands on. He says it will last me a while longer, but not forever. He went through his house looking for Swedish coins, found a handful and put them in my backpack. Said it might be nice to have change if I need to get a new trolley.

'I could just break one free,' I say. 'Chains don't last forever if you have a hammer.'

'Neither does anything,' he says.

We hug for a long time.

'All right,' says Georg again when we pull apart. He drops all my belongings back in the trolley and pushes it around as if to test the wheels.

'All right then,' he says again.

'All right.' I buckle the chest strap on my backpack and feel the familiar weight on my shoulders. When I turn around, his eyes have flooded and his bottom lip does a funny little dance. I don't think I'm crying, but my cheeks feel wet. We hug again for a very long time. The backpack makes it awkward. He forces his hands in between my back and the hard mesh, and I can smell nothing but him and the ocean. Scram barks and jumps up on us a couple of times, resting his head between our thighs when he can't get a reaction.

'No, Scram. Get down,' I mumble, but my heart isn't in it. It never really was.

'All right then,' says Georg when he lets me go. We go through this dance a couple of times. A very long hug. Then, 'All right then,' again. He hands me a note with the address of his house in Spain. He has drawn me a little map of how to get there from the church in the town centre. I fold it twice and put it in my pocket. It lies next to my stone and feels important. There isn't much else to say, so I smile, he smiles, and we're both really sad. I nod, and leave, and that is that. I take a step onto the bridge, and now I'm on my wa—

'Hey!' he calls, so I turn around. He is handing me something.

'I always thought you were an artist,' he says, and pushes the bag into my hand. I open it, smell it and know what it is. It's the sweet and spicy smell of Amsterdam and alleyways and neighbours I never really knew.

'I think you'll like it,' Georg smiles. 'Wait until you get home. Do it somewhere safe. But you'll like it.'

We hug, again, for a very long time. Like the hugs before, this is the first and the last. I start walking backwards, pushing the trolley with my back as I move. I wave and wave and wave until his truck is long gone, and I'm all alone again. Except for Scram. Except for Lady.

And except for the creature. I sigh.

'What do you want?' I call to it. It's slouching in the shadow by the end of the bridge. It doesn't reply but bares its teeth. It snarls, but I cannot hear it. The wind is picking up.

The shop was not a shop, but a service station. It promised to hold everything I'd need for a pleasant journey, but I didn't carry that sort of hope. I walked through it twice, trying to imagine what I would need for the two days it would take me to walk through the tunnel. 50.5 kilometres. I remembered from planning the Camino that the average per day was around 20 kilometres. As I wouldn't need to stop anywhere, wouldn't need to find shelter or be social for dinner, I figured two days would be more than enough. I grabbed a couple of water bottles. Some biscuits and some chocolate bars. There wasn't much in terms of regular food, but I found some Pot Noodles and figured I could eat them raw. There was a cafeteria, eerie in its emptiness. There were some foil-wrapped treats on the bar, coconut kisses and a carrot cake. The carrot cake was only a week or two past its best-before date. The coconut kisses had months to go. I grabbed some batteries, some antibacterial wipes, ran out of things to pick up, so I stopped.

Everything hurt when I walked. Making my way back to the tunnel entrance, my feet were already aching. I should have thought about it, but I didn't. I worried more about how to get into the tunnel itself. And it took time. Much longer than I thought. It was already dusk and damp and chilly when I stepped into the absolute dark behind the gates.

In the beginning, there was darkness. My head torch made the darkness worse. It illuminated the broad path in front of me, showed me rails and exit signs, promised me it was still far to go. I walked for an hour, then for one more. Another right after that. But progress was slow, and I was cold to the bone. My feet hurt. My hiking boots were rubbing and chafing. I thought back to the last time I had worn them. The prepping and primping I did. The plasters and petroleum jelly that were essential for me not to blister.

'You're right,' I whisper to Cleopatra's photo. Whisper, so as not to disturb the darkness. 'I should have prepared better. I'll sort it when I'm out on the other side.'

I walked until I was too tired, then I placed my sleeping bag down in the middle of the tracks. Although I knew I was in no danger from approaching trains, I couldn't make myself relax. I dragged my stuff down to the next service tunnel and went to sleep in its entrance, out of the tracks, out of danger, air smelling of iron and dust.

I had no idea how much time had passed when I woke up, but I felt awake, so I decided to start walking. An hour, maybe two, before I noticed the numbers on the wall. Somehow, the night had turned me around and I was walking back towards the entrance.

'You're right,' I whispered. 'I need to pay attention.'

I turned around to face France and tried to move quicker, but my feet hurt and made me groan. The darkness whispered its secrets back in a language that crept along my spine. Shivering, goosebumpy, crackling and cold.

'Cleopatra?' I tried after a while. 'Cleopatra?'

Empty. My hand was empty. I opened and closed it, again and again, but it didn't fold around the keyring. It wasn't there. I sat down on the tracks and searched the contents of my backpack. Thoroughly once, thoroughly twice. On the third try, I took out every single item, lined them up in an orderly row, made sure I knew what everything was, counting them, packing them, the keyring wasn't there.

Each service tunnel looked just like another. Where had I slept? Where had I been? I searched the tracks, back and forth, over and over, unsure how far I had walked in any direction. I inched the tunnel with my torch, willing it to reveal her face on the tracks. My pulse beat hard and fast like a drum, calling the darkness to war. My heart felt betrayed; I had lost my love once, and now I'd lost her again. I shivered and cried and told myself I would find her. But hope was bloodied, outgunned and outnumbered, fighting both darkness and time.

I tried, over and over, to tell myself to stop. Take a breath. Look closer. Go back to the entrance and try again. But I remembered talking to the keyring the night before. I remembered Cleopatra smiling to me as I fell asleep. And the fact that it was missing... Could something have taken it? Had something stolen it from me? I scared myself with images of creatures crawling through the dark. From the depths of my childhood nightmares, I pulled up memories of ice-cold faces, pale creatures approaching from behind, sharp claws and fangs hanging over my shoulder, darkness ready to pounce.

'There is nothing dangerous here!' I said out loud. Talking aloud made the tunnel feel smaller. I narrated my journey, explaining every motion, trying to scare the darkness away. It clung to me, crawled on me, drew out its horrible plans for me. Any second now, the mechanical pumps could run out of whatever it was that kept them going. Water could flow in from any direction, drown me down here with the keyring. This was wasting time, and I knew it. I had to keep going. I had to, but I kept searching nonetheless.

The darkness sucked me up. Diluted me, emptied me, left me translucent like a ghost. It called to me, tempted me, made me feel like bending my knees and searching the tunnel floor with my fingertips. It made me feel like I'd die without the keyring. It made me feel breathless.

'I'm sorry!' I called into the tunnel, hoping Cleopatra could hear me, wherever she was. 'I have to go now. I have to get out.' And I knew I shouldn't apologise, because this is what she would have told me to do. *Keep walking*, she would have said to me, holding her hand against my chest to make me feel my breath. *Don't waste your time. Don't waste your breath. Just walk.* So I walked, and there she was, on the tracks right in front of me. She was further up the tunnel than I thought I'd been, closer to France than I thought I'd come. She smiled to me as I approached. My heart calmed down.

'Welcome,' she smiled. 'Welcome back. I've missed you. Now, let's get you out of here.'

‘I’m losing it a little,’ I said. The light from my torch flickered and died.

14

The bridge is tougher going than I thought it would be. The wind whips and beats me as I walk, threatens to topple me over and wash me out to sea. Lady and Scram walk pressed to the ground and whimper. We inch our way over the asphalt.

I stop to put my raincoat on. It offers better protection against the wind, but makes me easier to push over. The wind forces its way into my ears, into my mouth and down my throat. It fills me with a chill I don't know how to shake. I'm not even a third of the way across. The ocean around me is wide, wild and beautiful.

Perhaps I imagine it, but the water looks clearer than it used to be. I know nothing has happened to the masses of plastic and waste that are floating around out there, but I still feel it's clearer, brighter, somehow. Maybe the lack of ships stirring it up has made it settle down into glassy depths, now frothy and crystal clear. Watching the waves makes me seasick, so I keep my eyes firmly on the road.

A gust of wind forces Lady to take two steps sideways. I lift her up and put her in the trolley. She curls up in the bottom and hides her nose under the tarp. I worry

Scram will have to go in as well, sooner or later. If the wind gets much worse, I may not be able to walk and stay steady myself. I may not be able to push the trolley. But these are maybes, because now I am strong. I feel it for the first time in my life.

My legs shove the road away under me. My arms push the trolley steadily forward. I lean into the wind and let it hold me up. Step by step, Sweden gets closer. Step by step, Georg becomes a memory on the other side. My resolve sings through my body like music. I am strong, I am strong, I am strong. An unexpected flurry brings me to my knees, and I brace myself against the trolley to keep it from crushing me. Scram barks and I scream, but I press back onto my feet and continue. I am strong, so strong, so strong, and it means something new all the time.

Sweden feels familiar. More familiar than Denmark. The edge of the bridge draws nearer and nearer, and I can already see how familiar it is. Almost home, I'm almost home. My entire body aches with the strain of crossing. In the back of my mind, I think that I might have to do it again. If my family isn't... But I'll be better prepared then. I'll have to find a better jacket. I'll have to make room in the trolley for both Scram and Lady. But maybe, maybe I won't have to. Maybe I'll never return.

The bridge and the road take me into Malmö. I haven't been in this city for ages. Not since the last time I took the bus to Germany, and sat for too many hours in a bus too full of people. It was so damp and warm that people's breath condensed and dripped down from the ceiling. The dampness covered the windows, the ceiling and the floor. We were swimming in each other's liquids.

People begged for the chance to leave and buy some water, get a coffee, get some air. But the driver pressed on, as the timetable didn't allow for hydration. I felt horrible then. Dehydrated, tired and short of breath, I thought it was one of the worst things I'd ever experience. I would sacrifice so much to be back on that bus. I'd love people's breath to drip down on me, now. At least, back then, there were people. At least back then, there was breath.

I have to be smart now, I know. I wish I'd asked Georg how he hunted. Maybe he would have known how to find me a gun. Maybe he could have taught me how to use it. But more than that, I need to find a map. And food and water, and a plan.

There is one road to Norway that I know, but I don't know if that's the quickest one, and time is of the essence. Half of August has already passed. The leaves have started to yellow here, and the air is crisp and dry. I pass a hotel, which is exactly what I need. The doors aren't locked. I wonder, as I place my backpack against the reception desk, if they did the same thing here. Told people to keep their doors open. That help was on its way. I wonder if there are people here, dead in their rented rooms. I hope, for their sake, that no one ever comes to collect what they owe. A lot of time has passed since they checked out. The thought makes me laugh, but I mean it completely. There isn't a joke in my mind.

In the reception, there are two city maps to choose from. One is surrounded by ads for restaurants. The other is a shopping guide. That's what I need. That, too, makes me giggle. I used to say stupid things, like, 'Shopping is like a slow death of your moral principles.' Now, I'm grateful for the shopping districts and how they provide what I need. Never what I want, though. Just what I need.

On the map, I circle a bookshop, a pet shop, a pharmacy and a sports equipment store. They're not too far apart. I leave my stuff in the lobby. I wish I was worried about leaving stuff behind.

The smell of death is everywhere, and it hits me again and again. The days by the sea have weakened my tolerance. The smell sticks to the roof of my mouth, fills my nose and lungs like mud. Some dogs down an alley are tearing a cat apart. Lady and Scram look attentive, on guard, but the others don't even look up as we pass.

I was planning to give Georg one of the MP3 players. Some music so he'd feel less alone. First, I was planning to give him the one with the Rush albums, the purple one I picked up in Belgium. But when I took it out of my backpack, the thought of the bag in the bus stop made me pause. Georg wouldn't know. He wouldn't know how the bag was filled with ten packets of mints, four packets of gum and a purple bottle of mouth spray. He wouldn't understand how the person who owned it must have been really afraid of bad breath.

He wouldn't spend time wondering if she was dating someone, was ill or had a confidence problem. Maybe it was a compulsion, like how I used to buy diaries I'd never use. Georg wouldn't know how everything in the bag was the same shade of purple as the MP3 player. The purse, the lipstick, the phone and the notebook. A favourite colour, no doubt. And Georg wouldn't know how neat the handwriting was in the notebook, or how the owner had scribbled flowers in the margins. Even if I told him all the details, he wouldn't truly know.

I considered the other music players in the bag. All 13 of them. But each of them belonged to someone, so they weren't mine to give away. For a while, I considered giving him mine. Something to remember me by. But as I held it in my hand and opened my mouth to call him over, from my selfish heart came an angry roar. This player held Cleopatra's voice, it held my favourite songs. It held the audiobooks I had listened to time and time again. I was angry, then, at Georg. Felt he was trying to steal something from me. But when the moment of anger had passed, I just pushed all the players back into my backpack and vowed not to think about it again.

The tunnel was endless and narrow, stretching out through too much darkness. I had slept thrice, but probably not for long. I should have been out by now, or at least, I thought I should. There wasn't much water left. There wasn't much food left. There were so many things I hadn't known.

I hadn't known my back would ache and make me slow and rigid whenever I took a break. I hadn't known my feet would bleed into my shoes, or that walking would feel impossible all the time. Not a single thought had I spared for the blisters on my shoulders and back. How my backpack would dig and gouge through my flesh, and press me further down into my boots. I hadn't known how long I would be walking through darkness, or how dark real darkness could be.

I hadn't brought enough batteries and was already on my final pair. I tried to ration the light as best I could. When I took a break, I turned the light on to make sure I started up again in the right direction. When I woke up, I did the same. I turned it on to see Cleopatra's face every now and then, just so I could remember who I was.

Sometimes, but only sometimes, I turned the light on when I heard the darkness whisper. Not because I thought something was there. Not because I thought something was hiding or lurking. But because I wish I *knew* that it wasn't. Wish I could look into the dark and say to myself, 'This is darkness. It hides nothing.' But even with the torch on, even when I pointed it into every corner, the darkness was stifling and slow to get out of the way. Still, shining the torch always helped for a second. Sometimes two or three.

The darkness was a trap. Nothing moved. I was hungry. I was thirsty. No one listened when I talked and no one made a single sound. Hello? Hello? Not a single sound, again. Then I ran out of light.

Whenever I took a break, I made an arrow of things from my backpack. I counted them methodically, made sure nothing got lost. When I woke up, I felt my direction. Made sure to stand up without twisting, walked along the wall and felt my way forward. There would be light. There would be. There would be light, I knew.

I wished I could see Cleopatra's smile, or feel her soft skin under my fingers. I wished I would find the exit. I hoped it would be filled with light.

Too dark. Too dark. I needed to get out. I needed to find the entrance or the exit or somewhere that wasn't here. The darkness scratched and squeaked now. Sometimes it brushed against my legs or ran over my sleeping bag at night.

I sang to keep myself company, but my voice was crisp and dry, and didn't carry at all. The darkness caught my voice and muffled it. Made every sound hollow and far away, except for the scratches, the whispers and squeaks—they were loud and everywhere. *I can't breathe for much longer*, I thought. *If I don't find air, I'll die in here.* My lungs filled with dust and silence. Drowning in darkness. Who even knew that you could?

I find a road map without trouble. They have one for Norway, too, and I bring them both. My mood is light. For the first time in months, I don't feel too bad. The world is big, and right now I'm safe. In a little while, I'll be warm and sheltered from the wind and weather. If I'm lucky, I'll be able to curl up in a soft hotel bed, cover myself in clean sheets and nibble away at pillow mints. Perhaps the hotel has a minibar in each room. Perhaps they have soaps that smell nice.

I skim the shelves of fiction. I recognise some titles because they resemble their Norwegian siblings. I pick out a couple from the English section. Easy chick-lit novels I've read before. If I'm lucky, getting into a hotel room won't be too hard, and then this is what I'll do: I'll snuggle up in the bed and read for a while. Think about nothing, and just read. I don't worry too much about the implications of choosing one book over the other. I don't worry about everything that will be forgotten. I don't feel the pressure or responsibility, don't feel I'm carrying the world inside my head. Today is a wonderful day.

The sports equipment store yields tennis balls for the dogs and some sports tape for me. My wrist is sore from pushing the trolley across the bridge, and I want to make sure nothing gets inflamed or angry. Scram is already playing with a ball; Lady watches him from under the counter. Everything feels familiar. I understand all the signs.

The pet shop reeks of dead fish, rotten water and mummified guinea-pigs. A fat tarantula crawls across the wall, and I keep it in the corner of my eye as I pick out some nail clippers and brushes for the dogs, a collar for Scram, some more toys, a bag of dog food, some dried pig's ear treats. I'm spoiling them, I know. But what else is there to do?

The tarantula moves slowly and deliberately across the wall. I don't know what it eats in here, but it doesn't seem to be suffering. Its hairy legs make me shiver, but I don't really mind spiders... or at least, I didn't use to. Perhaps we've turned back time far enough for my gut-instinct terrors to wake up. After centuries of slumber, somewhere deep in my DNA, a phobia of snakes, spiders and things that go *grrrr* in the night has been activated. The world's gone wild and I'm unprotected. Perhaps from now on, I'll forever shiver at the thought of that which slithers or crawls.

I wonder if this spider is the jumping kind. I wonder if it will survive, now that the window is broken and the cold welcomed in. Lady has found a dog bed and snuggled up inside it. Scram walks next to me, wagging his tail and begging for toys, for treats, for attention.

'Good boy,' I say and give him a dried pig's ear. He takes it over to Lady, who sniffs it but goes back to resting. I grab a couple of bags of fancier treats, in case she's too good for dried pork. She hasn't eaten much lately, and it worries me. Scram would be sad if something happened. Would he leave her behind if she got ill? Would he come with me or stay with her? Jealousy gnaws on my heart and makes me scowl. I'm being irrational, but what else is new?

I restock on blister plasters, although I don't know if I'll need them. I thought a few days off the road might leave my feet sore and blistered again, but the skin on my feet, shoulders and back has taken on the qualities of tree bark. It's rough, hard, and carries the memory of a thousand meetings with shoes, straps and linings. It has learned from experience, and protects me from gnawing shoes. I stock up anyway, just in case, and add some petroleum jelly.

When I was preparing for my pilgrimage, I learned there are two basic types of protection against blisters. Both seek to limit the friction between the shoes and your feet, but they approach it from opposite sides. One is to put barriers between the offending parties: plasters, extra socks, padding. The other is to eliminate the friction completely: make your feet too slippery, too soft and smooth for your shoes to catch. To do this, you have to smear your feet with petroleum jelly until your toes gurgle in your socks. This is the solution that works for me. It is disgusting, and makes me feel like my feet are always wet. But they're not, they don't bleed, and that's all that matters.

I've thought about this too often. How to avoid friction. How to avoid chafing that blisters and bleeds. I soak my mind in numbness, making it too slippery for my memories to catch.

My feet were bleeding, making my shoes wet and sticky, blood seeping down between my toes. Or maybe it wasn't blood. Maybe it was the liquid of a hundred blisters bursting. It pooled under my feet. My heels were rubbed raw, and I could no longer take my socks off at night in fear of pulling off whatever skin was left. *When I get out of the darkness*, I'd think, *when I get out of the darkness, things will change. When.* It had to be soon, surely. I'd been walking for days and days. I'd slept four times. Or maybe five. I needed water. I really needed water. I would need water so soon.

I used to work at a hotel as a night receptionist. It wasn't the best job I ever had, but it paid for my freelancing and it was easy enough. I'm hoping, as we return to the hotel, that some foreseeing soul has left the maintenance console unit somewhere I can find it. But of course they haven't. I search the reception and there's no sign of it, but what I do find is a backup key-reader. This is excellent news.

The hotel I worked for was relatively fancy. It was the kind of hotel where businessmen would take their lovers, and young couples would spend too much money on a room for the night. Our service motto was 'It can be done', and my manager had me go through extensive scenario training. I had to be prepared for every eventuality, he said, because when it happened, I would be the customer's only hope of leaving with their dignity in tact.

We had a fire once. One politician after the other came stumbling down to reception, undressed and wrapped in blankets. Their young secrets came a few steps behind, scared and clinging to bundles of clothes. We split them up without question before the cameras arrived. We sorted shirts and trousers from the uniform closet, and no one would ever know.

One of the eventualities I was prepared for was a long-lasting power cut. It has finally come in handy. For fun, I rummage around until I find a check-in form. I fill it out, meticulously, leave my telephone number and email address. For mailing address, I put my UK address rather than my Norwegian one. It only hurts a little.

The backup programmer is different to the one we had. It takes two C batteries, and I don't have any. There will probably be some in here, somewhere, but I can't be bothered to conduct another search. Scram and Lady are happy to come outside with me for another expedition, and we return in less than an hour with C batteries and the dwindling light.

The machine whirrs. The sound is so familiar, yet incredibly strange. It makes me long for laptops and heating fans. I don't know what sequence this hotel uses, so

I program a handful of cards at a time, and eventually I figure it out. The lock blinks green, makes a chirpy sound and lets me enter. I can hear the beeps from other locks down the corridor. Their batteries will go out soon, as these things do. But I only need one room, and this is the one. It's clean and spacious, and without the smell of death. By old habit, I check out the bathroom. I smell the soaps and the shower gel. There are teabags and freeze-dried coffee, and—blissful joy—there's a minibar.

I wonder if I should program keys for the top floors. See if I can find myself a suite. But the added luxury is worthless to me, and this bed is ready and here. I read until I fall asleep. None of the books make sense anymore.

15

I sleep better than I have in months. The bed is firm, the duvet soft, and the dogs are curled up by my feet. I don't mind the way they stain the covers. I don't even notice until I wake up. It isn't properly light yet, but I feel fully rested and ready to go. I spread out the maps and study my options. Try to remember all I've heard. There's the way I know. But that way means wolves, and miles and miles of forest roads and loneliness. Then there's the way that takes me too far north and too far west before circling back. That way feels safer but holds five days, at least, of wasted time.

Then there's the way I do not know and have not heard of. But which will take me up from the south and through the forest and some towns. It seems neither safe nor familiar, but it seems quicker, and I feel like the wolves would have better places to be.

I don't know why I have such a fear of wolves. There aren't even that many left in the woods, and I know that. I also know that there hasn't been a single confirmed wolf attack on humans since the 1700s, or thereabouts, and that there are plenty of elks and deer around for them to hunt. But I also know I'm all alone.

I don't really fear the wolf, but the Wolf: the myth, the force, the monster. The creature that stalks its prey and attacks when you start running. I fear the Big Bad Wolf who keeps me from my grandmother's house. The savage beast with the yellow eyes. And although I don't know the wolf at all, I think them both the same.

Scram and Lady. What use would they be against wolves? Would they protect me or run? Would they join them? Create a pack of their own? I don't know, and I don't want to guess. I want to go home, right now.

I draw out a path that takes me through as many villages and towns as possible. It zigzags and isn't efficient, but it's the best chance I have of survival. I've learned my lesson by now.

I try to calculate approximately how long it will take me, and I feel my spirit sink with the distance and the knowledge that it may be September before I reach the border. September is autumn in Norway. September can bite.

I saw light! There was light, and the freshest air I'd ever breathed. It broke its way down into my lungs and washed the darkness away. Outside! This was outside. The world had seagulls and sounds, the rustling had stopped and the dark couldn't reach me here. The light was so bright and so clear, it felt like a burning embrace. A scorching affair, a blistering kiss. Except, in fact, the light was the moon, and it was night. I wanted to laugh. Why would anyone be scared of the dark at night? Why was I, ever?

This darkness was thin and transparent and mild. It didn't whisper. It couldn't see me. It wasn't alive at all.

I couldn't stop walking. Needed water more than I thought I ever could, and I was tired. Every step I took snapped me awake from a microsecond's sleep. A deep pounding in my neck and shoulders. A cold jab in the small of my back. My body ached and hurt and begged me to stop, my head was still bleeding above my eye, or I thought it was, at least. There was no energy left to think, and that's how I knew I had to keep moving. If I stopped, there would be nothing more to do.

I walked through an already broken door. It could have meant that someone there was alive, but I didn't dare think the thought. I drank a bottle of Coke, which hurt so bad I thought I would faint. I fell asleep on the floor. Lying on my side, still wearing my backpack. Something was watching me from across the room. It didn't wish me well.

I woke up in a French petrol station. The shelves were raided of many things, but there was still Coke. I opened another bottle and drank it slowly. Ate a few sweets I could reach from where I sat. Gently, I removed my socks, and was glad I hadn't had more to eat. My feet reeked of sweat, of blood and infection. They were covered in pus-filled wounds and crimson blisters, my heels gushing and oozing. Not good. I had to be able to walk. Nothing in the world was more important. I considered my options.

There wasn't any still water left in the shop, but there were a few bottles of sparkling. Washing my feet didn't hurt more than I could handle, and the lack of grime made it easier to understand what I was looking at. I stayed in the shop for a couple of days. Ate chocolate, hot dog buns and granola from expired yogurt pots. Whenever it grew too quiet, I hummed or listened to a song or two. At night, I felt a presence, but it didn't make itself known.

There were road maps stacked in a display unit. I studied them closely and decided that Belgium would be my quickest option. I wouldn't have to walk for too long between towns, and it was infinitely quicker than walking up through Germany, which I had imagined would be my route. It embarrassed me that I had misunderstood the shape of Europe so fundamentally, but the silence had the decency not to comment.

I wished I had thought to use petroleum jelly. I wished I had brought bandages and blister plasters. I slipped my shoes on loosely. It hurt, but not so bad that I couldn't make my way to the nearest village with slow, uneven steps. I walked as if I was limping on both feet. Constantly trying to put my weight on the other foot, never really landing on either.

There was a bus parked by the road. There was a puddle of goo in front of the open door. Teeth, some of it, or so I thought. A skull, maybe a shoulder. Hair. Lots and lots of hair. I didn't kick at it with my shoe or poke it with a stick. Nowhere inside me was there a morbid fascination for this pool of putrid corpse. Where was the body? I didn't want to stick around to find out. The question placed itself in the back of my mind with the list of other questions I didn't want answered. They were having a conference, always murmuring. But the good thing about too many voices is that you can't hear any at all.

I leapt through the open door to look around for luggage or something useful. There was nothing of interest except the emergency hammer on the wall. It came off easily and felt good in my hand. I didn't stop to put it in my backpack. I just wanted to get away from the smell.

I jumped too high to get over the puddle. Too high, but not far enough. The backpack was too heavy and my shoes were too loose. I landed on my knees with a splash and a horrible crack. Something under my left knee gave way. Several sensations fought for attention as the thick, cold liquid seeped through my trousers. I ignored them all but replayed the crack over and over. It might have been skull bone splitting under my knee. It might have been teeth grinding against each other as I landed, a single last annoyance making her jaw clench and grind. One single annoyance that was all my fault. I slipped and stumbled onto my feet. Tried to get away. Slipped again.

'Aaaa—' I said. Because no other sound could cover the fear and discomfort I felt. 'Aaaa—' *Don't think too hard about it*, I tried to command myself. Get myself going. *Don't think, just walk, don't think.*

'Aaaaaaaaaaa—' I kept saying, fighting my gag reflex second by second. My hands stood out straight from my body, I bent forward awkwardly, trying to keep my knees from touching my trousers as I walked. My head was pounding and the back of my right hand hurt where I'd fallen. I looked down and saw a tooth pressed into my palm. It hadn't pierced the skin, just stuck to me.

'Aaaa—' I kept saying, until I was far away from the bus, still clutching the emergency hammer.

'Aaaa—' until the sound of the crack stopped ringing in my ears.

'Aaaa—' until I shook the tooth off and wiped the goo away.

'Aaaaaaaa!'

Sweden used to mean sweets and Gouda and trays upon trays of Coke. Food was cheaper there, so my family would drive across the Swedish border a couple of times a year to stock up. My sister and I would buy massive bags of pick'n'mix. We could get blue sweets in Sweden. Flavours and dyes that were banned in Norway. Sweden was wicked and wonderful.

Somehow, I feel I should take advantage of this fact now. Walk into a shop and fill my trolley to the brim with marshmallow strawberries, liquorice and jaw-breakers. But instead, I pick long-lasting canned goods and flour. I left my last batch of flour with Georg, showed him how to make simple breads over the fire. When he had his first taste of bread he had made himself, he was quiet for a long time.

'Things sure are different now,' he eventually said.

'Yeah.'

'Didn't think I'd taste...' And he left it at that. Or maybe I just don't remember. I showed him a few more ways. He wrote down the recipes, took notes about the gluten window and feeding wholemeal more water. I didn't think about my father but I could feel him looking over my shoulder, commenting on gluten strands and elasticity.

Lady tires easily. Even before we've left Malmö, she's whining and sulking and falling behind. I keep walking until Scram starts waiting for her, then I lift her up and drop her in the trolley. That works too.

Sweden feels like Norway and I can't shake the feeling that I'm almost home. I feel my parents at the end of the road. I can hear my niece's chirping laughter, and every step brings me closer.

'Dear God,' I say as I get ready for our dinner break. I'm pouring out food for Scram and Lady, and rummaging through the cans to find something I can eat cold. 'I know I said we were over. And I meant that. I still do. But I just thought you should know that if you've saved them... if they're all there, I'll turn back to you right away. We'll be the largest percentage of human population that ever believed in you. And I'll be part of it, happily. But you must have saved them. You must have saved them all.' Searching my heart, I know this is an exaggeration. Even if she's just saved one, I'd probably thank her forever. But if she exists, I'm sure she knows, and I can't make myself choose, so I stick with this prayer for now.

I made it to the nearest town and cleaned my trousers as best I could. I couldn't, for the life of me, stop shivering. Every muscle in my body seemed to spasm and pull to get away from my corpse-soaked knee. The chill along my spine wouldn't let go. My feet hurt so much I didn't know how to keep standing. Using the emergency hammer to make my way into a pharmacy, I found antiseptic cream and bandages and tried to wrap my feet in several layers of healing. It worried me how sore they were. If they didn't get better soon, I would definitely be too slow. What if I didn't heal at all? What if every day was nothing but feet and blisters and pain? Would I walk fast enough? Could I make it home before winter?

There were too many questions, and the smell of the puddle was still in my nose. I wished I could pull the keyring back out of the backpack, ask advice from the girl who knew me better than I did. But I didn't want her to see me like this, so I left the keyring hidden. I tried to sing but felt too much like gagging. I grabbed a big tub of petroleum jelly and left.

I limped across to a corner shop. The entrance was blocked and I had to step around a pile of dead to get in. They leaked and reeked in the spring heat. Stained shrouds that held little back. *Soon,* I thought, *they will merge with one another. Soon, they will be a hill of chalk and bone.* One body had rolled off the others. It was so small, so tiny, my heart flinched and hid. My eyes burned with the effort not to look at it, but dark brown curls flowed out of the stained wrappings and a purple hair clip was still attached. My eyes refused to let go.

Something had picked at the body, but only a little. There had been enough for them to choose from, and they'd had no reason to be greedy. Still shaking, I took a step forward. Vomit lurked in the back of my throat, peeked out through my teeth and waited for the right moment.

I closed my eyes and lifted the small body back onto the heap. It was so light and soft, I thought of kittens and baby birds. The face was hidden under shrouds, and I tried not to breathe at all. Tried not to disrupt the wrappings, tried not to inhale the small soul, if there was one.

I thought of my niece. From the minute she was born, she loved to lie on my arm and stare at the world. She'd press her back against my stomach and dig her fingers into my arm. Feeling me. Kneading me. Needing me. She'd search the edge of my sleeve until she found a way to push her hand in under the fabric. Always all about skin contact, the feeling of being close, near, together. I stepped away from the pile of dead. I made sure this little body wasn't alone. It didn't worry me to think I might not have reunited it with the right body. They were one, now, anyway. Close. Near. Together.

A dog snarled at me from across the road. It took a small step towards me, bared its teeth. A second dog, thin and scrawny, was cowering behind it. I took a step backwards and they both skulked away. The larger one kept an eye on me, backed off with its teeth still naked. My neck felt exposed but I fought against the urge to cover it up. *There will be so many more dogs,* I thought. *I should probably get a gun.*

The smell followed me into the shop and my knees finally gave in to the shivers. With my back against a freezer that smelled strongly of sour milk, I wrapped my arms around my body and allowed myself to fall apart.

Here are the pieces I fell into:

My one true love had maggots in her eyes, and had left me all alone, and I hadn't said goodbye.

The Channel Tunnel had stolen something from me, but I didn't know what it had taken or where it had gone.

I had to walk home. I had to. I needed to know if my family was still there, or if pieces of my life still remained in their house, and I couldn't think of the odds, or the distance, or the steps or the miles left to go.

Although I had spent years and years dreaming of being a walker, my feet did not want to carry me. They didn't even know how to. My family, my loved ones, who had waited with me, who had longed for me to lose the weight and regain my health and be the person they knew I could be—they might never know. To them I'd always be the failure, who couldn't lose the weight or regain anything at all. My feet wouldn't carry me. My feet couldn't walk.

My knees were red with someone's gloopy, sticky, muddy blood and humours. A someone whose body had disappeared. A someone whose skull I had crushed with my knee. A someone whose teeth were loose in the puddle of goo yet gnawed at my skin like rats.

I was all alone.

No.

I was all alone.

No.

I was all alone.

These were all truths I couldn't possibly believe, or think about for too long, or take on board as true. What point was there in walking—in doing anything at all for that matter—if any of this was true? It couldn't be true, because I was still walking, but I shouldn't be walking, because they were all true.

I picked the pieces up, one by one, studied them and tried to put them back together. I mixed up glue from anything I could find in my mind, splattered it on in thick gloopy strokes.

My one true love was dead, and I buried her in her finest dress. She loved me, and I loved her, and now I had her ring around my neck and her photo in my backpack. Many people had lost their loved ones before; I would survive without mine.

What I had left behind in the darkness would come back to me. The piece of memory, or personality, or whatever it was, would return. I would find it, I would get it back. I could wait.

I did have to walk home, but I had also always wanted to. This was the adventure I'd always asked for, my big hike, my pilgrimage. This would be impressive, and long, and my biggest achievement. If I could make it there. And I had to. I clutched the stone in my pocket. I could do this.

My feet would learn and my body would change. I would know, and that was something.

I would clean my knees, wash my trousers, forget the skull.

I was alone. That was okay, for now. I would find others. It was statistically impossible that I was the only one. Why would I be?

The glue was simple, just water and flour, but it held the pieces together for now. And there was nothing but now, anymore.

'So,' says Kobus, and a wave of relief rushes through me; he's been quiet since we left Denmark, but he hasn't left me. Not yet. 'I find it really interesting how you fear the forest. You said you grew up in the forest, yes?'

'Yeah,' I say.

'But still, you are more scared of the forest than being alone.'

'No,' I say, 'I'm not scared of the forest at all. It's what's *in* the forest that creeps me out.'

I can see the creature lurking in there. It keeps pace with us from a distance, a grey shadow weaving in and out of the trees, a constant threat in the corner of my eye. And there are wolves in there, too.

'But there is no forest anymore,' he says.

'What do you mean?'

'There used to be a forest because animals would shy away from people. They wouldn't come into the city or walk upon the road. So wherever the trees were thick enough, the animals gathered and you called it a forest. Everywhere they weren't, there was none. Trees in a city is a park. Trees outside is not.' I open my mouth to protest, but I get his point and can't be bothered.

'But now, there are no real boundaries,' he continues. 'Everything is the wild, and you're the intruder. The animals can walk into cities or towns, they can stand in fields or on the roads. They may not have realised quite yet, but they will soon. You're the anomaly, and they are the norm. Everything is a fucking forest, the way it's meant to be.'

'You know,' I say, chewing my lip. 'I never told you this when you were alive, but half of the time, I have no fucking clue what you're on about.'

'Oh, I knew,' he says, and I can hear him shrug. 'But that doesn't change anything.'

I think about it, for a while. 'I suppose,' I say, 'the city isn't really a city anymore. It's just empty buildings in a strange pattern.'

'Like fucking trees,' he says.

'Nothing like fucking trees. Nothing like trees at all!' The relief I felt when I heard his voice has already passed. I wished for comfort, not a debate. 'Because trees change and form and die and make new trees, but a dead building is just a dead building.'

'No,' he says, and I know he's fixing me with his stare and bobbing his head up and down for emphasis, 'that's exactly what buildings are. They are trees. Think about it!' I hate when he says that. 'One guy comes along, finds a nice spot of water and says, 'Here is my home.' He builds a building there, a little shelter. And the next guy, who doesn't want to be alone, places his shelter nearby, and in just a couple of moves, the first building has spawned a village. And from this village, some fucker decides he's too good for this place and goes down the river to start a town of his own. And his building spawns new buildings.

'The buildings change with time, they grow taller, wider. Perhaps people travel further before they set up their own. Perhaps a few of the villages merge together and create a city. Taller buildings in the middle, smaller and smaller towards the edges. But the centre keeps growing, so the edges keep growing. Cities are like cancer. They spread, they infect, they pop up unexpectedly. And all because of buildings.'

'They don't grow without people, though,' I say.

'Nah. Maybe you're right. Fucking people are like cancer, buildings are like trees.'

'Were,' I say, 'people *were* like cancer.'

'We'll see.'

When I walk through the next town, I try to figure out if the buildings are anything like trees. They are nothing like buildings, that's for sure. There's no protective invisible barrier between them and nature to say 'this is ours, this is yours'. Although I can step inside and keep nature outside, it's closer than ever before.

Or maybe I'm fooling myself. I can't keep nature outside, at all. All I can do is keep myself out of nature. I see an elk eat away at an apple tree. A hare nibble at autumn's last clovers. No one chases them away with brooms. No one disturbs their peaceful dinner. The garden and the forest are one and the same. I feel terribly lonely and small.

16

Of course my feet toughened up. Of course they got used to the strain. My skin grew thick and dry, and the wounds eventually healed. I met stray dogs that barked and snarled and raised their backs, but up until now they had kept their distance. I kept my distance too.

Occasionally, I felt the presence of the something watching me in the dark, but I shook off the feeling whenever I could. There was no point in driving myself crazy—there would be more than enough time for that. The silence was getting to me. I tried to whistle or hum when I could. I listened for birds and winds and animals chattering away. Sometimes I kicked up stones or ran my hands over fences, or played the pickets with a stick as I walked.

I accepted that my body would need time to adjust, so I walked slower through France than I'd planned to. Only a few kilometres a day as my feet healed. *You'll need strength for weeks*, I thought. *Take it easy, take it slow.*

I took breaks of whole days, sitting by the banks of rivers or resting in open fields. When it rained, I put my tarp up and read magazines I'd stolen from shops. But I tried to stay away from towns as much as possible. The smell was everywhere, but out here, there was also air.

I paid attention to the map but not too closely. If I did, the short distance I moved each day would worry me. I should have been halfway through Belgium by now but instead, I was here, still 40 kilometres from Bruges, right across the border from France. I'd certainly thought I'd be in Bruges by now, but if this was what needed to happen, this was how it would be.

The dog was huge, and startled me. Without any warning, it stood there, its tail wagging manically, its breath excited and fast.

'Hello! Oh, hello! Hello! Hey! Hey! Do you see me? Hey!' said its big wide face, and I couldn't help but smile. I walked past it without replying. It was a cute dog, but I was unsure how much I could trust its temper. It didn't seem all there. As soon as I stepped away, it ran a few steps, skipped awkwardly from left to right, then stopped to stare at me again.

'Oh boy! We walked together! HOW FUN WAS THAT? Want to do it again?' it beamed.

'Scram!' I said, waving my hands noncommittally. I stomped my foot a couple of times, tried to make it get out of my way. 'Shoo! Scram!'

It ran a circle around itself, wagging its tail so hard it lost its direction.

'What a wonderful combination of sounds and movements!' it seemed to cheer. 'Do it again!' I tried to ignore it for a while, but it ran around me, walked beside me, and every now and then it bolted forward a few metres then turned around as if to say, 'Come on! Come on! There is more road over here! I found some! Look! Look!'

It was a nice day. My feet weren't giving me much trouble and the dog's enthusiasm kept me walking for longer than I planned to. When I sat down for lunch, it walked around me, sniffing the ground. I was still a bit too nervous to eat properly, so I poured the rest of the tin of stew on the ground for the dog. I started walking again as it ate. Left it behind without a word. *What a weird dog*, I thought.

I heard it coming up behind me. *Whomp whomp whomp whomp* until it was next to me again. It was clearly looking for praise.

'I did it!' it glowed. 'I caught up with you right away! I'm a very good boy! Look! Look! I am such a good boy!'

I stopped and raised my finger. 'Go away, dog,' I said sternly. 'Go away! Scram!' I pointed hard down the road we came from. The dog looked behind us right away.

'What? What? What am I seeing? Is it a bird? Oh boy! I hope it's a bird!'

'Scram!' I tried again. It seemed to like the sound, and so did I. 'Go away. Shoo! Git! Go! Scram!'

I started walking again. The dog sat confused for the briefest moment before it jumped back up, walking.

'Oh boy! That was a fun talk,' it looked at me, 'but we're still friends, right?'

I shrugged and kept walking. The dog stuck around all day.

Sweden is easy walking. I bake bread most nights and eat it with tinned soup or stew in the mornings. The roads are good and I still float on the feeling of being strong. I take to sleeping in the road to save time, and a little to avoid the forest. Some days I move 50 kilometres without even trying. Others I take it slow and barely cut through ten. I give myself rest days. I play with the dogs. And every night, I take the note from Georg out of my pocket and read it three times. There is an address to a house in Spain. A village between Malaga and Marbella. A map to find the house if you stand in the town square with your back to the church.

'Hope to see you soon,' the note ends. I've read it so many times I can recite it by heart. The address has become a chant. A way to remind myself there's something behind me, even if there is nothing in front. I don't quite remember who Georg is. I remember the fireworks and the long hug at the bridge. There was something about bread and fire. Something about repopulation. He hopes to see me soon. But I'm in the forest and he can't find me here.

When I slip into this stream of thought, I know I'm getting lost. I bring the note out again and read the address; tell myself, over and over, that this is where I need to go if I can't find my family. That there are friends there. Life. But sometimes I bark at Lady to get her to keep up, and I can't remember what word I forgot. It had something to do with... another word, and yesterday is far away.

'So... the... all... interesting,' Kobus crackles.

'No!' I say. 'Be real!'

'So,' he tries again, in a voice more like his own. 'I find it interesting how you still haven't read the last chapter of the book you're carrying.'

'What book?' I say, because for a split second, I can't remember.

'The book you read to Cleopatra when she—'

'Shh,' I say and stare into the forest. 'There's something there!'

Scram and Lady feel it too. We huddle together and stare at the trees that are lining the field to our left. There's a something there. Scram growls quietly and Lady whines. I say nothing. I don't blink, I don't breathe, I don't move. There are a few cracks and snaps and shuffles. Something's watching us from right behind the bushes and trees. Something new. I take slow steps forward. Moving myself along the road. The snaps follow our progress, never letting us out of sight.

'Good boy,' I whisper to Scram. He stays close to me. Looks over his shoulder with every other step he takes. We walk like this to nightfall. Scram eventually relaxes, and Lady seems to have forgotten the whole thing. But I haven't. The creature is right behind us now. It stays on the road and keeps close, as if it, too, is wary of the forest. As if it, too, heard something it couldn't explain.

I don't want to sleep outside. I keep us walking until I find a house with a shed, not too far from the road. I step over the graves in the garden and shine the torch around inside the little building, which is just big enough to shelter us for the night. A few mice scuttle out of the light, but the ground seems dry and clean enough. I move all the bikes and family debris outside. Clear a space big enough for me and the dogs to rest comfortably. I don't make up a fire. Instead I fashion a small bolt to lock the door from the inside. The creature occasionally scratches the wall, trying to claw its way in. It doesn't worry me at all. I worry about whatever's out there, hidden between the trees, following us, stalking us, making the creature scared of sleeping outside.

'So,' says Kobus as I test the strength of my bolt by jiggling the door back and forth a few times. 'Do you remember that wolf conference at uni?'

'Yeah?' I say. It was a literary conference about wolves and werewolves. I helped out with registration, listened to a few of the panels, watched a few of the presentations. It was a decent weekend, all in all.

'Do you remember that talk about the wolves in Europe? And that guy who said that the cultural differences in how wolves are perceived lies in whether the wolf hunts the same prey as humans, or if the wolf hunts what the humans consider theirs?'

I'm quiet for a while. Something's wrong.

'Kobus?' I say. 'The conference... You weren't there.'

He sighs. 'Don't you fucking get it?' he says, annoyed and brusque. 'I'm not here, either.'

There's a loud roar outside. Something is fighting in the dark. I turn off my head torch and move slowly over to a crack in the wall. My heart's beating so hard it touches the wood. I press my eye to the gap and try to catch a glimpse of what's happening out there. Occasionally, I think I see the creature's tattered robe; sometimes, I think I see fur. It's chaotic, strange, impossible to wrap my head around. But whatever's out there is big, and strong. I can feel its ill will towards me; it radiates like heat through the wood.

Snarls, barks, howls and whimpers, then a bang! Something crashes into the shed, startles me and shakes the world to its core. Forms an earthquake that rolls through time. Shakes memories loose from my mind and traps them in the dirt beneath me. I hold my breath and cover my eyes, picture Cleopatra's face, think of home.

The creature's horrid breath blows through the walls. It's mixed with something new, something deeper and rawer. Moonlight bounces off sharp, shiny teeth, then off long grey claws. There are pools of blood. A yellow eye, then a dozen more. The stalkers are watching me like I'm watching them; they've got my scent in their noses and the taste of me on their lips. One of them is fighting the creature. The creature whimpers and falls.

Quiet. Absolute quiet. One second. Two. Footsteps outside make me back away. My eyes stay fixed on the small opening. The steps come closer. A deep sniffling through the grass. A huge wet nose pushing through, its nostrils vibrating, drawing in my fear. I think something giggles. I think they all giggle. A bright yellow eye appears.

'There you are,' evil growls from outside, and I scream like I haven't in months. The dogs bark and huddle against me. Whatever's out there throws itself at the door, again and again and again. Claws at it, pulls at it, drags, beats and pounds at it. I cover my head with my arms and sink to the floor.

'Go away!' I scream. 'Go away!' My voice trails off into high-pitched pleading, but whatever's out there doesn't listen. It slams and slams and slams again. The makeshift bolt jumps in its groove. It will let them in. Eventually. Soon.

'So,' Kobus shouts over the deafening noise, the barks, the growls and the pounding. 'Do you know what I find fucking interesting?' There are more of them now. More of these stalkers. They scratch at the walls. They run at the door with their full body weight, weakening the bolt, wearing it down. Long, slim claws poke through cracks, nowhere is safe, not here, not for long. They chatter and giggle in a language I don't understand.

Howls go up in the forest. Deep growls under the full moon, my death waiting for me in those jaws, in those hands, in those claws. Blood is leaving my head, and fast. It pools in my belly to hide from whatever's coming. Something is coming. I'm dizzy; I know I'll faint.

'What?' I whisper to Kobus.

'That you remember so much from the conference, yet treat the wolves like this.' He yells this at the top of his lungs but still, I can barely hear him. Everything turns a deep red black, the world is quiet and soft.

Eventually, I grew used to him. It was Belgium that gave me the idea—that I could repeat all the stories I knew to Scram, to help myself remember. *Remembering is important*, I thought. *If Lilly's still alive, I need to give her these stories. If she isn't... I need to keep them all.* This became the thought that lingered in the back of my head.

'I need to remember everything.'

So I told him one story after another until I ran dry. But in the middle of the second retelling of *Cinderella*, an abrupt stop. Wait. Think. How did it go, again? The glass slipper was Disney, I was certain of that. But the squirrel slipper, was that the folktale? Was it the folktale where the stepsisters cut their toes and heels off to fit the shoe? Or was that in *Three Nuts for Cinderella*? What was it in the three nuts again? The first was the hunter's outfit, the second was the ball gown... But the third? The wedding dress? Was that it? Or was there a scene I couldn't remember?

All night, this churned in my head. A burning question I couldn't contain: *what do I do if I never remember?* Should I make something up? Would it matter that I forgot the details, if I remembered the basic lore? That is, after all, how fairy tales used to stay alive, being passed from generation to generation. Each generation adding a detail and forgetting a few, always twisting around the same basic premise. The story-thread beneath.

But there would be no new generation after this. That was the problem. My story would be the final version, and I wanted to get it right. Sometimes, I felt like that's what I lost in the tunnel: the details of my memories, the third nut for Cinderella, the sound of Cleopatra's laughter, my mum's voice, Lilly's first word, the faces of friends I held dear. My memories had outlines, colours and shadings, but none of their detail or depth.

I hoped they would come back, soon. That I hadn't lost them forever. If I allowed myself, even for a second, to think that these details wouldn't come back, my knees would buckle and I would stop walking. I knew this to be true the same way I knew I would surely die if I stopped breathing. It was the same thing. Whatever watched me from the darkness knew it too.

When I wake up, Scram is watching me with his head on his paws. Lady is fast asleep, but bright sunshine falls through the shed walls and tells me it's morning. We've made it through the night, somehow, we've made it through the night. Nothing in the world can entice me to open this door. Not a single thing in the world can make me step out into that sunlight and face the stalkers and their claws. Or so I think, for a while. But it's all quiet out there. Scram is calm and seems eager to get going. And I need to pee, and I don't pee inside. Not if I can help it.

There's no reason to be rash. I open the door the tiniest bit, ready to slam it shut if there's the slightest change in sound or movement outside. There isn't.

There isn't a single scratch on the door. Not even a tiny groove to show where their claws dug into the woodwork. The bolt did rattle and I thought it would fall off, yet today it seems sturdy and whole. There aren't any splinters. There's no blood. I fully expect to see the creature lying in a cold dead heap in the grass, but there's nothing and nothing at all.

I step around the shed a couple of times, searching and studying every inch. But even the grass is thick and tall; it's not broken or bent to the ground. I dig into my backpack and search for the keyring. I don't know where it is and I can't find it on the first search, so I pull out the small notebook instead. I stare at Cleopatra's sad, tear-rimmed face.

'Hon...' I croak, 'I'm losing it. I really am losing it.' And her sad eyes agree with me. She wishes she could turn her head away and not meet my gaze anymore.

'I'm sorry,' I say, 'I'm so sorry.' I open the book to write in last night on the list. But I have to flip through so many pages before I find an open line, and I could have sworn I'd only used a page or two. I don't recognise my handwriting right away, either. It's sharp and small as if it's crouching down, ready to run.

'Georg snores,' I have written. I struggle to place this in my memory. Georg. On the other side of the bridge. 'Cut my arm on broken glass,' I have written. Surely, that hasn't happened. But I study my wrist and see a long scar, pink and shiny in the midst of my tan. I hide the book in my backpack and notice I'm already holding the keyring. It was in my hand all along.

'Baby,' Cleopatra whispers through the photo, 'just breathe. You'll be okay.' But her eyes aren't quite convincing. I think she might be lying.

17

Scram kept being there when I woke up, and I started to enjoy his company. We walked into Antwerp together; he was light and eager, I was dark and reluctant. I tried to figure out where the Norwegian Sailor's Church was—I was there, once, when I was eight. My uncle had worked for a Belgian shipping company, and my mum and I went to visit him during the '94 Winter Olympics.

The early '90s was an excellent time to be young and positive and from Norway. Norwegians were best at *everything.* We were superb in ski sports, wonderful at football, tremendous at women's handball. I was so proud, walking around Antwerp then. I thought everyone could see that here came a Norwegian, like the ones who won all the medals on TV.

I remembered a market full of spices and pastries, and a statue shaped like a severed hand. It was one of two, or so I remembered. One showed a Roman soldier flinging a giant's hand. The other showed just the hand, softly cupping whichever tourist was presently sitting in it. I found a map of the city and located the first of the two. I stared at it for a long time. Tried to dislodge its memories from my mind.

There were memories about chocolate pralines, and lacework in Bruges. There was something about a restaurant selling pittas, and another celebrating the Danish fairy tale author H C Andersen. I decided it was better to leave Antwerp alone. There was too much that threatened to stir up and change. My mum reading to me at bedtime, my uncle letting me ride on his shoulders through town. My uncle's friend, who had an extra toe and showed it to us at dinner, making my mother squirm.

I filled my backpack with all the food I could carry and grabbed—for the first time—some dog treats. The days were long and lonely, but as long as I kept talking to Scram, it was easier to make them pass.

Talking dwindled as the days went on. It was harder to find something to say. My words got stuck between my teeth; I confused myself by speaking Norwegian while thinking in English, or the other way around. Twice I yelled at Scram because he didn't answer me. He didn't seem to mind, but I sure did. When we approached the Dutch border, I had given up trying to find new things to say. Scram didn't mind this, either.

In all of the Netherlands, we didn't see a single milkmaid. Or maybe we did. Everyone looked the same after weeks in the rain and the sun.

I hear them behind me all the time. They're in the forest somewhere, stalking us with all the patience in the world.

Scram seems to have given up on them and doesn't turn to look anymore. Lady whines and begs to sit in the trolley, and seems more scared of the forest than I am. In the trolley, she sleeps soundly, oblivious to what's going on back here. I wish I could do the same.

Fear makes me walk faster, and Norway is close now. I wonder if they'll follow me across the border, or if Sweden is their only turf. Every now and then, I see the creature limping behind us on the road. Far behind. Further and further behind. Whatever it fought has made its mark, but the creature is still holding on.

Being scared is exhausting. The hairs on the back of my neck are constantly rising in terrified shivers. My heartbeat is fast and if I don't pay attention to my pace, I start running. I have to keep myself from fleeing. From abandoning the trolley and the dogs to the stalkers. From running until I can't run anymore. I need to slow down, need to walk steady.

I know, I think, that they aren't there. As much as I can feel, hear and smell them, I don't think they're actually real. Or maybe they're just ordinary wolves, waiting for a glimpse of weakness. This could be true, but that wouldn't make it better. Or maybe they're just ordinary men, making sure I'm alone before they pounce.

But I know they aren't. I know they're nothing. I saw their long, pointy claws, and bright eyes, and horrible, terrible, snickering grins. Sooner or later they'll come for me, and I don't think I'll resist them. I'll let them bite into my flesh and rip me to shreds. I'll listen as my bones crack and snap in their mouths. Listen to the pitiful yelps of my body, and then to the silence that follows. This is what I know. I just have to keep them off until I also know, for certain, who else is in the world. If my mum has made jam and my father made bread, and if my niece wants anything specific for her birthday.

I clench the stone in my pocket and the tiny blue socks. It won't be long now, I think. It really won't be long.

I sleep inside when I can. I don't go into people's homes, but I occupy sheds, garages and barns. Most nights, I pretend not to see the horrid faces staring through the windows, or hear the scratching and banging as they try to get inside. I get used to them, and some nights I even sleep an hour or two at a time. Other nights, I faint in terror. Those nights are okay too.

The creature has taken to sleeping on the roof of whatever shelter I find. Most nights, I try not to let it affect the type of dwelling I pick. But sometimes, only sometimes, I make sure I choose one that's tall enough to let it sleep in peace from the stalkers. It still limps, when I see it, and it's much slower now. Whatever they are, they got it good.

The trolley's getting more difficult to push, especially at the tempo I want to walk. The rubber on the wheels has nearly rubbed off and one of them keeps sticking. It upsets me that I have to change it, but I can't have it slowing me down. For some reason, I have a handful of Swedish change in my pack. I must have picked it up along the way, or brought it with me from an earlier shop. Everywhere I go, there are enormous supermarkets with lines upon lines of trolleys outside. I try them out in the car parks. Transfer all of my belongings from one trolley to another, push them around lampposts and along the outlines of dead parking spaces. None of them feel better than the one I have, so I just leave them behind.

I keep looking for them now. My eyes dart here and there across the landscape to see if I can find another shop. The hunt keeps me distracted, and I enter a jungle of business parks and storage units. Thicker and thicker is the growth of buildings, until everything seems familiar and strange. Memories wash through the streets, but I struggle to place them in my mind. That is, until I see the posters for the amusement park.

The hunt for a new trolley has led me north quicker than I thought. I'm still in Sweden, but this is Gothenburg. The city my grandmother loved. The city I loved with her. She used to bring me here every other year or so. We used to eat at the same restaurants and sleep in the same hotels, every time. We used to visit the sawfish in the aquarium and stroll around the amusement park. We spent way too much money trying to win gigantic boxes of chocolates from the carnival games. We argued about fashion and immigration, and whether she was hard of hearing or everyone else was mumbling when they spoke. Now, this city is all around me. Empty and towering and wild.

'What do you think, Lady?' I say. Scram is sniffing a fence further up ahead, and Lady is standing in the trolley. She looks like a pirate, scanning the horizon for land. 'Do you think we should rest for a day again? Have a little break?' She doesn't respond, but she rarely does.

The dead welcome me to the city centre. I make my way to our hotel, but when I get there, I don't want to enter. The bookshelf lifts and the metallic butterflies hold too many memories, and I don't want to let them out. I feel better knowing they're safely behind the locked door and unbroken glass. But there's another hotel, the one we stayed at only once. The one where the lift was small and impossible, where my grandma couldn't hear a word anyone said; there was music everywhere and drunk people in Christmas jumpers. This was the year we went there late, the year without roses.

Everything feels different. This city brings the past much closer to me. It lingers on the little bridge we passed to find my grandmother's favourite shop. It stretches up and over the tallest ride in the amusement park. The one she refused to try, but loved when it was dressed up like a Christmas tree. The one I always thought I'd dare to try, not this time, not this time, but next time, maybe. The past hides in the windows of the shops I once visited. It dwells in restaurants I recognise and familiar cracks in the street. And because the past is present here, everything hurts more. I think about Georg, and wish I hadn't left him. His face is lost, but I can hear his laughter. Or maybe that laughter is mine?

Breaking into hotels is easy. They were never designed to keep people out on any permanent basis. This one's no different. It's on a corner and its main entrance is a revolving door. The locks are easily broken. Of all the hotels I ever stayed in, this was the only one to disappoint me. Its horrible lifts, its complete lack of facilities, its horrific air of resignation. And yet, this hotel was good to me. It gave birth to many great ideas and filled my schedule that winter. My grandmother was miserable here. Nothing of her personality lines the halls. I'm happy to be back in this silence.

I can't be bothered walking further than the fourth floor and I can't be bothered with locks. I picked up an axe in a woodshed, somewhere. For self-defence, of course, but it's excellent for breaking down doors, too. Scram and Lady whimper and walk away from me as I swing the axe. The noise is hard and rugged, and I hit metal in the middle of the door. It doesn't last too long. The room is just like my room was back then. This one's named the Orca, mine was the Starfish, I think. Mine had a painting of five red starfish above the bed, minimalistic and interpretive, as these things often are. But in this room, there's a photograph of an orca underwater. Its face is tilted slightly towards the camera, curious and playful. I check the little fridge, but just like I remember, there's nothing in there except space for you to store your own drinks. I take off my socks and leave them in the fridge. They smell too bad now, and it's time to change.

Again, I smell the soaps in the bathroom. These do not smell nice. The generic 'fresh' of discount air fresheners all around the world.

I use the toilet. It feels strange and cold. The first month or so, I would seek out porcelain. If possible, take a dump somewhere the cistern was accessible so I could fill it with water and wash away my filth. But it seemed so wasteful and lonely. I've left a trail of faeces across Europe. In porcelain, bushes and streets. Short-lived proof I was actually here, feed for whatever comes next.

They have cheap toilet paper but it beats leaves and grass. I still notice, though. I still notice how it's not soft and four-plied and nice. *What strange creatures we are*, I think. What strange creatures indeed.

The dogs are going crazy outside the bathroom door. They scratch and bark and whimper. The separation confuses them—they don't remember doors. But I enjoy this moment of peace. I have chosen these seconds of loneliness; they weren't forced upon me.

And for the first time since I left England, I study myself in the mirror. It's not that I haven't seen mirrors, there's just been no reason to look into them. I've known the truth of most things.

I'm not there in the mirror. This woman, this person, is wild and strange. She has a short beard under her chin and in patches along her jaw line. Evidence of a hormone disorder that's no longer treated or cared for. She's stopped tweezing and waxing, threading and grooming. She doesn't care at all.

I strip off my worn clothes and inspect the rest of her. She hasn't shaved any part of her body for weeks. Months. Her breasts and even her belly are covered in hair she would have spent ages hiding in the time before the End. Now, she doesn't seem to notice.

She's got two bright scars on her forehead and scalp. Her hair seems to split awkwardly across them, unaligned and uneven. Her body is lean and tight under too much loose skin. Her tan lines still visible, but softer than they used to be. As I watch her with admiration and concern, she watches me back. She's careful, measured. Calculates the risk of me intervening. She's allowing me close, but not too close. She's keeping her secrets, and I don't mind. Who am I to judge her, anyway?

As I stand there, listening to the dogs panic and my heart beat, I decide to become that woman in the mirror.

Leaning in through the glass, I dive into her eyes. I swim through her mind and see how she's been wrestling against nature. There's no reason to resist it. It has already won.

Her memories are boxed away in neat stacks along the edges. There are gaps in the system, big folders missing. Some have scratch marks along their sides, bite marks on the shelves and pages ripped and torn. No wonder she doesn't trust me. There are crayons and paper on the floor, and I draw her a couple of bright memories and stick them in the biggest holes. A sun and some eyes, a heart and a blue sky. Childish and pure, but it's the best I can do.

One of the boxes has a hole in the lid. Bits and pieces of fabric and thread poke through. I pull at a corner and the box explodes, shooting hundreds and thousands of clothes in the air. There are goth dresses and tie-dyed shirts. There are sleek dress-suits and dirt-covered over-alls. A huge white wedding dress with fairy tale arms, and a smaller wedding dress that smells of hope and red wine. I recognise them all. She's kept my clothes in a box, collected every style and phase and image I ever wanted. All were important. None of them me.

A crayon drawing sinks through her soul, and I grab it, bring it with me to the surface. She has drawn Cleopatra's face, eyeless and maggot-eaten. I grab a blue crayon and cross them out. Doodle hearts in their places, hearts in her eyes. That's what I'll remember. How she loved me with her eyes. I crash through the mirror in the back of her mind; our nose and forehead bleed from the impact but neither of us mind. We've been reborn the way we wanted to be. And now it's time for new clothes.

18

Germany came with rain and mud and scorching hot days with a blasting sun. There was more variation here than in the Netherlands. There were forests and fields and curved, pretty hills. There were villages hidden behind towns, and towns gliding into cities.

At night, I talked to Cleopatra's photo. I told her about everything I'd seen that day, and how far I hoped to walk tomorrow. Scram sniffed the keyring and gave it a lick every evening, as if he wanted to prove we were a weird little pack. Me, him and the keyring. Cleopatra would have liked that. We always wanted a dog.

I longed to get to Hamburg, but I didn't know why. Perhaps I felt like after Hamburg, I was really heading north. Perhaps I was just surprised I'd made it this far in the first place, and needed to superimpose that relief onto a place—something outside my body, something I still needed to reach.

'So, I read this really interesting thing,' Kobus said. It was a wet day, and I had mud up to my knees. My steps were heavy, and my mood miserable. My shoe had a huge gash in it and with every step, new rainwater swished and swooshed its way in. I'd have to find new shoes soon. That worried me. *If breaking in new boots is as painful as it was breaking in my feet...* I thought.

'Oh yeah?' I replied. Scram startled at the sound, and I started coughing.

'Yes. Ages ago now,' Kobus continued. 'I sent it to you, remember? It was around the same time I told you about that weird dream I had. The autopsy. Remember?'

'Yeah?' I did, kind of. Kobus didn't buy it.

'It was when I dreamt about watching an autopsy of Leonardo da Vinci. We were all gathered around the autopsy table like in Rembrandt's *The Anatomy Lesson.* The light was fabulous, and da Vinci looked like a sleeping angel on the slab, all bright and luminous, surrounded by dusty mortals.' Kobus was using his 'poetry voice', the voice that meant he was exploring some idea he found beautiful, something literary and magnificent, but not quite tactile or rational. He went quiet for a bit. I wondered if I should point out that the mere fact that da Vinci was being dissected meant he was mortal too, but decided against it.

'I kind of remember...' I said eventually, to break up the silence.

'No, you fucking lie,' he said. But there was nothing mean or ill-tempered about it. He just pointed out the obvious, and did it in the manner most suited to him. 'You don't remember. Don't worry. I'll remind you.' He cleared his throat. I strained my ears to hear his steps behind me. They weren't there.

'Many of the brightest minds of history were gathered there, shouting and cheering for the surgeon—who was dressed in an executioner's hood—to make the first incision. To show us the beauty of da Vinci's mind. They all wanted him to spill da Vinci's knowledge out onto us; imagined it would flow from his brain like a fountain, and that we could drink it and toast with it, get drunk on his understanding of the world.

'The surgeon sliced through his skull like butter and exposed the brilliant mind. It was soft, pink and transparent like jelly. Right under the surface, hundreds and thousands of small lights blinked and slid through the mass. It was like watching traffic at night, from a height, far above a busy city. Trails of light, reflecting off our faces, making us the illuminated. It was the most beautiful thing I had ever seen and I immediately felt an enormous sense of shame. A bitter disappointment in myself for having wanted to steal the brilliance of something so pure. So true. So valuable.

'Not everyone was satisfied, though. "Slice it!" they called. "Release it." And even though I knew we weren't worthy, and even though I knew it was wrong, I called out too. "Slice it! Release it!" And the greatest fucking sadness came over me. Because in the glow from the brilliant mind, I knew the knowledge couldn't be understood in bits and pieces. I knew a slice of the mind would not be a slice of the knowledge, it would be a fucking nothing at all. I saw the shining network—intricate, like a hive—and I knew with absolute certainty that in isolation, not a single part of it would make sense.'

It sounded like he was crying, but it might have been me.

'The surgeon cut a thin slice through the entire brain, and the crowd cheered as he held it up. The lights in the slice sent rays down to a dozen other points still in the skull. The slice came away with some difficulty, held back by the lights. They were tough and stringy like caramel, but as it got pulled further from the skull, they turned thin and brittle, like spun sugar or glass. The connections cracked as the surgeon tried to release them. Dozens of lights went out in the brain, and the slice in the surgeon's hand was nothing but grey matter now.

'The crowd hissed. I could feel myself baring my teeth, snarling at the surgeon. "That's not real knowledge," we shouted. "Give us knowledge we can keep! Something we can absorb and understand!" But all the while, I cried inside, because I knew we'd gotten it wrong. We had committed a crime. We had lost our chance.

'The surgeon sliced and sliced, and pulled strings of light from the head until they cracked and snapped into thin, dull splinters. I wanted to murder him. We all did. And it took the full weight of my will to turn my back on them all and leave the theatre. The howls behind me were fucking horrible. I heard them roar and leap and dig their fingers into the surgeon's flesh. He screamed. But not for long.' Kobus went quiet.

'Wow,' I said. 'That's intense.'

'Yeah,' said Kobus, and I could hear him shrug. 'Anyway.' And then he was onto something else, while I was left in the theatre, watching the surgeon die. I struggled to rejoin Kobus's rant.

'So I read this thing, around the same time I told you about that dream. I think I emailed you the article. It was about these monks who would spend hours upon hours, even days and weeks, designing these intricate patterns of brightly coloured sand. And when they were done, covering entire floors with perfectly symmetrical works of art, they'd scoop them right back up.'

'Mandalas,' I said. 'They're called mandalas.'

'Okay,' he said, 'anyway, I read this article about them.' He went quiet.

'And?' I said when he didn't continue.

'No, that's all,' he said and was gone again.

I wash myself thoroughly in bottled water and generic 'fresh'-scented soap. I leave my tufted beard intact. It doesn't bother me today and it won't bother me tomorrow. I wonder if Georg commented on it. If he offered me his razor or offered to help wax my cheeks. I don't think he did, but I can't remember.

The dogs are happy to be outside, and we walk through the ghost of this city. I break into what used to be my mother and sister's favourite shop. The one where all the clothes are loose and colourful and made of organic cotton, or Swedish linen, or wool from happier sheep. This new body is ten sizes smaller than my last one, and it takes me some time to find the right fit. I think in light layers. Loose-fitting burgundy tunic outside a turquoise singlet with stars, both in organic cotton. I pull mustard-coloured harem trousers over indigo-and-black striped leggings. A loosely knitted jumper on top, and a green scarf to protect myself from colds.

I leave my dirty clothes in a bin next to the counter. From their large display, I pick out four pairs of bamboo socks. I've heard they're better for your feet. Purple and red and blue. One pair with stripes, three with flowers. I pin my braids together on top of my head and wrap them in a blue scarf. When I look in the mirror now, the woman and I are the same. We're earthly and ready and free. She smiles at me, and I try to smile back. I wish Cleopatra could see me now. Scram nods approvingly and widdles against a rack full of dresses. Lady rests on a coat that has slipped to the floor, doesn't look up, just taps her tail once when I say her name.

It hits me then. The magnitude of it all. Every mirror in the shop opens into a million other shops filled to the brim with clothes for no one but me. A burst of anxiety shoots through my spine and spreads through my body. All the identical dresses. Anxiety coils around my nerves and squeezes. The hats and scarves and socks that no one will ever wear. My hands are tingly, cold, numb, nothing like my hands at all. Perhaps it's the woman in the mirror. Perhaps I've become her too soon.

The vibrant embroideries on all the coats twist around me and bring me to my knees. I'm all alone but surrounded by the clothes of a hundred women I'll never meet. Loneliness tightens around my lungs until every breath is a wheeze. My chest shatters into millions of snowflakes, falling quietly around me like time. I kneel on the floor. Scram comes over and sniffs my face. His paws make no sound against the linoleum and I can't hear his sniffles or breaths.

'Kobus?' I gasp. 'Say... something.'

'Interesting...' he murmurs, but it's all inside my head.

I gather my voice in a box in my chest. Heat my words up like popcorn and wait for them to pop. They grow and grow as tears stream down my face and my lungs scream for air and everything grows black and tunnels away from me. Then my words burst into a roar, and I roar until the snow melts and my heart is gone in the thaw. There's nothing left do to but walk. I bring up a memory.

'Hey,' said the girl who looked like Cleopatra. Her voice made my heart flutter, and I stepped guiltily into my bedroom and closed the door. I clutched the phone so hard to my ear that I thought she might feel it on her side.

'Hey you,' I said. We were quiet for a while. Only her breathing on the line.

'I've got something I need to tell you,' she said, 'but... it's going to take a little time, and you can't interrupt, okay?' She sounded nervous. It had only been a few months since I left England the first time. I missed her so much I felt on fire all day. I drank too much water and went swimming in the sea.

'Okay...' I said, 'but... if you're ending this... just...'

'Just listen,' she interrupted me. Hectic. Soft. 'Just listen, okay?'

'Okay.'

'I'm really scared of this. This... thing that we have. It terrifies me that I haven't grown sick of you yet, and that every time we hang up, I think of another 20 questions I wish I'd asked. It scares me that I want to spend all my time with you, because being alone and independent is very important to me, and it has been for a long time.

'I still don't know if I will... you know, be any good at this. I still don't think I'm girlfriend material. But I want you to know that I'm in. I'm all in. I think I love you. And if I don't, this is certainly the closest I've felt, and I don't know if I'd even want something else. You can take whatever time you need to figure things out. I'm here and I'm yours if you want me, and if you don't.' She went quiet, and I said nothing for a long time.

'I really miss you,' I said.

'I miss you too.'

'Talk later?'

'Sure.'

'Okay... bye then?'

'Bye,' she laughed.

Neither of us hung up.

I replay this memory as I walk back to the hotel. Passing bridges I know and shops I have been to. And I replay it as I step past the rose garden where my gran loved to wander. This town is full of memories, but I think of that phone call and nothing else.

It doesn't hurt like I thought it would. There's no shooting pain or river of sadness, just the numb pain of pressing your fingers against an old bruise.

At the end of each day, my feet were white and wrinkly. I washed my socks when I found water, and dried one pair at a time by hanging them from my backpack while I walked. They were rarely clean. They were never dry. Even when I left them in water overnight to soak, they dried to reveal hard, crisp cotton: worn-down fibres dressed in petroleum jelly and sweat. I needed new ones.

Perhaps because I was lost in thought about my feet and socks and jelly, or perhaps because nothing like this had ever happened before, I completely ignored the sound of Scram barking. It didn't register at first—I was far away in a world where nothing ever really changed. The fourth and fifth barks registered as mere annoyances, but the eighth dragged me out into his world.

'What?' I said, and looked up. The dog in front of us was not one of the timid starving dogs I'd met before. Neither was it the hungry domesticated dog turned wild I had encountered in the cities. This was a savage dog turned king. His pink gums shone against his slightly yellowed teeth. Big slops of drool fell to the ground as he approached. I was on his turf, I could tell. And he wasn't going to allow me safe passage.

'Go away!' I shouted. 'Go away!' But he kept walking towards me, his head low and his ears flat against his head. I picked up a rock and threw it at him. Scram barked angrily and stood pressed to the ground. The dog didn't care. *He's going to kill me*, I thought. *This is how I'll die.* But I had my knife in my pocket, my hand wrapped around it without telling me why.

'GO AWAY!' I shouted as loudly as I could muster. 'OR I WILL HAVE TO HURT YOU!'

No, I said to myself sternly. *Don't hurt him. He's just following his instincts. It's not his fault.* But the dog came closer and there was rage in his eyes.

My knife flew through the air before I could stop my arm. The silver blade shone as it spun, quickly, deadly, then stopped. It wasn't a perfect hit. I had aimed for its legs, wanted to maim it, scare it, make it leave. But he stared at me in confusion and hurt.

'How could you?' his one eye said. 'You were on my turf!' My knife stood proudly in his other eye. Deep. He toppled over to the side and didn't make a single sound. Scram whimpered, and so did I.

'I'm sorry boy,' I said to Scram, and patted his head over and over, 'I had to...' But I saw now that I didn't. Behind the dog was another corpse. The flesh, what little there was left of it, was brown and shrivelled and old. It still had its clothes, and was eerily intact. Rotten, yes, but not eaten, and I had just killed its guardian. A loyal dog protecting his master, for months and months, by the look of it. I could have walked around. I should have walked around.

I make myself a drink in the bar. A little something to calm my nerves. The drink is too sweet and sticks to my insides. They don't have a great selection of wine, but I pick the nicest one I can find, light a candle on one of the tables by the window and drink from a beautiful glass. I pick an MP3 player at random and turn it on. Wham. Mariah Carey. Show tunes. It will do. There's music in my ears, and I look out onto the shopping street with all its empty promises. I imagine people and trams and cars.

Later, I bring the duvet and pillows from my room down to the lobby and go to sleep in an ocean of cushions. I read Georg's note over and over. Try to remember if he's real or imagined. Lady is licking her paws and grooming her fur. The sound is comforting and aggravating in equal measure. Scram eventually finds his way over to us. He rests his head on my chest for the first time in many days, or weeks, or even months, and I stroke him gently, scratch him behind his ear and whisper, 'Good boy,' until we both fall asleep.

19

I abandon the trolley outside Gothenburg and immediately feel homeless. I pack what I can in the backpack, preparing myself for leaner days. Lady may not make it. I can't carry too much dog food, and she's still not used to our way of improvised living. I'll let her try.

I walk on the train tracks, heading to Norway. It's not the easiest way, it's not the quickest way. It's neither the way I know to walk, nor the way I *should* walk, but it's the way I've chosen and I'm happy with that. It's impossible to get lost, as long as I keep checking the map whenever I walk into a new station. Without the trolley, I make good time.

As soon as I left the city, I felt the stalkers pick up my trail. The creature runs in front of me, terrified. It keeps looking over its shoulder but never at me; it fears the stalkers, like I feared the creature, and our mutual fear keeps us far apart.

The evenings are still long, and I walk until I can't. Most nights I find shelter, but some nights I'm too far from where people were, and on those nights I sleep in my new tent. I listen to the stalkers sniff their way through the forest. They've not caught up with me yet, but they will.

I hear a wolf howl somewhere far away, and I wonder if it fears the stalkers too. The howl might be a warning, telling other wolves to stay away. Or maybe to come, come here and gather, prepare for a mythical war. *Come*, it howls, *come, come*. Or perhaps it howls go. *Go! Go!* Elks trot through the woods with crashes and snaps. Twice I hear a boar grunt in the dusk, and I see its enormous dark outline against the darker ground. Owls hoot and bats flutter; mosquitoes sing around my head. I hear a bear, I think, but I tell myself it's definitely just another boar, as I'm already afraid of too many things.

I wake up one morning and have started bleeding. It's my first period since the baby died inside me, and it's thick and heavy and full of clots. Too heavy to just let it flow, too gloopy and clotty for tampons. I've already got one pack of pads, but I run through them quickly. I'm bleeding so much. I've forgotten to stay on top of my iron tablets, and to catch up, I eat too many. It makes my stomach hard and my faeces dark, but I don't feel any shame.

I worry about leaving the pads behind, worry about leaving a blood trail for the stalkers, or for animals, or for something else completely. For days, I wrap them up in leaves and grass and whatever I can find. I carry them all in a bag, and I never feel comfortable letting it go. Eventually I throw it in a car park dumpster and light the whole pile on fire. Perhaps there is magic—blood magic—afoot, or perhaps it's just the break from my routine, but either which way, the fire is cleansing, and I walk on feeling stronger and clean.

Having a period used to be such a significant thing; a shameful, hard and difficult secret. We hid it from our fathers, our brothers and boyfriends. We'd blush dark crimson if we bled through our clothes. We'd pretend like we weren't in excruciating pain, or grumpy, or moody, or sick of it all. I admired the girls who came after me, who openly asked for tampons at restaurants and discussed their flows out loud. My grandmother had to dry her pads in the shed to avoid embarrassing her brothers. It all seems rather stupid now.

The cramps aren't too bad, and the period comes and goes without issue. I consider making a mark on a calendar, but what does it matter when my period comes?

Some days I walk too far and there's no food or shops to be found. I fill my bottle in streams and rivers to make sure we won't run out of water. Through the many packings and re-packings of my backpack, it's a wonder the iodine tablets have made it this far. I crack them into bottle after bottle, white scraps of hope in an endless ocean of things that could kill me. But I don't worry. This is Sweden, almost Norway. The water is clean and fresh and tastes of mountains. Scram drinks anything, and Lady prefers puddles to streams.

I walk onto a farm, mostly by accident, in the middle of a pine forest. I strayed from the tracks to find some water and without warning, the farm was there. House, barn, shed and storehouse, all so Swedish they could have been painted, red and white against the trees. There's even a Swedish pennon swaying from the flagpole. I hum the Swedish national anthem. I don't remember the words.

The unkempt grass is alive with the last frogs and adders of the season. They jump and crawl away from me. Scram chases frogs towards the barn; Lady studies an adder sliding towards the rickety shed. The open space in front of me makes me fear the woods behind us, so I run towards the main building, looking over my shoulder, again and again. Nothing comes. Of course it doesn't.

Through a window, I see a man hanging from a beam in the kitchen ceiling. His skin is brown, dried and shrunken. Raisin, raisin, well-hung man. Corpses like that smell of sour dust, marshes and spoiled meat. Things that go 'ooooh' in the night. There aren't many, but I've seen a few. I head towards the storehouse instead.

'So, I read this really interesting article,' says Kobus.

'Oh?' I say.

'It was about a suicide forest in Japan. A forest so thick and dense, the authorities couldn't keep up with clearing it of bodies.'

'Yeah,' I say, 'I was the one who told you about this. *Jukai*—sea of trees.'

'That's right,' he says. His voice is in front of me, walking towards the storehouse with me. I can see his footsteps in the grass. Clear indentations where he's placed his large feet. That's new. 'They could only clear it of bodies once a year, finding 50 or 70 or over 100 at a time. Bringing them down to friends and families; letting them know for sure what had happened.'

If I keep his footsteps in the corner of my eye, I can almost see him. His skin, sunken, and lips, blue. This startles me. His voice is unclear and his accent is fading. I try to recall it clearer, try to make him speak up, but instead he just laughs.

'Fuckin' hell,' he says, and then he's not there.

I try not to think about my parents, but something about this farm makes it hard to avoid. My father was a rational man. And when he wasn't, he still thought he was. His constant awareness of everyone else's irrational behaviour made him constantly ignore his own, and I would have resented this trait in him, deeply, if I didn't see it so clearly in myself.

My mother, however, was made of everything soft. She was made of hugs and cuddles, and a repertoire of lullabies you could never reach the end of without falling asleep. Even if you tried. Even if you pushed your eyes open with your fingers, and thought about something else. I used to try a lot.

When I was little, she would spend what felt like hours—probably minutes—drawing simple patterns on my forehead with her fingers. With each repetition, I would sink further and further down into the sweetest dreams and quietest slumber. Her skin smelled of lotion and strawberry jam.

She believed everything she said very firmly as she said it, but if you contradicted her, she was easily swayed. This is not to say she was indecisive, no: she made decisions swiftly, but made new ones just as fast.

We often held large parties. My father and his sisters held committee meetings over how best to solve the coffee-and cake portion of the evening. They discussed movement flow and numbers. Should the cups be stacked in the kitchen, or placed with each seat at the tables?

'It's impractical, having to carry a full cup back from the kitchen,' one of them would say.

'But we don't have anyone to pour coffee by the tables,' another would answer. Theses debates never got heated, because they knew one thing to be absolutely true: no one was as good at throwing big parties as they were. This had been their house for generations. The cake forks had been in the same drawer since my great-great-grandmother's wedding. They knew how to do this, and they'd get to it in a minute.

In the background, my mum would place the coffee cups in neat stacks in the kitchen, pour sugar in bowls and uncover the cakes. She would issue each saucer with a silver teaspoon and fill extra coffee pots for the tables. Perhaps it wasn't optimised for movement flow, but this was my mother's kitchen now. In all secrecy, she kept a couple of cake forks mixed into the cutlery drawer.

In my mum's kitchen, things got done. Perhaps not perfectly, but to my mum, done was better than perfect. Done meant the coffee could be served. Done meant there was time to help old ladies back to their seats with their coffee and cake, and some small talk on the way. Done is better than perfect, she would say. And this became my motto, too.

My mother could be infuriatingly oblivious to the world around her. She could stand in a gale storm blowing straight from the north, see a microscopic cloud in the south and, without fail, say, 'Here comes the rain!' But she was soft and honest, and incredibly clever with numbers and people and all sorts of crafts. Despite all evidence pointing to me being my father's daughter, I secretly hoped to turn out like my mum. She was an excellent person. Was... I mean... She is. She is. There's still time. I don't want to think about this anymore.

The smell in the storehouse is from a different kind of death. Anger and murder, excitement and blood. Carcasses hang from the beams. Except, really, they don't any longer. They're pooled on the floor, pools that once were bubbling and oozing, and now are dried and crusty. Antlers poke out of the pool like a grow-it-yourself deer of some sort. This doesn't interest me.

On a bench to the left, however, the only place in the room that is not smothered in blood and grime, there's a huge compound bow and a range of angry-looking arrows. Thank you. Thank you. Thank you. On closer inspection, there are two types of arrow. The narrow, pointy kind I recognise from archery with Cleopatra, and another type with triangular razorblade heads. Hunting arrows. I knew they existed—I've seen them in horror films and once, I heard a bow hunter talk at length about how much more exciting it was to hunt with a bow and arrow than a gun. Hunting arrows. Illegal in Scandinavia, I know, but they're still here. I don't believe in signs, but this is one. A sign, a hint: something is coming.

I spend two days on the farm. I sleep in the barn, which is dry and musty. The stalkers haven't found me yet, or perhaps they fear the bow. I practise with the simple arrows, which are a bit long for me but I can't afford to care. It takes me ages to find the right stance.

My forearm bruises from the wrist to the elbow, but it doesn't hurt, so I persevere. The creature watches me from inside the house. It stirs the air, making the hanged man's rope sway and creak. I never look.

I was never bad at archery, but I'm not amazing. After two days, I can hit the target every time—rarely the bullseye, but rarely the edge, either. My arms are sore and tired, but I keep trying. With each shot, I step back a little. I can quite confidently hit a bucket-sized target at 15-metre range. It is a good beginning, but it's far from enough. I can't wait much longer, though. I have to hurry home.

When my niece was born, my grandfather was 98. He was a farmer through and through. His body, now worn and slouched, still held strength many times the strength of mine. He kept driving the tractor around my father's farm until he was 96 and the doctor no longer let him. Growing up with him next door was a harsh lesson in work ethics.

I don't think my grandfather ever *tried* to be a good worker. I don't think he put any pride or effort into being hard-working, helpful or resolute. In his world, there simply was no alternative; if you had the ability, you had the duty to utilise it. If you could help, you helped, if you could sing, you sang, if you could work, you did, and everyone could. I've often wondered how he'd feel about all the talent I've wasted. I have wasted a lot.

My niece was born with the tiniest, frailest hands I had ever seen. Few things ever touched me more than seeing her three-week-old hand grip around his ninety-eight-year-old index finger. Her soft pink skin against his gnarly yellowish hue; his wrinkles and scars against her unbroken newness. This thought hurts. I'll never see anything as new and unbroken again.

'So,' says Kobus, and I can feel him walking next to me. There's a slight chill in the air, a nip to say that winter is coming. That autumn is here. The long, Scandinavian summer evenings are migrating south these days. He doesn't say anything else for a while, and I don't prompt him.

'The dream I had,' he says, finally. 'What do you think it means?'

'What dream?' I say, because I don't know what he's talking about. More and more often, I feel he's coming at me from an angle I can't quite see. As if he remembers things I don't, although I know that's impossible. Or perhaps it isn't. Where did all the knowledge go? All the information gathered inside people's heads, all the information of the internet, the unread pages, the libraries and vaults—where is that information now?

I know, because my father raised me well, that energy cannot disappear, only change. Perhaps the information is still here but in a different form. Perhaps, somehow, the ghost of Kobus has tapped into the traced outline of Kobus' memories. Perhaps my memory has tapped into the knowledge and wisdom of someone else; chosen Kobus's voice to convey it. Maybe I am talking to a new ghost now. I can't really know and I don't really care. It's nice to hear his voice.

'The dream with the autopsy, remember?' he says and I nod, because now I do.

'I don't know what it means,' I say. 'Did it have something to do with the mandalas you talked about? The patterns of sand made by monks?'

'I don't think so,' he says. His voice is weaker now. As if I can't quite place it in his mouth. 'I still think it's a fucking waste of time, though,' he says. 'Bloody fucking hours of work just to be whisked away. And that's why it is so beautiful. The meaningless of it all. That,' he says, and I remember how he'll be bobbing his right hand up and down in the air to emphasise his point, how his eyes will be digging into me, his smile will be widening, his head will be dancing. 'That,' he says again, 'is better than a million fucking mindfulness bitches talking about being in the moment. That is the difference between measuring time—' his hand will be shooting out in front of him now, and he'll be weighing the imagined moment in his hand, 'and fucking being in it.' I finish the movement for him. Push a finger into the palm of my hand, cup it as if I'm four years old and this is a precious, smooth and beautiful stone.

'Exactly,' he says. And I know I did well.

20

For days, I can't lift my arms. My shoulders are stiff and sore; my bruised arm hurts like hell. I'm extremely hungry. It's been way too long since I last saw a shop, and the backpack is all out of food.

In the mornings, I thread myself into the straps of the pack while crouching low to the ground. I rock back and forth until the momentum can heave me up on my feet. My back aches, my arms tingle, my right elbow is hot and swollen. I let them rest. There's nothing else to do.

I don't even notice crossing the border. Like God, the border is gone now that there's no one left to believe in it. But when the tracks next take me into a larger station, the name is Norwegian and I've been here before. Everything's suddenly familiar, the corpses feel like family, and I would have known how to pronounce their names.

I catch a glimpse of myself in a window, and for a second think I see someone else. Her body is lean, scrawny in places. Her head is slightly too large for her lollipop neck, and her eyes a bit too huge for the sunken cheeks. What big eyes you have, Grandma. I must remember to eat more.

It takes me a long time to break into the shop—a familiar shop, a chain I have heard of. I read all the magazines and newspapers I can find. The same news I once read in English, but in reverse. The doctors, the evangelists and the hindsight lenses, they're all the same.

I read glossy magazines about celebrities I once knew the faces of, and eat food made by brands I grew up with. My stomach jumps at the first bites, dissolves them and burns them instantly. So hungry.

The creature has collapsed right inside the door. Its chest is heaving with uneven breaths. It's limp, weak and broken. I search the shelves for my favourite chocolate, kick it across the floor in case the creature's hungry too. There's still no sign of the stalkers. Scram and Lady eat until they throw up, then slowly eat some more. I haven't really noticed how skinny they are. I don't quite understand how it happened.

The phone turns on with its loud little beep. September 10th. It's late. Too late. I've wasted so much time. What have I been doing? I try to trace my steps through Denmark and Sweden. It should have just been a few weeks. Where did it go wrong? What did I do in Denmark? Where have I been?

I need to move. From here, I'll follow roads. I find a new trolley and fill it with food. Mostly dog food. I haven't been treating them right. The trolley is heavy and awkward to push. I miss the old one with a homesickness I can't explain or let go. Lady's happy to be back off her feet, and I am almost home.

I don't know where the elk came from, if it walked out in front of us right now or if it's been standing there, watching, as we approached. Scram sees it first and tenses. Lady sees it and doesn't care. I see it, and time slows down.

It's very early, still. Dawn is hard and clear and solid like glass. As I push the trolley forward, it cuts through the air and ploughs through the morning, making a groove we can walk in. As I stop, the air surrounds me like a bell jar.

I feel the bow against my back. It's been five days. The bruise on my arm still throbs under my skin, but I'm ready. My muscles screech and I take aim.

'Baby?' she says, and the arrow goes flying over the elk's head. The elk doesn't mind. I spin around, stare in between the trees. She's here! The girl who looked like Cleopatra is here, just behind what I can see.

'Sweetie?' I say, then cough sandpaper out of my throat. I must remember to keep talking. 'Honey, hello? Hello?' I want to shout but can only whisper.

'I wouldn't starve,' she says, and her voice is right next to my ear three years ago. We're in the bathtub, drinking wine and talking about survival. 'If I was dying and there was nothing to eat but meat—of course I would eat it. I wouldn't die to save a pig or a deer. I suppose I would even hunt, if I absolutely had to.' I don't move, I don't breathe. I don't want this to end. The water is warm and smells of lavender and cinnamon. I can feel her stubbly leg against my stubbly leg, I can feel her nose against my cheek.

'Besides,' she continues, 'it's not like I don't like meat. I do sometimes think, "hey, bacon would be nice." The thought of eating an animal is absolutely repulsive to me, so I don't. But like, if they get this synthetic meat thing going, I would eat that. Bring on the bacon! Even if the very first cell they grew it all out of was an animal cell. Just because, you know, it would save millions of other animals.'

I know what comes next. I'll argue that millions of other animals will not be born in the first place, because they're no longer needed. And she'll argue that this is a good thing, but eventually get sad because I turn the discussion into something it was never meant to be. I'm hoping my brain will leave that part out, so I wait for one second. Two. Three. But when I don't say anything, she doesn't reply, and I want her to speak, I need her to stay. My Cleopatra. The girl across the room. I try something else.

'Do you not think I should shoot it?' I say, and the forest comes back, tree by tree. Her leg slips away and the water is ice cold.

'You need to take care of yourself,' she says, 'it's important.'

'Why?' I say, whinier than I intended. I want her to comfort me. I want her to stretch out her tiny hands and touch my cheeks and brush my neck. I want her to stroke my forehead the way she does, the way that reminds me of my mother's touch. I want Cleopatra to comfort and read to me. I want her to be here. I want her. I want her.

'Baby...' she says. I know she'll do her little head-shake. The tiniest movement that signals I am being silly.

'Did you love me?' I say. I don't know where it comes from. She doesn't reply, not at first. The water and the cinnamon fall away completely. It's just me and the elk, Scram and Lady. I listen to the wind in the treetops.

'Of course she did,' they whisper, but I don't trust them. How on Earth would they know?

I look through the new trolley. It has food enough for a couple of days. More for the dogs. I don't *need* to kill the elk. But I do need it to move. Eventually, it does. I can still smell Cleopatra in the air. I take a few steps but the smell grows fainter, so I stay absolutely still.

'I can't answer your question,' I hear her say, so softly I don't know if I'm imagining it.

'Why not?' I say. My voice breaks into tears. I want to beg her to say it again, to tell me she loves me and that everything will be all right. But all I can say is the same thing over and over. 'Why can't you say that you loved me? Why not? Why not? Baby, why?' And eventually, I hear her somewhere inside my left ear. Just the whisper of a wish, nothing more.

'Because you're not quite sure,' she says. I clench my jaw and walk.

I think I've always dreamed of walking. As long as I can remember, the thought of open fields rolling out around me, the thought of seeing them, taking them in step by step, has fascinated me. I loved seeing tracks shooting through forests and woods, seeing paths clearing their way through shrubbery and straw. I loved wooden bridges over streams, stone steps lining a hill, a viewpoint seen from far below. They all called to me, sang to me, told me that I should be moving. That I should step into the wild and explore. Lie on the ground and listen.

But even so, I spent an awful lot of time on planes. High above the ground where I felt lost, dislodged and strange. I would stare down at the world below and try to envisage every step of the roads beneath me. I imagined seeing the cars and trees, valleys and rivers up close. Around me. Above me. Under my foot. And I always wanted to be there.

As soon as I started hiking, as soon as I started crossing the fields and valleys, standing on the bridges and climbing to the viewpoints, the whole world turned into a map with a 1:1 scale inside me. A map of all the places I was at the moment, and those were my favourite kind.

I also spent a lot of time on trains. I would stare out into the night around me and try to imagine living the thousands of lives that passed by. Each window along the tracks held a day I never lived. Sofas I never bought. Friends I never met. My entire life, I stared through windows next to train lines, trying to catch a glimpse of something different to what I knew. People cooking and watching TV. People crying and making out.

I once saw a penis at Elephant & Castle. It was displayed proudly, like a gift to the world outside. The man who owned it held his hand around it, terrified it would fall off and crawl away. It couldn't compete with the glowing lights of the London Eye, or the hundreds and thousands of lives I wished I could try on for size. All of them bigger, so I left him alone. It's not like he needed me, anyway. I'm sure he imagined we were hundreds and thousands of applauding strangers down here, in the trains, when really, there was only me.

I have commuted thousands of hours on buses. Slept my way through mile after mile of bad Norwegian roads and dull English highways. I listened to audiobooks, the same ones over and over. Sleeping through different parts each time.

I used to go *home* on a bus... A bus with drivers who recognised me and knew which of the luggage holds my suitcase should be in. A bus that took me from my life to my old life, from my husband to my parents, from my new self to my old. A bus that carried me through the landscape that told me I could have walked, if I wanted to. That nature was right there, right outside my window, waiting for me to step out of the bus and move through it. I wish there were buses now.

I've decided to sleep in a bike shed. The creature's already asleep but I'm sitting outside, watching the stars. There are satellites moving up there. Hundreds of them, I suppose, although I can only see two. They glide through the sky and disappear in the night.

I show them my breasts as they pass above me. I doubt they notice and I know they won't tell. Even if they did, no one would listen. Scram barks at a mouse that nips at my backpack, Lady rests her head in my lap. I stroke her fur softly. She's so tired, she seems ill. I worry, but not too much.

I call out Cleopatra's name but get no answer.

'Kobus?' Everything quiet.

'God?' The stars twinkle and giggle in the sky.

Outside Hamburg, I stood in the rain, howling against the cold and the wet. Something was wrong, something was lost. And there, across the field, I saw myself. A part of me, an important part of me, stood there, shy and worried, and stared at me.

She studied the tattoos, the one I got when I married and the one I got when I was free. She took in my new, tight muscles, firm and lean, wound-up springs under my skin. She was judging me, had left me behind to see us from the outside, consider my body, my soul, my condition—but on her own. Without me.

She watched me shiver, writhe and convulse against the cold. Anger welling up inside me. She'd left me here, without the ability to move or walk. Left me to wait, trapped, open and ready for her to get back inside us, to let us be one and whole. But left me without the ability to choose.

Scram could tell. He whimpered somewhere beside me, noticed I wasn't all there. Anger. So angry. I was so angry that hot tears mixed with the rain. White heat burned and glistened under my white cold skin. I glowed like coal and embers, furiously waiting in silence. Eventually, she slid back into our body, and I was whole and me again, but there was still so much anger, somewhere, deep in the back of our mind.

I forced up images of things we should be dealing with. Cleopatra dying. The potential emptiness of home. The fact that we might be walking for no reason and the facts of the things we'd forget. But somehow, she was stronger. She kept these thoughts at bay. The anger burned like a single candle in an endless night, it wasn't enough to break through.

It happened more and more often. She'd start walking, blocking me out, and hours later I'd wake in a landscape, strange and new. I'd have passed cities and towns, corpses and misery, without even knowing, without being told.

I wondered if she knew what she was doing. If she consciously kept me from myself or accidentally shut the doors between us. But when I woke up, I could never remember. No matter how much I searched my mind, no matter how much I pushed or begged, she never let me remember how we got there in the first place.

It's a new morning and I've slept in a barn. Waking up, I know I'm almost home, a fact that rings through my bones. If I walk hard, I can get there tonight.

I notice my own procrastination but I can't make myself move. I spend ages repacking my backpack, shutting out the feeling that I should leave some things behind. I empty out all the water bottles and refill them with water from a stream nearby. I crack iodine tablets I know I don't need, watch them dissolve in the crystal-clear liquid.

I make a bread dough that I'll let rise in the trolley. I'll have to stop in a few hours to bake it. I'll need it either way. Whether or not I make it home tonight. Maybe I'll be eating on the porch. Tonight. If I make it home, if, but only if I do.

This is anxiety. I recognise the heavy pendulum behind my lungs. It pulls me down, drags me to the ground; its slow swaying makes me nauseous and uneasy. It keeps me from knowing where my centre of balance is, a little to the left, a little to the right. My palms prickle and go cold. There's a bubbling sensation behind my ears, on top of my scalp, right under my skin. Take a deep breath and swallow.

'Hey,' says Kobus. 'How are you doing?' His voice is clear and his accent soft. He sounds like me, I think. I don't think he's ever asked me how I'm doing before. I stop and wait.

'How's life?' he says instead. That's more like it.

'I'm nervous,' I say.

'I get that, you have a lot riding on getting there. When will that be? Today? Tomorrow?'

'Tomorrow,' I say, and pick up the pace as soon as I've said it out loud. I'll sleep somewhere close by tonight. Walk into the farm while it's still early morning. Have the whole day to...

'Alright,' he says. 'So. Why am I here?'

'I don't know,' I say, 'I think I just needed someone to talk to... I'm scared.'

'There's nothing to be scared of,' he says, 'the truth is already true. You're just going to know what it is.'

'Yeah...' I say. It is true. My family is either dead or not dead. That won't change by me getting there, but still... 'Hey... Kobus?'

'Yes?'

'You haven't sworn once in this entire conversation.'

'Huh,' he says. He sounds sad, I think, or maybe it's just me. 'I guess you forgot.'

I walk until it's time to eat and bake my bread. I do it in the manner of Norwegian campers everywhen; I clean twigs and sticks of bark and dirt, and twist my dough around them. I bake the breads slowly. Turn them occasionally, make sure not to get them too close to the fire. They hang above the flames like worms on hooks. They try to catch their breath, and swell with yeast and heat and time.

My mind is about 30 kilometres further north-west. It's walking through the grass outside, looking for my mum. It's opening our front door and taking that first breath. It's asking God, or fate, or circumstance, what that breath will smell like. Dust or death?

Half my breads are sooted. The other half are burned.

21

The rage was half, the other was sadness, and that was all she left me. This was what she had been practising. She'd perfected the art, over days of confusion, and now she'd fractured us, split us apart, left me behind and gone.

There was rage, there was sadness, and then something else. Something softer and weaker I held, but didn't recognise.

Somewhere close to Denmark. Somewhere in Germany. Sometime after Hamburg. She split me off and abandoned me. Carried on without all of herself. She took our body and left me, and all I could do was follow. Try to catch up and force my way back in.

The rage was strong and spiked and metallic, so hard I could touch it. Twine and sinews under my fingers. Armour of sorts. I slid inside the sadness, took it on as form. Coated myself in the anger and it shaped itself close, claws and teeth. She hadn't made it too far, so I caught up quickly. Saw myself across a field of bloated dead cows and a few survivors. I approached her slowly, but the rage ran wild. I lost control. The closer I got, the angrier I let myself become, and my form grew, my fangs grew, my claws pierced the sky. I was rage.

I could imagine myself attacking our body. I would break it, ravish it, make myself taste it, devour the full force of our anger and fear. I would push all the loneliness to the surface. Make us go mad with the certainty that nowhere, no matter how far I walked, would I ever find enough to get back what we'd lost. I would drive us insane, make our body turn south. Walk south, walk far, towards heat and survival. I'd push out the memories, wipe out the past.

I picked up the pace, ran towards her, ready to pounce, rip and tear. I slowed down only to make our body fear, quiver. I wanted her terrified and weak.

She was talking to the ghost of Kobus. Listening to him go on and on about one thing or another. I felt no love for his memory, I only had burning. The rage of all the times I'd felt like screaming in his face, the rage for him thinking the death of his girls was his decision to make. The rage that he left me behind.

Grief drove me forward, hoping, maybe, that if I got there fast enough I could catch a glimpse. See his stupid staring face and hear his sarcastic laughter. I missed him and I hated him for it. Then, the something else… the little something packed inside me, the little parcel of softness I couldn't identify, reminded me that Kobus made me a portion too. That he gave me the option to follow him, to bring Cleopatra with me to a swift and scheduled end. When I got close enough, she had turned our back to me. She clung on to Scram for dear life, leaving their throats open to me, giving me the option to tear them both to shreds.

I hid in the tall grass.

I recognise the landscape around me. I pass my old college and decide it's time to stop. I'm too close already, and it's nearly dark. Soon, I'll pass my cousin's farm, soon I'll pass my best friend from childhood's house. Soon, I'll walk the road I walked when I ran away from daycare at the age of six. I'll pass the shops I know and the houses of everyone I grew up with. I'll pass the church I once worked for, sang in, loved, got married in. The church I spent 33 of my first 35 Christmases in. My grandfather's grave. My primary school. I'm too tired for all of that today. Soon it will be tomorrow. I break the window of the library and get all the way inside before I remember it stopped being a library many, many years ago.

The creature gave up somewhere along the way. I heard it whimper and sigh, and when I turned around to look, it had collapsed in the middle of the road. Its fur was blood-soaked and glistening, its legs bent at unnatural angles. *Roadkill*, I thought. It had been a long road to get here.

At first, I thought I'd leave it. Every instinct told me to walk, leave it behind and forget it. But the stalkers might still be out there, somewhere, and the creature hadn't actually hurt me, not yet. It shrunk in my arms, shivering slightly, and it easily fit in the trolley. If nothing else, I thought, it would keep Lady warm.

Now, it stretches its broken bones over the side of the trolley. Slumps onto the floor like so many rags. It fights for breath, drags itself across the floor and disappears through the door. I let it.

I eat burned bread and feed the dogs all they can eat in pet food and snacks. I spend ages on their fur with a brush I got in the pet shop next door. Lady loves the grooming. She sits so proudly and snootily, stares at me with a face that says, 'Finally, you odd little human, you're doing what you are supposed to. Where are my nice collars? Where are your diamonds? Are you going to sort your own fur now?' I grin at her silly little face.

Scram tolerates the grooming but he doesn't enjoy it. I don't know why I do it anyway, I just know I want them to look their best. I want them to look as if I've taken great care of them along the way. As if they're not too thin and partially feral. As if it isn't completely my fault.

I don't sleep much, but I didn't expect to. Perhaps my parents are in their bedroom, now, just a few miles away, wondering if I'm still alive. Maybe only one of them is, or maybe everyone is. Perhaps my sister and my niece have moved back into the main building to keep the little family close, to save on resources as much as possible.

Maybe Lilly is asking them, 'Where's Auntie?' and perhaps they're saying, 'She'll be here soon.' But I know they won't be, they're too realistic. He'll have explained, I'm sure, that I'm dead, and that she'll never see me again. What a surprise I will be.

We can plan her birthday, which is only a month away, and I can bake her a cake again, like I used to. I drift in and out of these thoughts, and sometimes I think they're real. Sometimes I can hear Lilly's laughter, which is probably three years too young, and probably just a memory anyway. Sometimes I can taste strawberry jam, or hear my father reciting *Peer Gynt*. The world smells of homemade bread and my mum's meatloaf and body lotion. I think I'm crying, but when I get up, I don't remember.

It's getting lighter outside.

I might as well go home.

She carelessly dropped pieces along the way. I followed close and kept finding chunks of us left behind. Entire people ripped from our memory, conduct and care abandoned for dead. She got wilder, less human, and I feared it would be too late. That no matter how hard I tried to shove myself back inside, I'd no longer fit or make sense. She cared so little. She walked around naked. Shat on the road. Ate with her hands and wiped them on her thighs. She kept forgetting to brush her teeth. Her breath stank worse than mine.

I absorbed what I could. Each new piece I found, I tried to find a place for. I locked some between the anger and sadness, wrapped some around the softness in the middle. But much I had to abandon, too. Some things belong somewhere deep beneath the skin, and I had no skin to offer.

Multiple times, I could have attacked, but the softness in the middle wouldn't let me.

'We can merge when we get there,' it would tell me, 'but first, let her get home.' It sounded like a good idea, and I kept myself at bay.

She found something in Denmark. I don't know what. Something that shielded her from me for days. She was talking to herself, and replying, I think, or perhaps she didn't and I imagined things. I had no ears, I had no eyes, I had no senses at all, just feelings. Feelings, feelings and a purpose. Feelings, feelings, patience and a purpose. Feelings, patience, rage and a purpose, but I didn't quite know what it was.

It's cold. Very cold. It's cold the way only Norwegian mornings in autumn can be cold. The air is so crisp I hear the starlight shudder through space and fall. I breathe small needles of frost. They puncture my lungs and run through my blood; my breath comes out shortened and hard.

Every stream and river crowns itself with white mist, sends its mist across the fields, claiming territory for itself. It grabs it, tries to keep it, but a yellow salmon line on the horizon tells me the sun is on its way to claim its territory back. I claim nothing, I just walk.

I do not look to my cousin's farm. I don't look at the houses of people I once knew. My eyes don't register the shops or the crossings, or my mother's old workplace down the road. I just walk. Push my trolley down roads I know, roads I know so very well.

There are bodies here, too. For some reason, it never crossed my mind that I would walk past bodies here. Here, where the bodies are people I once went to school with. Or children or cousins or parents of the same. It's important to me not to recognise anyone, so I do what I can not to look.

The quietness is bigger here. It stretches from place to place, from name to name. I get to know it from side to side, because now it's in my life. The quietness isn't just here, it's everywhere, and growing. It stretches past the house on the hill, the symmetrical house and the alpaca farm. It stretches past my niece's daycare, and all the way to the bus station in the town, past it to the big city, and further on and on to the mountains, to the sea, to the snowy plains up north. No matter how far I send my mind across the landscape, I know the silence still wraps around it. I can feel the entire world, now. My heart is a void.

'So,' says Kobus. 'I read this thing...' But I don't have anything else to fill the silence with, so I just let him walk with me for a while. I wheel the trolley off the asphalt. Barely a kilometre and a half left on this dust road I once walked home from school. Perhaps I imagined it wouldn't have changed. That it would be hard and compact from cars rolling over, or wet and sloppy from the rain. But the rain has washed the hardness off and it's dried again, flat and unstoppable. It lets my trolley pass, but just barely. The wheels clog, drag the sand and gravel along, but it keeps rolling, it moves. The walk doesn't take me forever and the trolley doesn't force me to stop. No matter how much I wish I could, no matter how scared I am.

I think I noticed the stalkers before she did. I felt them gliding up behind us, following in our wake and giggling at my misfortune. They attacked me. Viciously. But I had already started forgetting, so I snarled and bit and clawed them back. I don't know what I lost. I don't know what they took from me.

I was already ill when they came. The abandoned pieces I picked up along the way had infected me, poisoned me, left me feverish and weak. I don't know what they did, or why.

I also don't know where the stalkers went. Perhaps they ran ahead. Perhaps they lost our track. I don't believe the latter, but I can't believe my luck. I've felt the determination in their consciousness—there's nothing but survival in there. The stalkers want to live, that's all, and survival's a dangerous goal.

After the fight, she looked out for me, pitied me and kept me safe. I made one desperate attempt to merge us, but instead of falling back into her, she fell into me, stole my form and shape for a second, dragged out what she wanted and left me with the rest. Again.

But she kept me alive, let my broken body sleep close to where they slept. She didn't come near me but let me approach. I forgot that we were one and I was grateful that she let me. I was grateful she was there. The memories stayed quiet in my body. They had no consciousness to rise in, so they kept themselves asleep. I was only angry, sad or soft and too tired for them all. Perhaps that's what she knew, and why she let me sleep so close.

I think, perhaps, I was dying. Perhaps the things I was made of could only be contained outside the body for so long. Or perhaps my parts just didn't add up, a mathematical equation with too many variables, no answer and no one to mind. Either way, I didn't hold together. I don't know what she saw, but she touched me, then. Let me rest in the trolley, and brought me closer to home.

She wasn't us anymore. I don't really know who she'd become. I ran away. Hid in the forest. Ate a deer or two or three, regained my strength and fuelled my anger. It was almost too late. She had almost won. But there was still hope. If I could get there before her. If I could only find a way in.

The farm is like it's always been. It lies surrounded by our fields. They have been sowed but not reaped this year. I know what that means, but I'll think about it later. The main house looks like home. So much so that it makes my heart beat faster. It's so tall, so wide and holds so many rooms; each of them, I know, holds thrice as many stories.

My sister's house is next door. It used to be my grandparents' house, and was built from wood my grandfather salvaged from a school. That school was built with wood from a chapel, a chapel that was built on the grounds of another, and now it's my sister's house. It lies silent and low in the landscape, an afterthought of the forest and fields.

All the buildings are like I left them at Christmas. The gazebo, my little oasis, greets me with its windows dark. The barn is red and solid like a rock. The little red drying house—the house where two hundred years ago, my ancestors would have hung hams and onions from the rafters—the house where five generations of unused items are held—the place where the things we don't care about live a good life—this house stands there, next to the gazebo, and knows nothing of the emptiness outside.

There's life on the farm, I can see it from here. Seven magpies are perched on the roof. I can hear their squittering squattering squawks cross the landscape. Three fat elks are eating their hearts out in the fields. It's not at all an unusual sight, I used to see elks a hundred times a year. But the silence encases the washed-out world, and they seem serious, ominous, territorial and huge. They've planted their flag in our fields, and I no longer have any right to the ground. In fact, standing here, it surprises me that I ever thought I did.

22

The magpies don't fly off, even as I walk past the barn, even as I stand beside the birch that marks the split in the road, even as I clear my throat a couple of times. They sit there, squawking, indifferent and aloof. They know something I don't.

Where should I go first? My parents' house, or my sister's? My parents' house is straight in front of me. Every second, I expect the door to burst open and my parents to stand there. I expect it any second now. Right now, it will open. Just see. Right now. Here they come. Right... now!

Any second, my mum will run out and hug me with her soft cheeks while crying her soft tears and looking at me with that soft little look that means she loves me in the softest way. My father will cry too, but differently. They will draw me close and kiss my face and call me 'their girl'. Maybe. They've never done that before.

They will tell me who's dead, and who lives. My mum will have jam, maybe talk about which berries they've picked and which had too dry a summer or too wet a spring.

My father will show me the preparations they've made for winter. They've probably reaped just one area of the fields. Of course! An area I can't see from the road. Grain enough for personal consumption, and enough to sow next year.

They'll have dug a potato cellar. Brought potatoes home from the shops before it was too late. Put the farm back to how it was 150 years ago, functioning and independent. A fortress of survival and seasons and things that grow tall in the night.

My father will have filled the tanks with diesel. My mum will have made a hoard of all the yarn and fabric she could get hold of. They'll have found her a vintage sewing machine, or my father will have built some sort of bicycle-driven dynamo to power the one she has.

Any second now, he'll show me everything. They just need to notice I'm here, and they will. Any second now. Watch. Here they come. Just wait. Any moment. I've fixed my eyes on the door.

I kick gravel up as I walk; I call out, 'Hello? Hello?' I listen to my echo rolling through the valley and wait for it to die before I call hello again. There's no movement in the windows. No shuffling of feet from inside. Perhaps they're resting, or reading to one another in the living room. Maybe my mum's upstairs, sewing. Maybe my father is in his office, reading or soldering, or building something useful for the winter.

I feel so light and grateful: I am finally, finally here. I wonder if my sister is. I wonder if my aunts and uncles will have gathered here on the farm. I wonder if our mattresses, our duvets and spare linen will all be pulled from storage and placed side by side in the dining room. I wonder if our farm is now a safe place for survivors.

Perhaps they're all having dinner, right now, dunking freshly baked bread in my mother's potato soup, telling each other that they know I'll get here. Since the rest of the family has survived, I must have survived, they'll say, and if there's one person they know can handle being on her own, it's me. They've seen little proof of this before, but now they'll sense it. They'll know it in their bones.

I'm so happy. So light. I can see them all there, around the table, right inside my mind. Any second now, someone will spot me, and everything will be safe and home.

I leave the trolley and run. I run up the steps to the front door, and grab the door handle, pull at it. 'I'm here!' I shout. 'I'm here!' I shake and tear and pull the handle, but the door's locked and cold. I ring the doorbell. Over and over, the way we did as children, the impatient, annoying way of us and other kids in the neighbourhood. Ding dong, ding-ding-ding-ding-ding dong!

'Mum?' I shout. 'Dad?' It's okay if only they have survived. Only my parents and my sister and my niece. I'll teach her to swim next summer. Teach her to make bread on a concrete slab. I'll tell her about whales, and how all of us dying might have saved the planet. I'll make sure she knows about porpoises, bread and Kilimanjaro. I'll make sure to tell her all I know about fairy tales and songs.

I don't know why they can't hear the doorbell. I try knocking. Maybe they're sad. Maybe they're sitting in there, crying over all they have lost. Maybe they think they're imagining the sound, and that even if they went to check, nothing would be on the steps except the ghost of summers past. Maybe there's just one of them left. My father. My mother. My sister. My... well, she wouldn't survive on her own. I hammer on the door.

'Hello? Mum? Dad? Anyone? Hello? I'm home! I'm here!'

They can't hear me. Maybe they think the sound isn't real. Maybe they're haunted by ghosts, the same way I've got the stalkers behind me. Maybe they think I'm some dark spot in their mind, ringing the doorbell, slamming my fists into the door. Perhaps they ignore me to stay safe and sane.

'It's really me,' I try, but if I were an apparition, that's just what I'd say.

There's still a spare key under a flowerpot in the barn. I haven't been in here for years and years, and it smells damper and colder than I remember. I call out for my father a couple of times, but there's no reply. Sometimes, if he's working on something, he won't hear you right away.

It's then, just as I walk back from the barn, that I see them. The six wooden crosses in the grass behind the house. I catch them at an angle, hope it's a mirage, twist and turn my head, shake it, no. But no. But no. They're there. They are really, really there.

They already look old to me. Wooden, withered, worn. I was prepared for this. I was. But a cold sensation spreads like liquid fire through my mind, topples down my heart and penetrates my soul.

The emptiness inside me is replaced by something else, and it feels as if my body will be crushed beneath its weight. The crosses startle me, stun me, and lock me into this one moment. I can't move. Can't turn. There's nothing at all but the crosses and they're eating me alive. I hear footsteps in the gravel behind me.

These are slow, deliberate footsteps. They approach without caution or fear. These are not my father's heavy even trots. They are not my mother's hectic steps, or my sister's replica of hers. They don't create the light and easy tapper of my niece.

These steps bury into the gravel and cut through it with precision. They push the stones away and leave deep scores in their wake. They get lower. Slower. Ready to pounce. My chest is pushing its way through my skin, blowing up like a balloon, crushing my heart into smithereens, choking me, drowning me, claiming me. Five thousand seconds, compressed into one. I feel sick; my mouth swims in stomach juice. I can't spit it out. I can't move at all.

The beads on my forehead grow icy cold in the light wind. My eyes flicker from one side to the other. I need to see what's coming. I need to know what...

The pain of the attack is everything.

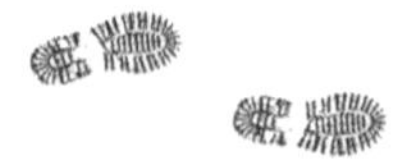

I leaped and jumped and bit and clawed. I dug myself through our skin and pushed away the foreign parts. There was hardly room for me in there, she'd dismissed the guards of anger and sadness, taped across the doors, closed the wards down, turned off the lights. But I burrowed inside, ripped through the tape and screamed as I tore anger and sadness apart and sent them to their rooms.

I dug my claws into our brain. Forced her to absorb me. Bond. Feel our wrath. Despair in every breath.

I pushed our memories back into their slots and myself into myself, until there was only us completely. I felt all of our truths tumble back into my consciousness. I didn't know if we could handle each other anymore, but it was too late to go back, too late to escape. Too much. Too much! There is nothing left but grief and grief, and we are all alone. There's no one here. We've lost it all, and I scream, I scream and scream.

I crash to my knees. The scream fills me completely and I am nothing else. I scream the magpies away. The elks startle and run. Scram and Lady run to me, bark, yap, jump and growl. Scram is frantic, desperate, pushes me with his nose and jumps his front legs from side to side.

I can't stop screaming. My eyes fill with tears, and I miss Cleopatra so much I don't know how to make it fit. The balloon in my chest has burst, and my crushed heart reminds me that it was crushed all along. It's been nothing but splinters since she died in my arms. This scream isn't even a new scream. It's the echo of the scream I screamed back then. It has run across the Earth and made its way back to me, and now I keep it going.

I grab hold of Scram. Drag him closer. I'm gasping for breath. Sob deep and wet and long for my mum.

'I'm sorry boy,' I whisper. 'You're so thin. I'm sorry, I'm sorry, I'm sorry.' He licks my face in forgiveness and it makes me cry even more.

Wave after wave of anger and sorrow wash through my body like tides. The anger makes me scream and slam my fist to the ground. I yell myself hoarse and dry.

The sadness makes me scream, plead and beg and bargain. It isn't fair. It isn't fair. This is not how it's meant to end. *Where's my hope?* I ask the gods. *Where's my hope?* There has to be hope, there has to be! It's a fundamental function of the universe, I've believed this since I was a child. If everything else breaks down, there's always—at the very, very least—hope.

But now I see that the universe has given up; it no longer plays by the rules. It's played tic-tac-toe against itself, my family as markers, six crosses in a row. Or six I can see from here. How many more are hidden behind the house? And who dug the last grave? Who is buried here, in my home? Who have I lost?

Everyone, of course. That's the answer. But I still make my way to the graves. As I feared, there are two more I couldn't see. Eight graves. Seven of them are completed. Dug and filled. Crosses for each. A devastating treasure map. X marks the spot, marks the spot, marks the spot. But the eighth grave, the one in the middle, is not filled. Only dug. The shovel still lies beside it, resting and rusted. I know I have to look inside and I know what I will find. Whomever was the last survivor might have lain themselves down to die in their grave, the same way I did, ages ago.

The placement makes me think it was my dad. The eighth grave peeks out between the houses, taking in the view of our little valley. He loved that view, and he would have wanted it.

Looking down into the loam will teach me things I don't want to know. Did he die recently or long ago? Would I have met him if I had gotten here sooner? If I'd walked faster. If I hadn't procrastinated. Was he already dead when I left home? Was all this walking for nothing, doomed right from the start?

But what if it isn't my father? What if it's my mum, or my sister? Or what if it's my uncle down there? What if he was the only one left and the one who had to bury himself? Maybe my father and he prepared the graves as soon as they realised what was happening. Maybe they helped each other bury their loved ones, as long as they both were around.

Or maybe they were the first to go, and my mum had to organise the burials. Perhaps she stood, day after day, with the shovel in the ground to atone for surviving. The way I've walked across time to do the same.

Who could they be, all eight? The eighth is the last survivor. I'll find out when I look inside. But first, but first...

The seventh grave, under the willow, I can't think about just yet. That leaves one for my mum, one for my sister, one for each of my aunts, one for my grandma and one for my uncle. Or one for each of my grandmas. But I doubt they both would have survived very long into the second wave. One was so frail, the other so lonely. I'm not sure my father would have told me in our last conversation, if one of them was already dead. Or both of them. What could I have done? What would it have mattered?

Maybe there were strangers. Someone they saw lying limp on the side of the road and decided to offer a proper grave. Maybe one of the neighbours spent their last few days on our farm. Maybe.

I steady myself and turn my head to the seventh grave. It's so small my heart breaks, and its cross is more detailed than the rest. I know who's buried there. I cry for her. I cry for them all. I'm disappointed, and hurt, and scared, and angry.

There might be no one left. I get that now. My survival may be nothing but an anomaly. I *get* that now. I thought I'd got it ages ago. I've been telling myself, many times, that I might be all alone. That my house may be empty, or full of the dead. That there may be no one left but me. I look into the eighth grave. I need to know. I get it now.

There's no one there.

The key sticks as much as it ever did. It holds the feeling of being 12 and coming home from school early, or being 19 and coming home late. It holds the brief second of fear that you're locked out, that the door will not open at all, then the deep click and incredible ease with which it slides open.

The air smells of death. I leave the door agape to let the fresh air in.

The dogs wander as they please. They don't care that I go inside, and I'm glad they don't follow. By old habit, I slip off my shoes. Now that I step on ground I know, I can tell how hard my feet have become. I can barely feel the grooves between the tiles in the hall. I can barely feel the heat from the flames under my feet.

The kitchen door has a special sound. I know it well, and I'm home. The smell gets worse, but even though this is the smell of someone I loved's dead body, my nose is hardened and doesn't care. The kitchen is tidy and clean. A thin layer of dust has formed and sealed the cleanliness inside. The flowers in the windows are dry as chalk. The clock on the wall is ticking off empty seconds on a never-ending list.

I know it by the smell and the mood in the room. There's a body here. This isn't the smell of the dusty dead, nor the round and all-encompassing smell of rot and quick decay. This is the sour, marshy smell of the slowly drying. My least favourite kind. The body isn't in the kitchen, why would it be? I'm sure it will be in the living room.

If I close my eyes, I can imagine the scene without looking. If it's my father's body, it will be in the green leather chair. Stretched out under the grey and black blanket, the one of the roughest wool. It will look like he's napping. It will look like it's 1995 and he's too exhausted, napping in a quiet cocoon that doesn't allow us to turn off the TV or change the channel in case he might wake. A quiet cocoon that needs to remain the same until he wakes up.

Quite possibly, he'll still be wearing his big woollen slippers. As if it is still Christmas and he's gone to bed too late. Quite possibly he'll lie with a book still in his lap, as if it's right after dinner and he was just going to 'read for a while', the way he often introduced his post-dinner naps.

But it might not be my father. If it's my mother's body, it will be on the chaise longue. As if even after he died, she doesn't deserve the full comfort of his chair. She'll not be wearing a blanket but she'll have wrapped herself in scarves and knitted jackets. She'll be on her side with her hands under her head. As if she's just come home from work and wants to 'rest her eyes for a bit'. But it won't be my mother. I know that. As soon as I saw the open grave in the middle, I knew. As soon as I smelled the body in the living room, I knew.

I take one step.

'Dad?' I call into the living room. I step forward, eyes to the ground. Don't want to see before I have to. One foot in front of the other. Walk until I know I'm standing right next to his chair. I think my insides are dissolving. I feel acidic and molten from my neck to my pelvis. Swirling and uneasy. I think I might drown if I don't keep swallowing away the spit in my mouth.

I swallow and swallow and swallow. I close my eyes, raise my head, and fix my eyes behind my lids. Stare to where I think the windows are. Make sure I look up high. Rather too high than too low. My eyes open slowly. Comically slowly. The soft pretend-blink of being 14 and thinking it makes you cute, or mystical, or interesting, or anything but who you are. Blinking softly, like a movie star. Look one way when the lids are going down, another when they open. Blink.

I look straight ahead. I see the unkempt hedge and the forest. A single goshawk circling, a candyfloss cloud, trouser-clad legs in my peripheral vision. Legs with grey woollen slippers. That's all I need to know for now. My stomach is hard as stone, or maybe it's just my heart. It threatens to pull me to the ground and never let me rise again. I close my eyes and back out slowly.

I keep my eyes shut until I'm outside and can sit down to watch the goshawk. I watch it for a long time, trace it with my eyes until it disappears over the forest and stops circling back at all. My eyelids are heavy and swollen from the crying. My insides are still like water. I might seep into the soil and disappear into the ground. Perhaps I should run away. Instead I fall asleep.

I wake from a sound I've heard so many times, I used to ignore it completely. The metal hooks on the flagpole's string are ringing gently against the pole. The *cling cling cling* is a song I used to be able to hear far and wide, and now, the soft evening breeze plays it to me. It has sung me home, I realise now. I've heard it all the way from the crossing, I heard it while I walked. It formed a steady rhythm for me to follow. *Cling, cling, cling cling, cling, cling, cling, cling.* It's almost dark, and the shadows are deeper than they used to be.

Scram and Lady are sniffing away, somewhere in the dark blue light. Perhaps they've caught the scent of me, the way I used to be, or perhaps they're exploring the tracks of badgers and foxes and voles and mice. I walk across the overgrown lawn and open the door to the gazebo. The air in there is damp and stale. The only trace of death is the slight sting of dead wasps and flies, a whisper of the acrid smell that hordes of dead insects leave behind.

I carry the table and chairs into the garden. Stack them in the overfilled drying house and push the bolt across the door. It takes me forever to find the spare key to my sister's house. She is, was, careful, and would move the hiding place from month to month. She wouldn't tell anyone where it was unless she needed someone to lock themselves in. And then, as soon as it was used, she would move it to a new spot.

I'm getting annoyed. Why? What's the point of this constant vigilance? Her house is so far away from the others. Anyone who wanted to break in for reasons of theft or greed wouldn't bother with the key. Not when she has such big windows. Not when my parents' house is right next door, and bigger, and brighter and old.

'So what's the fucking point?' says Kobus, and I laugh.

'Hey,' I say. 'Welcome. I know these aren't exactly the circumstances you wanted to visit Norway and my home under, but you take what you can get, right?'

He laughs, and I laugh, and he helps me look. We find it eventually. Taped to the back of a birdhouse. The birdhouse is halfway up a tree, and Kobus tries to assure me she wouldn't have put it there.

'It defeats the whole fucking purpose of a spare key, if you make it too hard to get,' he says, but he didn't know my sister. To her, the point of a spare key was that no one would ever find it. But my sister didn't know me. The anger burns away some of the darkness, and I see things clearer now. I wish I didn't.

I lock myself into my sister's house. I close my eyes and hear my niece's quick footsteps running towards me. She's two years old, and I'm her favourite superhero.

'Auntie!' she calls, and she jumps into my arms, digs her hand in under my sleeve, and says she has to show me something in the living room.

'Hello!' calls my sister from the kitchen. 'Tea? Coffee?' And she'll be knitting in the sofa, and *Frozen* will be on the TV for the fifteen-thousandth time today.

The clocks are ticking away just as dutifully here. It's messy. My niece's toys and books are shoved aside. There are dishes on the counter. Grey, hard slabs of what may have been bread.

The velvet squid lies forlorn and lonely, perched on the corner of a table. I bought him before she was even born. When she was still an idea. When my sister would refer to her as her belly squid, and I would taste the feeling of being Auntie for the first time. I bought him because of his long arms. Great for hugs, great for pulling along when she started walking, and great to suck on before she was old enough to realise how gross it is to suck on fabric.

I pick him up and smell him, deeply. My nose searches for a hint, a trace, a shadow of any of my favourite people. I sniff a knitted scarf hanging over the back of a chair. I sniff my sister's coat and my niece's pillow. They all smell like dust and the sadness inside me. The sadness turns with each deep breath I take. As if it has dislodged now, and blows through my body like tumbleweed.

I grab my sister's guest duvet and pillow from a cupboard; I go through her sheets and find the ones I think she'd least mind me using. I look through her cupboards and smile to myself. They're chock full of reserves. Boxes and boxes of tinned goods and chocolate. There's a whole closet shoved to the brim full of toilet paper. My sister knew which way the wind was blowing. Gallons and gallons of fresh water in the cellar, an oasis in a desert of concrete. My sister knew about what-ifs. I take a couple of tins and a bunch of chocolate from the kitchen. I can hear her shortened breath from the corner, know she thinks I'm taking too much, wishes I wouldn't dig too far into the reserves, just in case... just in case.

23

Once upon a time, this stretch between my sister's and my parents' house used to be a path through a jungle. But it wasn't my sister's house back then. They weren't even houses, as such, they were people. On one side stood my grandparents, on the other stood my parents, and in between them was this path.

There were mice in the grass, and sometimes frogs. Once, a badger ran across the road in front of me and I thought I'd faint from fear. My legs moved like drum sticks back to my grandparents' house, which I refused to leave until my father came to get me. I was a very nervous child.

In the mornings, I could see deer and foxes and elks walk across this road. The road, itself, was wild. And then I had to pass the drying house, which loomed over the path on its high pillars. The darkness underneath held scrap metal and abandoned lawn mowers, pieces of broken porcelain and old bones.

I once found a jaw down there. Its glistening teeth poked up from the ground, white and threatening. I thought my father had killed a man. I cried for days, too scared to tell anyone but firm in my belief. When I saw his strong muscular back bent over a bread dough, I could imagine him breaking a grown man's skull against the concrete slab by the drying house. I imagined his eyes, black and angry. I imagined the blood so clearly I could smell its irony tang.

Finally, after days of torturing myself, I went to my father to confess.

'I know what you did,' I said. I started sobbing hysterically. It took him a long time to calm me down enough to explain.

'I know you killed the dead man under the drying house.' I remember the look on his face.

'There's a dead man under the drying house?' he said, and his body tensed as if internal springs had suddenly been wound.

'Yes,' I sobbed. 'He's dead because you killed him when you smacked his head against the slab.'

'Show me where he is,' he said. Moving quickly, decisively. But I knew, because I was a very smart kid, that if he'd buried him under the drying house, he already knew where the body was. Therefore, I reasoned, my father was leading me in under there to kill me, too. He had to make sure no one knew what he'd done. To me, that made perfect sense. After all, I didn't want my father to go to jail. And I didn't even trust *myself* with this secret. So why on Earth should he?

My father half ran, half scurried across the garden, slipped down the small slope where the gazebo now stands, looked in under the drying house, slid in under, stood bent in the darkness and scanned the dirt.

'Where?' he said. 'Where is he?' I walked over to stand with my back against the slab. Closed my eyes and sobbed.

'There,' I said and pointed to where the white teeth still stood out of the ground. My father went over, pushed his toes at them. Sighed. He dragged the jawbone out of the ground and held it up along his cheek.

'Look,' he said. 'Do you see how long it is? Do you see how big the teeth are? And do you see how they are all in a straight line? It's a pig's jaw,' he said. And I looked and looked and could see it was true.

'Oh,' I said, still sobbing with every breath. 'Do you promise?'

He turned it over in his hands a couple of times. If I imagine it now, I can see him crossing off a mental checklist: too short and the wrong teeth to be an elk, too long and narrow and the wrong teeth to be a fox, wrong shape to be a badger. 'Yes,' he said, 'I promise... Why did you think...?' He looked at me. 'You've had a lump in your belly for days, haven't you?' That's what we called it, walking around with worry or sadness, a lump in our belly. Emotional cancer. I just nodded. 'Well, I'm glad you told me. If there had been a man,' he said, 'we would have had to call the police.'

I wiped my tears and drew a couple of clear breaths in between sobs. 'Even if you were the murderer?'

'Yes, even if I were the murderer. No one should get away with murder.'

'What about God?' I asked, because I was that sort of child.

'Well...' he said, 'I suppose God doesn't really murder people...'

'What about all those soldiers who drowned when the Red Sea wasn't open anymore?' I asked.

He didn't laugh and he didn't frown. He just thought about this for a little while. Then shrugged. 'You know, I don't know.'

He smiled, and held the pig's jaw out in front of me. 'Do you want to keep it? It's really old, but you should give it a good clean if you do.'

I nodded. 'Yes please,' I said. And for years to come, I wondered why God got away with murder. My father had said no one should, and I always believed in my father, who's now in heaven.

Kobus is already sitting outside the gazebo, waiting for me.

'Do you know what I find fucking interesting?' he says while I'm still approaching.

'I know a whole lot of things you find fucking interesting,' I say. I'm tired.

'I mean right now.'

'No?'

'Okay. Let me tell you.' He clears his throat and stretches his legs out in front of him. Makes himself comfortable. 'In all this time you've been walking, you've been talking to me. Correct?' I had forgotten this trait, the way he would get to his point by making declarative sentences and asking if each of them was correct.

'Yes,' I say.

'And you always used to believe that men and women are the same. That one gender isn't better than the other. Correct?'

'Yes.'

'Then how come,' he says, and although I'm still a few steps away, and although it's dusk and he's not really there, I can see his smugness shine like a beacon, 'you only give a man a voice?'

'What do you mean?'

'I am a man,' he says.

'I'm going to need a little more than that...' I say, because I struggle to see his point in this light.

'Of all the people you could bring forward. Of all the women in your life you could recall. Your partner was a woman, yet you only speak to me, and you mostly think about your daddy. Why do you think that is, if not because you find us better company for the apocalypse?' he asks.

'Because it hurts too much,' I say.

'What?' He sounds surprised. I blink away tears in my eyes.

'Because I am used to you speaking at me, having the same conversations over and over, and I'm used to being intimidated by the memories of my dad. They are no different now. You are no different. But Cleo... my mum... I can't recall them the way I can you. I can't give them words as easily, because every conversation was always new. And it hurts too much to think of Cleo! It hurts!' I'm crying now, and it takes me by surprise and knocks my breath away. 'It hurts! It hurts! I miss her more than I miss you!' I shout this last bit. I don't know where it's coming from, but I know it to be true.

I wish I could bring up Cleopatra's voice and talk to her now. I wish we could walk through the landscape together, and that her voice would be as clear as his. But her words were measured in life and can't be careless in death. It would break my heart to have her half. I want her back, or not at all. I miss her completely.

Kobus is quiet for a while, and I calm down. I take a deep breath and shake my head.

'Sorry,' I say. 'I miss you too. Just... differently.' He nods and I remain quiet until my heart slows down.

'So,' he says, 'what now?' He fixes me with his 'important underlying message' stare and leans back against the wall. I shrug.

'What do you mean?' I say.

'They're all fucking gone. You are alone. What will you do?' He was always very direct. He always jumped to the solutions, left no time for wallowing in the problem. I remember that now. 'You could stay here...' he says, and looks around. 'Could be a nice fucking castle for a lonely queen of the world. Fucking sit here and make the animals your subjects, and point out to the sunset every morning and say, "Sun, rise." You will have plenty of room,' he says sharply. 'Fucking massive, this house.'

I blush. 'Oh yeah... about that... I meant to tell you...'

'No, no. I understand. It is inheritance and tradition. It is farmhouse-sized because it is a farmhouse. I get it.' He nods.

'Must have been fucking great being a child here,' he says after a long while. I'm making dinner, trying not to think too much. I sit with the velvet squid in my lap and stare at the boiling stew.

'It was,' I say. 'It was awesome.' I stare a while longer, and then I smile. 'I used to pretend I was the last person on Earth,' I say. He smiles at me. 'I used to pretend there was no one else and I had to carry water from the well to the farm. But I wasn't allowed up to the well alone...' I stir the stew a few times.

'So what did you do?' Kobus asks eventually. It's rare for him to be curious about my stories, but I push that knowledge away. It's good to see him.

'Well,' I say, 'I had to keep a sense of proportion... naturally.'

'Of course, only a charlatan wouldn't,' he says, because he understands these things. But wait, that isn't his catch-phrase. I think it used to be mine. Or actually, I stole it from a TV show. But I don't care. The point still stands.

'So, I filled this massive bucket with water, and dragged it halfway up the path to the well. Far enough that it was a bit scary, and there were many frogs in the grass, but not so far as to break the rules. I never broke the rules,' I say.

'How things change,' he says.

'How do you mean?'

'Man.' He used to call me that a lot. That is 100% Kobus. 'You're walking around with a bag full of weed,' he says.

'Oh yeah!' I say. 'Do you want some?'

'Don't mind if I do,' he says. I have never rolled a joint before, but Kobus shows me how. It gets all too thick in one end, and too thin in the other, and too loose and too tight at the same time, but it will do. I light it on the camping stove, which burns off half of it and makes the rest taste faintly of gas and barbecue, but I don't care.

'Anyway,' I croak. I've never smoked, not really. I have pretended to smoke, but never inhaled. The smoke burns and tears at my lungs. Why anyone ever chose to get used to this stuff is beyond me. 'I then had a well.'

'Yeah?' says Kobus. He takes deep drags and smiles blissfully. I think I've reunited him with an old friend.

'But I still needed a bucket to carry the water in, which needed to be small enough to be a bucket in proportion to the bucket that was the well...' I shake my head. 'Does that make sense?'

'Yes, proportions, yes,' he says. The world smells of sweet spice and student hallways.

'So I carried this tiny doll's cup back and forth between the bucket and my house, and poured the water into a bigger cup. I imagined it to be a bathtub, maybe, or something else to store water in. And I could play that game all day. I imagined being all alone, and I made myself so lonely and sad that I would cry while walking back and forth on the path, carrying water in a little doll's cup.

'Once, my mum heard me sobbing as she came outside to put out the laundry. She asked me several times what was wrong, but all I could say was, "I don't like being all alone." And...' I don't know how to explain the rest. But this is Kobus, and he knows me already. 'And, well... nothing much has changed. Really.' I take a few more drags. I feel nothing.

There are candles on the table in the gazebo. I light them and we take the party inside. I know we are a glowing globe against the darkness outside now. It's just me, Kobus, Scram, Lady, Velvet Squid and the world. My little family.

I've never been this thirsty. I drink and drink and drink until I'm out of water and have to go back to my sister's for more. The night seems to be slower than most nights. Probably because I'm home. I stare at all the pictures, shine on them with my torch. Everyone in my family was so beautiful. I never really appreciated that. They all had such life in their eyes. They all smiled with so much love.

I open her freezer. It smells of rotten food, as I knew it would, but I find a box of my mum's strawberry jam and bring it with me. A gallon of water. More chocolate. All the candles I can fit in my pockets.

Kobus is giggling, carrying a single bar of chocolate through the night. The gazebo is beautiful and I place pictures of my parents, my sister and my niece, my grandparents, my aunts and my uncle, my great-grandparents, my grandfather's siblings, all around the gazebo. Each of them gets a designated spot on a windowsill, and they're all so fucking beautiful, I could laugh or weep or sing.

I pick the mould off the strawberry jam, and the bits underneath are fine. I eat it with my fingers, and it tastes like childhood and home. It claws at my heart and makes me remember things I thought I'd forgot, so I dip chocolate in jam and think about things that hurt.

I think about never seeing my mum again. How I'll never again get one of her soft hugs. How she'll never send me a text with ridiculous punctuation or talk to me in unfinished sentences.

I think about never again hearing my father recite the priest's monologue from *Peer Gynt*. About never again being angry about his stubborn certainty. I think about my sister's nervous laughter and her endlessly patient advice. I think about the way we used to make up songs when we were children, and the way we used to sing the same song over and over, in the back of a tired old car.

I think about my niece's loving hands cupping my cheeks, and how she'd rub her nose against mine. And the loss seems so much darker than before. I start listing details, the smallest things I can think of, things I will miss about the ones I love. And I tell them all to Kobus, who cries on my behalf, and I cry, and Scram cries, and Lady whimpers in my lap.

In the end, I pull the keyring out of my backpack. I haven't seen it for a while. Then I pull out the angry notebook, and I regret ever disliking the picture. I would give anything to have Cleo's sad face in front of me. I would love to reach out and comfort her. I remember her smell now, and the small birthmarks on her left arm. The ones that perfectly resembled the big dipper and the ones that looked like a flower with one petal drifting away.

I remember the way her fringe never did what she wanted it to. And the way her ears felt impossibly small. I remember how she'd always tangle her feet with mine when she was sleeping, and make happy little sounds when I drew her close to me. All of these tiny details are written in her sad face. I can't believe I didn't see them before. I can't believe I almost forgot.

I cry until I fall asleep. And I wake up with a hole inside me. A hole that threatens to swallow me, but feels better than what came before.

I hear them in the distance. The stalkers are giggling from across the field. Every now and then, I feel like I can see them between the trees. No doubt they'll attack, sooner or later, no doubt they've had a plan all along. They'll be back with their piercing claws and dripping teeth and leering laughter, but I'm dangerous now, because I have lost everything. And someone who has lost everything has nothing left to lose. I am, however, tired, and need to make a plan.

There's plenty of wood in the shed. There have been a few warm winters, but my father has still made his yearly quota. There are pallets and pallets on the barn floor above. It's birch wood. Dry and compact. More than enough for a freezing winter. Probably enough for three or four of the type we've had the past few years.

I should bury my father. Clean the living room, thoroughly, with bleach. Then I should make myself a bed in there, and move down the books and clothes from my room.

Maybe I should drag in a chest of drawers, or the box we used to keep cushions in for our garden furniture. I can keep my stuff in there, and only need to heat up the living room and kitchen. The tanks are full of diesel. My father has thought ahead. I could drive the tractor up to the shops. Bring home all the canned goods they have.

Next spring, I could walk to the neighbouring town. It's only a few hours' walk, and I'll probably miss walking by then. I can walk there with a trolley and empty the shops, trolley-load by trolley-load over the course of the summer. Perhaps I can even build myself a better trolley; there are tires and wheelbarrows and scrap metal enough on this farm, and the next farm over, and in the rest of the neighbourhood, too.

Frost should still be a while away, so I can dig myself a potato cellar. I can bake bread in my father's baker's oven. Even with no harvest or sowing, there'll be some grain coming up next year. The crops will have dropped their seeds on the ground, and some of them are bound to return. If I read my grandfather's old books on farming, I'm sure I can figure out how to keep a field going. Just enough for me and the dogs. Or two fields, perhaps. One for sowing, one for eating.

We can stay in the house, the dogs and I. If it snows, we can dig ourselves a trench to the wood shed. Or I can spend the rest of the autumn moving wood from the shed to the wet room. In fact, I could fill the hallway and the bathroom. Or the entire basement, for that matter. But I don't like the basement. It has mice, and sometimes frogs, and darkness. I am still five years old, somewhen, inside.

We can keep track of the days. At least for as many years into the future as the calendars in my mum's office will allow. I know her almanacs used to have a ten-year diary. Ten years is an endless amount of time, and I can't imagine anything lasting that long. But we can keep track of time. Cross off days as we go. Celebrate Christmas as best as we can.

I could drag a Christmas tree down from the woods, decorate it with the same decorations we always have. For a week, I'll fire up hard enough to keep the dining room warm. I'll light candles in all the windows and sing the Christmas verse.

This thought chokes me up. The Christmas verse. The song we know my great-great-grandmother sang in 1861. Which we think her mother sang before her, and maybe her grandma, and maybe as many generations as it would take to get back to its first appearance in a Danish book of hymns in 1589. The song my grandfather sang every Christmas Eve his entire life. The Christmas song I have sung, almost every Christmas. The song our family kept bringing forward, generation after generation. The song that will die with me.

But then again, all songs will die with me, unless there are other survivors out there, in which case, the songs will die with them. But they don't know this song, I'm sure. And not all the other songs I carry. I sing it once, just to make sure I remember. I sing it once more, because it is nice.

We could celebrate Christmas. Walk up to the church and ring the bells the old-fashioned way. Make sure Christmas rings in the way it's supposed to.

But why...? Why would I keep that part of tradition? Why would I celebrate the birth of a baby who died with all the other babies 2,000 years or three months ago? Why do I care if Christmas rings in, when there's no Christmas to go home to? No boiling potatoes or unbelievably dry turkey to eat. None of my mother's meatloaf. No tangerines or dried dates or homemade marzipan shaped like butts, because my father is also five years old, somewhen, inside.

But whether or not we do Christmas and Easter, we could wait around for spring to come. We could look out the window, daily. Wait for the return of the swifts and the swallows. We could prepare the farm for another spring, another summer, another autumn. Get wood in for a new winter, grain cut for yet another spring.

I could reduce our existence to the bare necessities. It could become our creed. I'd be like an animal. Free and liberated in the knowledge that all I ever had to do was survive.

Perhaps I could read every book in the house. Finally learn to play the guitar. I could write a masterpiece and read it for Kobus in the evenings. We could get another dog or two. Find a surviving horse somewhere, build a sled for winter. I could stay. In a year, or two, or five, the loneliness will surely become familiar. We would keep each other company and find new memories to live on. My new little family, loneliness, and I.

24

I spend the day doing chores I don't have to do. I use a scythe to cut the high grass in front of the house. The swishing sound of the rake is soothing, and the piles of grass smell of childhood and summer. The grass is wet and sticky but I work until I'm done. I never walk behind the house or let my eyes turn to the crosses that gleam in my peripheral vision.

The mailbox is empty, as I suspected it would be. No one has made the flowerbeds bloom this year. No one has trimmed the hedges or dragged last winter's gravel off the lawn. It takes me all day; I get sweaty and cold. Light rain hangs in the air like a damp blanket, not falling at all. I keep walking into it on my way back and forth, I push my way through and feel it begrudgingly move to the side. Subconsciously, I look for the tunnels, the holes left from where I've passed through before. With my eyes closed, I walk forward; I try to guess when I cross my own paths, try to feel for changes in the clouds of water that brush against my face.

When evening comes, I light up my father's baker's oven. Not the big one in the cellar, but the small one in the garden. I make myself a huge loaf and dip pieces of crisp crust into honey I nick from my sister's house. That's when they come. I hear their swift footsteps in the fields. I hear them giggle and pant, shove each other out of the way, fight to overtake each other, competing to be the first one here.

It's dark, and I can't see them. There are more of them now, I'm certain of it. I shine my torch into the field but only catch a reflection or two from razor-sharp claws or teeth. Their breath hits me like a warm tide. I'm so sad, so angry, so ready for them. Scram is barking like crazy, Lady runs into the gazebo. Kobus, who's been with me all day, talking about nothing in the best possible way, takes this opportunity to disappear into the rain like a ghost.

'Right,' I say to myself. 'Right.' And then I drag Scram with me into the gazebo and close the doors. Close the curtains. Close my eyes. They're upon us. Clawing, screaming, howling with laughter. They think I'm hiding. And I let them, for a minute, maybe two or three.

I imagine the worst-case scenario. Blinded by anger and fuelled by adrenaline, I miss and hit Scram, or Lady. That can't happen. I pour some treats onto the floor and give them both a good cuddle.

'It's okay,' I say, 'it's going to be okay.' But I don't know how to solve this. If I go out there and die, then they'll be stuck in here, dying. But if I leave the door ajar, I'm sure they'll come out and try to defend me. I wish Kobus was still here so he could let them out should something happen. I make a choice.

I step outside and close the door firmly behind me. They're already on top of me, a swarm of searing pain and overwhelming frustration. I can't even catch my breath.

But I am furious. I'm so enraged, I feel it should melt the skin off my body. They may not be at fault. They may not be the ones who took everything from me, but there's no one else to blame and nothing left to lose. I lash at them, claw at them; every muscle in my body howls, and I howl. The sound staggers them for a moment. Just a couple of seconds, they lean away, try to put their resolve back in order. Even revenants long for survival.

Seconds are all I need. I hold the bow out from my body, feel the arrow sing between my fingers. My anger vibrates through my arm and out into my fingers. It polishes the arrow and makes it hum. My bow is a mortal weapon for immortal things. The nearest stalker stares me straight in the eye, and the longing and strangeness in its gaze doesn't faze me. I've seen it all before.

The arrow stands between its eyes, and the stalker's shriek is universal. From all over the globe, from every star and tree, from every grave and pile of corpses, the shriek is the same. It shatters every window in the world and makes me shatter, too. But I don't care, and shoot another. A third, a fourth, I shoot and shoot. They come from every angle, and I shoot until I'm out of arrows.

I still attack the next. I jump on top of it, rip its throat out with my bare teeth. Feel gushing blood under my tongue and a ripped-out tube of some sort hanging limp from my lip. I do not care if its purpose was blood or wind, it's empty now and I spit it out—jump to the next creature in line.

There's nothing they can do but hurt me. Their claws leave wounds, and sure, I bleed, but there's already been so much blood, the memory of all the blood out there runs out before my own. One bites my shoulder and I hear bone crack between its teeth. But my other hand finds the creature's eyes and pokes and digs at them like pecking birds. Eventually, it lets me go. It starts running away, cowers, limps, tries to get away with a shard of life. I don't let it. This is it. This is where I make my stand.

I fight until there's no more air in my lungs or in the world around me. I fight until every shadow is grey and empty. I fight until I'm out of fight, and out of enemies and hope. The sky has cleared and the stars are flowing across like big burning seconds of time. Big burning warnings, or markers, or signs. Big burning omens. I don't listen to their song. The end is, as always, near.

I wake up cold. A raw chill has crept up from the grass beneath me, run through my joints and lined my mind with frost. I stand up and stretch. Yawn, then jump up and down a few times. It's a beautiful morning. My body hurts and creaks and sputters, but as soon as I move, blood rushes to all the forgotten outliers. The tips of my fingers, the heels of my feet. Every artery holds, every vein does its job. I'm strong, I'm whole, I'm alive.

There's the taste of blood in my mouth. The lawn is riddled with arrows, dug deep in the ground. One has gone through an upstairs window of the house, or so I assume, as the window is broken and wasn't before. There are no stalkers to be seen, and not a single giggle in the air. When I turn around, however, I see one limp body on the ground. Blood-soaked fur, paws pointing out into air. A neck that never held a collar.

In my mind, I turn to the gazebo a million times, see the door open and realise what I've done. A million times my heart bursts, before I can stop and take in the facts. The fur is the wrong colour. The gazebo door is shut behind me.

It's a wolf. A real one. Not a fairy tale Wolf with cruel intentions, not a werewolf with humanoid features and means. It's a lone wolf. Young, by the looks of it. The gaping sore on its neck leaves little doubt of what I've done. I can't stop staring. I remember the feeling. I remember the fur in my mouth and the hot pumping that followed. I see the bruises on my arm and I remember how it tried to bite me, but couldn't, not quite. I run to the newly trimmed hedges. I vomit and gag and gag.

'That,' says Kobus, who sits on the steps and watches me solemnly, 'was fucking vile.' I don't answer, because I can see right through him. I think I always could.

When I open the gazebo, the dogs cower away from me. Stare at me with fear and doubt in their eyes. But I sit down and reach out my hands, and they come to me, obedient and loyal. Neither of them has touched the velvet squid.

I bury the wolf in the garden by the others. A ninth grave. I don't make it a cross, but bring up a big white stone from one of the flowerbeds. It resembles the moon a little. I'm sure the wolf won't mind.

My father's body is harder to move. It stirs up unsettled emotions inside me; I cry when I put him to rest. I make him a cross, because he would want one; I say the words I remember, and sprinkle his grave with ashes and dust.

I dig another grave. A small and shallow one. From my backpack, I pull out the angry notebook. I pull out Cleopatra's favourite earrings, the sweater that no longer smells like her and the necklace with her silver heart and our wedding bands, dangling loosely. I bury them with tenderness.

I make a cross for the grave and decorate it with things from the house. Flowers I used to put in my hair, the silver brooch from my national costume. I find silver paint in my mum's office and write Cleopatra's name in beautiful letters. I make a bouquet of the flowers and pin the silver brooch to the cross. I hope it will last for a while.

The next grave is even smaller. I bury the pair of blue baby socks and place velvet squid on top of it. I think of the hopes I once held for my baby, and let them fall to rest. My niece would have been a proud cousin, and she'd let Emma play with velvet squid, at least for a little while. I don't give Emma a headstone. Just four glass birds from my childhood collection. They catch the light and shine like rainbows. The squid wraps his arms around them, and I know he'll care for them well.

I bury the tape from the sports shop in Germany. I let Laura and Opa's voices lie together forever, and hope they feel whole and found. I place my mother's hiking boots on top of their grave. They're almost unused, and still shine a little. I imagine Opa would approve, being buried under the family seal, so to speak.

I bury the poster of Anya's band and play 'Pretentious' one last time.

I bury the letter from the woman with the horse, add her MP3 player and a strip of the reins I cut off. I give her a Barbie horse for a headstone and move on to the next.

The Belgian woman's lipstick and music, my gran's silver mirror for a stone. The hours pass and my backpack empties. I have picked up hitchhikers all over Europe, and now, I'll leave them behind.

I can't stay.

There are 52 graves in the garden. Some, you can hardly see. My backpack is emptied of all that's not mine. What's mine is the keyring, the iodine tablets, the unused notebook with the photo from Rome, a book, a piece of paper with an address on it and a picture I take from the living room.

The picture is only a few years old, from Christmas, and we are all there. Cleopatra and I, my sister and niece, my parents, my aunts, my grandparents and my uncle. It took us four tries to get the timer right, and by the end of the session, half of us were laughing, and the other half annoyed.

There's a ripple of emotion through the picture. Cleopatra and I can barely contain our laughter. We look strained and happy and in love. My mum is talking, the way she always was when we took pictures, so her mouth is O-shaped and her head tilted backwards. My gran looks shy and flustered, my grandma and grandpa are holding hands, smiling their soft, loving smiles.

My father has raised his hand to tell us all to be quiet and stand still, his smile plastered across clenched teeth, the way he smiles in every single photo. My niece is bored and leaning away from the rest of us, leaning down to pick something up off the floor. One aunt is laughing, the other is stern, my uncle is somewhere else completely. It's my favourite picture of my family. It shows us like we really were, the way I nearly forgot.

I walk through the house and let myself feel the longing and sadness of every room. I play the piano for a while. I knit a few rows of my mother's half-finished project, wish I would ever become as good as her.

I read a couple of pages from some of the books I always meant to finish. Others I leave untouched. I clean the living room and brush up the glass from the broken window, cover it with a green tarp and nail thick boards across it from outside. It will keep the house intact for a few years. For long enough, at least.

I skim through my old diaries and weep for the person I used to be. The dogs love playing with my niece's toys and we cuddle in front of the fire at night. I wonder if Lady is pregnant. I kind of think she is. I wouldn't mind a bigger pack.

Every now and then, Kobus interjects, but I don't answer him. Most of the time, I don't even hear him, just see his lips move in my peripheral vision.

I tidy up my sister's house as well. Make my niece's bed and place her favourite toys on the shelves. I hang my sister's scarves in the hall, and do the dishes in bottled water.

It takes me a few days to build a new trolley, and it ends up being a cart. Bicycle tires on a big plastic storage box. I leave the winter coats it used to contain on my parent's bed. No one will mind if the moths eat them now.

I pump up the tires, locate my father's tire repair kit and my sister's bicycle pump, and pack them both in a bag. Perhaps, somewhere, I'll find better ones, but it's good to be prepared.

It's a simple design, the cart. I can change the wheels if I need to. It rolls easily enough, if it's not too heavy, and I can pull it along or push it in front of me. It requires a bit more arm strength than the trolley did, but I'm strong, my backpack is light, and this is the best solution.

I sleep in my own room. Lady and Scram rest on the rugs on the floor until I fall asleep, then they curl up at the foot of the bed. I pretend to fall asleep right away, because I miss them when they're not there.

I go through my mother's closet and find practical clothes that fit. I boil water and have a proper wash. And then, September is over.

It's time. I know it is. I have known it's time for a while now, but the world is calm and not in a rush, so I've waited until I can't. I lace up my hiking boots for the first time since I got here. My feet feel at home, and they're longing to walk. I put on proper clothing, must keep myself warm. I pack most of my sister's reserves into the cart and fill my backpack with the bare minimum of clothes and gear. The dogs can tell we're moving, and they leap ecstatically and chase each other around. Clouds are drawing in from the north, and there's movement in my body.

When we walk outside, my sister's old cat steps out of a hedgerow. It doesn't care that we're here, but the dogs care about its presence and I think they'll chase her. I jump in front of them, bark once, then growl, bare my teeth as they cower and stop. They watch the cat disappear back into the hedge, obeying my order not to follow.

I have one last stop to make. I kneel at Cleopatra's grave and clear my voice. I open *The Hobbit* where my niece's photo marks the spot, and clear my throat again.

The last chapter is beautiful. I read it slowly, the way Cleopatra liked, with the singing voice and lilting intonation that I always used when reading Tolkien.

I realise, at the same time as Bilbo does, that maybe my family presumed me dead. Maybe one of these graves is mine. Maybe my mother buried some piece of jewellery, maybe my father put in the copy of *Peer Gynt* that has my college bus pass as a bookmark and where we've written little notes for each other in the margins.

Maybe they sprinkled my grave with ashes and dust, and divided my memories between them. Maybe my mum remembered my crafts and cooking, my father our discussions and fights. *The Hobbit* is tattered and worn now. Scarred by months in my backpack. When I finish, I bury it with the photo still inside.

'So,' says Kobus. He's standing right behind me, just out of sight, and his voice is more a whisper than a drone. 'What's the plan?'

'I don't know,' I say, taking a long look at the keychain before threading a cord through its loop and tying it around my neck like a tag. 'There are some things I would like to see again. The clock tower in Prague, for example. And some things I never saw that I would quite like to find. I've never seen the *Mona Lisa*, the Sagrada Familia or the Sistine Chapel. I never saw *A Huguenot, on St. Bartholomew's Day*, even though it's my favourite painting. There are things, out there, I'd still quite like to see.'

'Oh yeah?' he whispers.

'And there's this address,' I say, flipping the note between my fingers, 'and if Georg was real, I would quite like to see him again. And if he wasn't, I would quite like to know.'

'I understand,' he says.

'And when all of that is done,' I say, 'there are still things... I have a word to find that I lost along the way. And I've never tasted ouzo, or seen a zebra in the wild.'

I turn around to face him, and he shimmers like snow in the air.

'I think, though,' I say, 'that I have to leave you here.' He nods a little, or maybe his image just flickers.

His car keys are still in my backpack. I bury them in an unmarked grave. He already knows where he is.

I've made a little basket in the cart for Lady. She sits there now, ready to go. Scram sits obediently beside me, but looks up every other second.

'Can we go now?' his eyes say. 'How about now? Now? Ready? Can we go?' I smile and touch the stone in my pocket. It feels lighter now than it was before. I pull a yellow tennis ball out of the cart and throw it down the road. Scram licks my hand before setting off after it, and we're on our way again.

Writing a novel really takes a village, and I want to thank everyone in mine.

THANK YOU

… to you, for spending your limited time and concentration reading my book. I firmly believe stories belong to their readers, and I'm so happy you picked up mine.

… to my first round of test readers: Candice Barlow, Tielman de Villiers, Asher Fok, Furbene, Michael Kobernus, Pernille Velling Krogeide, Silje Lier, Lars Lindberg, Sara, Ann-Charlott Sommer-Ekelund, Julie Sommer-Ekelund, Greger Stolt Nilsen and Linn Tesli. You read an early version of this book in 2016 and treated it with so much kindness, thought and – when needed – blunt honesty. Your feedback was crucial to the shape of the finished story.

… to Manuela Hotvedt, who volunteered to help a complete stranger with a "may-never-actually-happen project" by translating a handful of random sentences into German. Thank you for your generosity and time.

… to my writing colleague, idea bouncer-backer and oldest friend, Rut Granli. You read this book when it was about to be lost forever and demanded it stay out in the open. The way you root for me, fangirl my writing and will jog across the woods just to tell me how much you like it means everything to me.

... to Dr Anna Tripp and Dr Pat Wheeler, who are both awe-inspiring academics, lecturers and people. You rolled into my life right when I most needed to challenge my internalised understanding of the world. Your classes and guidance helped shape the ideas that became this book, and the 'me' who wrote it.

... to Dr Rowland Hughes, whose class on literature, spatiality and nature writing gave me a world in which to place my story. Thank you for introducing me to creative non-fiction and getting us ever so slightly lost on the Icknield Way.

... to my MA class, particularly my beloved Scooby gang, the 'Masters of Articulation': Callum, Danielle, James, Janette and Tielman. I hope we keep meeting up until we're all dust. An extra thank you to Tielman for our hilarious, interesting and frustrating conversations, and for letting me completely distort them to give Kobus a voice.

... to the author Evie Wyld, for showing me that you can put your weird in your writing without breaking the genre.

... to my parents, for never making me feel like I was too weird to be loved. I am sorry for all the worries I've caused you, for that time you had to come pack up my flat in Kristiansand, and for not learning to drive sooner. I refuse to apologise for anything else. Thank you so much for your love and encouragement.

... to my brother, who, despite this being a work of fiction, will feel left out since the main character doesn't have one. You will notice that none of these thanks are directed at our sister, which means you're special. Thank you for giving me my wonderful nephews, and for being cool and stuff, I guess.

... to my mother-in-law, whose friendship and support has made my life in England so much happier and brighter.

... to all my friends for being my friends. Special shout-outs to Anniken, Cally, Candice, Clair, Dave, Greger, Jen, Robin, Sue and Tim. I love you all to bits.

... to my sisters-in-law and brother-in-law for your friendship and encouragement, and for giving me my nieces and nephews. (Also to my sister. Let's see if our brother notices).

... to my brilliant editor, strictest critic, biggest fan and wonderful wife Nica. Without them, this book would be nothing. Thank you for being the best company. You're the wisest editor I've ever worked with, and the kindest person I've ever met. I <32 you. (Editor's note: Not a typo.)

And finally,

... to my former selves. I'm genuinely sorry, but thank you for holding on.

If you loved *What Survives*, you can support Amelia by leaving a review online or recommending the book to a friend.

For more from M. Amelia Eikli,
visit www.ameliabilities.com
or follow her on social media:
@ameliabilities

Printed in Great Britain
by Amazon

36768343R00175